Temptation

by

Brenda Huber

Chronicles of the Fallen, Book 3

This is a work of fiction. Names, characters, places, and incidents are either the product of the author's imagination or are used fictitiously, and any resemblance to actual persons living or dead, business establishments, events, or locales, is entirely coincidental.

Temptation

COPYRIGHT © 2020 by Brenda L. Huber

Cover Art by *Rae Monet, Inc. Design*

The Wild Rose Press, Inc.
PO Box 708
Adams Basin, NY 14410-0708
Visit us at www.thewildrosepress.com

Publishing History:
Previously published by Samhain Publishing, 2015
First Black Rose Edition, 2020
Print ISBN 978-1-5092-2813-3
Digital ISBN 978-1-5092-2814-0

Chronicles of the Fallen, Book 3
Published in the United States of America

His loyalty to his brethren was the only thing keeping him from falling over the razor's edge of a treacherous cliff, however precarious his balance was. He owed them that much. So he would take this last mission. For them.

He didn't have to like it. He just had to finish this.

But once this was done, once the Halfling was secured, he was through. He'd go find this Maggie Michaels. He'd bring her back and leave her with Niklas or Xander, let one of their women take care of her. And then he'd end this pitiful excuse of an existence. He refused to return to Lucifer, whether the ruler of Hell would accept him back or not. And he feared if he stayed this course much longer that was exactly what would happen.

Oblivion—death for the soulless—was waiting for him, and he welcomed it with open arms. He refused to live another day longer than absolutely necessary, let alone another century unable to touch or be touched.

Oh, he'd go down like a warrior. He'd find the biggest, baddest nest he could, shimmer into the middle of it, and take out as many of the bastards as possible before he bit the big one. But he just refused to do this anymore.

He, more than anyone, knew you didn't have to be alone to be lonely.

Pushing a hand through his tangled hair, he heaved a defeated sigh. "Tell me where to find the Halfling."

Praise for Brenda Huber...

THE SEER:
"Thrilling, dangerous and seductive... Brenda Huber has done it again with her continuation of a fantastic plot, amazing characters and sizzling passion."

~Fresh Fiction Reviews

THE SLAYER:
"With danger, passion, sexy demons, and a lot of action, *THE SLAYER* by Brenda Huber is a new favourite of mine."

~Fresh Fiction Reviews

SHADOWS:
"Brenda Huber is an author to watch. The way she paints a scene is fantastic..."

*~Catherine Bybee, New York Times and
USA Today Bestselling Author*

"Huber's serial killer is truly twisted and readers will be guessing the person's identity until the last pages of the story..."

~Romantic Times

MINE:
"The turbulent, fast-paced plot leaves readers holding their breath while turning the page..."

~Coffee Time Romance

Dedication

I would like to dedicate this book to my readers.
Thank you for finding me.
Thank you for staying with me.
Thank you for becoming part of my world.

Acknowledgments

I would like to thank my editor Callie Lynn Wolfe. There are no words to properly express my gratitude for all you've done to give this series the chance it deserves. And also, heartfelt thanks go out to all the other authors of Holly's Hellions who have not only provided me with insightful nuggets of advice and wisdom, but also helped me feel like part of a community. It truly does take a village.

The only way to get rid of a temptation is to yield to it.

~Oscar Wilde

~~

Feel free to yield all you want, but I'm not goin' anywhere, darlin'.

~Gideon, Demon of Temptation

Prologue

Gideon tore through the jungle. The sharp edges of broad leaves slashed him, ripping his face and neck. Gnarled, hanging vines caught his pumping arms. Tangled roots and slick, moss covered rocks made every racing step treacherous.

Sweat drenched his body. His clothing clung in the oppressive humidity. He'd sprinted, more or less, the last eight miles, and his breathing was ragged. His heart pounded inside his chest like angry war drums. Not from his exertions, but from overwhelming excitement.

The Mayan ruins of Calakmul, the Kingdom of the Snake, flashed in the distance, bobbing in and out of his line of sight as he darted, jumped and weaved his way through the overgrown jungle. Indescribable power radiated from the Amulet of the Gods, drawing him inexorably onward, urging him faster and faster.

Gideon's stamina was nearly limitless. But the heat, the nightmares that had plagued him with increasing frequency, and the extensive injuries he'd sustained less than an hour ago in a fierce battle with a nest of Animagi were beginning to sap his strength. It'd been too long since he'd fed, and his wounds weren't healing anymore—not like they should be. Even now, blood seeped from the ragged hole in his shoulder. Blisters from a lucky plasma ball seared his side, raw and oozing. Dizziness washed through him in waves, but still he ran. Hope, a ruthless and unforgiving taskmaster, rode him hard.

A fresh surge of foreign energy ripped through the air without warning, something familiar. Something evil. A whisper of awareness shivered along his nerves.

Another demon was near.

Determined to get to that amulet first, Gideon burst from the choking vegetation near the base of crumbling steps, so close to his goal he could taste it. The power of the amulet hissed through the air, sizzling energy that pulsed with a life all its own. He'd sensed it the moment he'd shimmered into the jungle several miles away, knew it would have been the same for whoever else it was that was there with him. The closer he got, the more powerful the draw.

The amulet was his last hope, the only possible loophole he'd been able to come up with in the two hundred years since Lucifer had compounded his curse, twisting an already impossible situation into something heinously cruel. He'd already been stripped of his angelic gifts of precognition during the Great Fall by the very angel he'd once called brother. But then Lucifer had seen fit to punish him twice over for disobedience, cursing him to never again have physical contact with another—any other—while in human form. In demonic form…well, that was a whole other messed up situation. Lucifer's curse had been the last straw, the thing that had driven him to join Niklas, Xander, Mikhail, and Sebastian in rebellion.

It's so close!

A plasma ball whizzed past his head, exploding in a whoosh of flames and shattered rock, obliterating a column of ancient inscriptions. Crouching, whirling about, he ignited his own plasma ball and scanned the lush greenery around him. His breath wheezed in and out. Sweat dripped in his eyes, plastering his hair to his cheeks and neck. He did a quick visual search of the foliage at the base of the ruins, but he couldn't locate his attacker.

Gideon leaped back into the edge of the vegetation. He glanced up the steep stone steps. Steps stained by the blood of countless sacrifices. Soon more blood would join with the rest—*his* blood—a gruesome offering required to obtain the amulet he wanted almost as much as he wanted redemption.

But that's not strictly true, now is it? his conscience argued.

A flicker of guilt speared him. If he were being truly honest, he'd admit he wanted that amulet even more than the forgiveness he'd worked so hard to earn.

God help me.

A small alcove at the top of the temple offered concealment and a vantage point. He gathered his strength, corralled his focus, and shimmered to the top of the steps, to the entrance of the alcove. A plasma ball exploded near his shoulder, spraying him with razor sharp shards of rock, slicing fresh wounds into his flesh. Dust plumed in the air. Gideon darted into the alcove. His chest heaved as his gaze whipped around the room. The chamber was large, an altar placed dead center in the space.

Power radiated from the base of the massive stones, throbbing in the air. Hope all but choked him, surging wild and greedy. He was so close, the thrum of the amulet's energy vibrated in his very bones. His hands shook with excitement. This was it. It had to be.

The answer to his prayers lay only a few feet away. With the sacrifice of his blood, with the incantation—*please, God, let me have translated everything correctly*—the amulet would allow him to touch others once again, let him *be* touched after an eternity without the simple intimacy of contact.

Gideon took a step forward, his sole focus the massive stone slab atop the altar. He began reading the carvings aloud, searching for the correct stone, the right marker. The air in the corner began to waver and he read faster. Words, phrases jumped out at him.

Yes. Yes this is it. This is what I've been searching for.

Determination shot through Gideon like a river of lava, molten and unstoppable. He would not be thwarted in this. He would not yield.

He felt the stirrings of the monster within and fought to keep control. He could not morph. Not now. Mindless, unbiased destruction would not benefit him. Quite the opposite. In his demonic form, he might be just as likely to destroy that which he desired most and not even realize it until it was too late. It was just too much of a gamble.

No, he would not morph.

And he would not fail.

A demon solidified in the corner.

Mortikaï!

One of Lucifer's cruelest soldiers, the Captain of the Prison Guard for Lucifer's personal dungeon, stood before Gideon in all his demonic glory. Massive body, grotesquely deformed face, bald head and pointed ears. His flesh was gray, pockmarked and lumpy. Gideon could smell his putrid breath from this distance. The scent of death and decay. Gideon pushed down the urge to morph, mindful of his resolve to remain in control of the beast within.

He was fighting a losing battle.

Gideon had never had a personal bone to pick with this particular demon, no axe to grind, no grudge held. But the Captain of the Guard, Gideon knew, had always seen things differently. He'd resented Gideon's rise through the ranks of Lucifer's army. He'd watched Gideon with a jaded eye, waiting for the moment the Demon of Temptation slipped and fell from favor, like a vulture waiting for a wounded animal to stop kicking before it moved in to pick the bones clean. Mortikaï's mere presence threatened everything Gideon had been trying to accomplish. Fury flooded his veins.

"I know what you seek, Temptation," Mortikaï sneered in the ancient Demonic language, his voice deep and layered. Plasma balls hovered over the open palms of his massive hands.

No!

How had he found out? How had he learned of the amulet? Gideon had been so careful in his inquiries, covering his tracks, and, yes, even killing a few demons that'd asked too many questions or seemed to take a little too much interest in his business.

"How accommodating of you to meet me, then, to offer yourself up for my blade," Gideon taunted, careful to keep his mind off the object of his deepest desires. Though he had no proof, he'd heard rumors Mortikaï could read minds, rather like Sebastian had been able to decipher a being's deepest desires before the Great Fall. "And that's *former* Demon of Temptation, by the way."

"Ah, yes. You are of the Fallen now." Mortikaï

spat on the floor, punctuating his disgust. The droplets of spittle sizzled and bubbled like acid on the aged rock. Gideon considered his best plan of attack. Mortikaï had few weaknesses. Having become his unwilling target, Gideon had made sure to catalog them all. Something he'd willingly take advantage of in the ensuing battle.

"Such a pity. Heaven won't take you back, and all of Hell is out to kill you," Mortikaï mused with mock sympathy. "Did you know the Dark Prince raised the bounty on you and your legion of traitors yet again? Still not worth quite as much as the Slayer or the Seer, but you'll bring a hefty sum all the same."

"Too bad you won't be collecting," Gideon taunted. "You know, being dead and all."

"Such a waste, Temptation. You were as a god. Now you are nothing. Less than nothing, so pitiful you must rely on legend and human magics to fix yourself."

Time stood still as Mortikaï's greedy gaze slid to the altar, caressing the stone hungrily. A kernel of panic, cold and hard, formed in the pit of Gideon's stomach.

No, it wouldn't go down like that. Not if he had anything to say about it. Mortikaï wasn't going to touch the amulet. Gideon wouldn't stop now, wouldn't be defeated. Not when he was so close. Fierce, focused resolve pushed aside all common sense and rational thought, burying the fury and the panic, until he was the brutal, unfeeling killer he'd once been, honed in the fires of Hell.

He fought to remain in control, struggled to keep his temper in check. Because if he slipped, even for a moment, and the monster inside him won, all could be lost. *He* could be lost.

"Perhaps I'll keep the Amulet of the Gods for myself," Mortikaï said, gloating.

Just like that, the monster raged free. Pain ripped through Gideon as muscles and tendons tore and reformed, his frame growing larger, more powerful. Blood gushed inside his mouth as his teeth shot long and jagged, tearing into his lower lip. Not just fangs as most demons possessed, but a complete mouthful of lethal daggers. His claws burst forth like steel talons. Searing agony split his skull as horns sprouted, lengthened, spiraled up and back.

Temptation savored the pain, reveled in the agony. He thirsted for blood. Wouldn't stop until he'd drenched himself in it. Somewhere, deep in the back of his mind, a niggling tendril of something tugged at him. A concern. A goal.

But he couldn't recall what it was. Only that an enemy stood before him, waiting to die.

His roar of challenge echoed throughout the jungle, sending shrieking flocks of birds flapping into the brilliant blue sky. Startled animals screamed and chattered. Somewhere in the distance, another large predator roared in reply.

His enemy hurled plasma balls in quick succession. Temptation dodged and rolled, firing his own molten missiles. He shimmered behind the demon, tossing another plasma ball, but the demon vanished and reappeared across the room. In anticipation of his opponent's next move, Temptation shimmered near the doorway, solidifying a split second before the demon.

Temptation launched himself at his adversary's back. He bared his sharp teeth and went for the demon's throat. But his opponent twisted at the last second, and Temptation missed his target, sinking his teeth into the tendons where neck joined shoulder instead.

His rival's body convulsed, and the demon roared in pain as acidic blood filled Temptation's mouth. Tearing loose, he spat out the foul-tasting flesh and blood.

The two massive titans crashed to the floor, grappling and clawing, landing bone-crushing blows with massive fists. Temptation reared back as he pinned his foe to the floor, his arm slashing down toward the demon's throat, claws fully extended in what was sure to be a decapitating blow.

At the last second, the demon vanished. Temptation's knees connected with solid rock and his claws gouged deep furrows into the ancient stone. He whipped his head up, his senses throbbing and overloaded because of the amulet's proximity and power.

A plasma ball skimmed his already injured side, searing away clothing and flesh. Another plasma ball slammed into the massive altar nearby. The corner exploded in a spray of dust and sharp shards. Another plasma ball, another explosion of rock dust and jagged projectiles. All too soon, his challenger's game became apparent. And Temptation began to remember his own purpose. There was something in that altar he needed.

But slowly, blast by blast, his enemy was demolishing the altar, and with it the incantations inscribed in the ancient stone. Bit by bit, he was whittling away any chance Temptation had of fully understanding and harnessing the powers of the Amulet of the Gods.

And there wasn't a damned thing Temptation could do to stop him, aside from kill him. Heaven help him, he was trying. Rage fueled his demonic body, driving the last meager shreds of logic and reason to the far recesses of his mind. He increased the speed and ferocity of his attack.

Another bolt of fire shook the altar, causing the top slab to teeter and crash to the floor on one side, revealing a hollow in the base of the stones. Before Temptation could react, his challenger shimmered to the altar. He plunged his beefy fist through what was left of the secret vault, his triumphant gaze locked on Temptation. And as his foe straightened, his bloodied fist lifted to the sky, the glint of gold and bloodred rubies sparkled from between his clenched fingers.

Temptation conjured a black athamé and let it fly. The ten-inch blade buried itself deep in his opponent's chest. The demon staggered back a step, his roar of triumph cut short as he clutched the hilt of the athamé with his free hand. His ghoulish face registered first shock, then agonized pain. A trickle of blood gathered at the corner of his mouth. Temptation pushed to his feet and called forth his sword. He would take this bastard's head.

That belongs to me!

Temptation stormed closer, his chin dipped to his chest with murderous intent. His challenger staggered sideways. His hip caught the edge of the slab, sending the massive, off balance rock crashing the rest of the way to the floor. The impact reverberated through the thick soles of Temptation's boots and up his calves. The demon met and held Temptation's gaze. A bloodcurdling smile twisted the demon's thick lips, giving Temptation a moment of pause. A moment of unease.

His foe began whispering words in a furious rush, his volume growing with every syllable. As the meaning of his words registered, Temptation's eyes widened in horror. The demon was summoning Hellfire. Temptation lunged forward, hand outstretched. But he wasn't fast enough. Before he could reach the demon, a blaze erupted in the palm of the demon's hand. A blaze so hot, so bright, so blinding, Temptation instinctively threw up his arm to shield his face.

He lurched forward once more. Something about that piece of gold and glittering stones was important. He couldn't remember why, but the power in it drew him with such strength he couldn't resist.

But he was too late. His challenger had disappeared, his shimmer trail rapidly fading. And on the ground where his foe had stood just a moment before lay a ball of blackened gold and crushed ruby. Melted and deformed. Without a trace of power left. The sight of that melted lump brought clarity. Temptation let go, and Gideon took control once more. In a rush of blinding pain, he morphed back to human form.

Unable to breathe, unable to fully process what had just happened, Gideon fell to his knees. The sword clattered to the floor at his side. His face twisted in shock. Trapped in immutable horror, Gideon scooped up the mangled ball. He held it before him in shaking hands.

Everything he'd hoped and prayed for…gone. He let his hands fall to his lap, his fingers limp, and he watched as the ball thudded to the floor and rolled lopsidedly away. As the last shreds of hope disintegrated, Gideon dropped his head forward. Despair the likes of which he'd never before experienced rocked him. He was hollow. His guts ripped out. His purpose lost. He was wrecked, beyond destroyed.

Here and now, he could finally admit the truth. Forgiveness was not for the likes of him. He'd never believed he could be redeemed. He'd never again see his Heavenly home. Never again feel the warmth of God's grace and love. All that had been left for him was the promise of the amulet. And that was now lost to him.

He had nothing. Not false hope. Not a purpose for existing. Not even the hope of one day feeling the comfort, the warmth, the basic sensation of physical contact without destruction.

Tipping his head back, drowning beneath the despair welling up inside him, Gideon released his raw grief in a howl so frightening the jungle for miles around fell utterly still.

Chapter One

Three weeks later

Gideon ripped himself free of the nightmare as his cell phone screeched. He rolled to his back and scrubbed both hands over his clammy face. He was covered in a cold sweat. His ragged breath sawed in and out, burning his lungs. His eyes were gritty. His head throbbed like an abscessed tooth. In short, he felt like something the cat had dragged in. Something that, if it wasn't already dead, damned sure should be.

So, all in all, about the same as normal.

Xander, Gideon surmised by the ringtone. A ringtone he'd once found amusing, given Xander's recently whooped status. Now he couldn't give a shit one way or the other. The phone went silent—*thank God*—which was a good thing as he'd had no intention of answering it anyway. Unfortunately, Gideon's ears continued to ring, an insistent accompaniment to the throbbing in his temples.

He glanced first at the heavy watch on his wrist, then at the bright sunlight pouring in through the crack in the drapes, and he stifled a groan. Two in the afternoon. By now he should have been up, should have been back out on the streets. He should have been chasing down those ever-elusive relics. But he hadn't shimmered home and crawled into bed until…well, he wasn't even sure what time it had been this morning. At least, he was pretty sure it had been this morning.

Or had it been yesterday?

Ah, hell. What does it matter anymore, anyway?

Gideon rolled to his side and sat up. He braced himself on the edge of the bed as he hung his head. A stifled curse slipped from his mouth as he lifted both hands to clutch at that foreign-feeling appendage attached to his shoulders.

He waited until his head—or the room, one or the other—stopped spinning before he tried to stand. He didn't even want to consider how much whiskey it had taken for him to hit the state of numbness he'd found last night. But, judging by the raging hangover he was contending with, it must have numbered in cases rather than bottles.

Oh dear Jesus, his mouth tasted as if something had crawled in there and died. By the swollen, furry feel of it, the *something* was his tongue.

Groaning, he braced a hand first on his dresser and then the wall as he staggered to the bathroom. Once there, he splashed water on his face. It took a long while, standing over the sink with the water running, before he could work up the effort, or the courage, to look in the mirror. Squinting against the sight that met him, he groaned, then winced at the pain that small sound had caused.

One step at a time, he reminded himself.

He brushed his teeth. Twice. Just as he reached to turn on the shower, his phone began its shrill serenade once more. Gideon cringed. Niklas's ringtone this time. Grimacing, he ignored the phone and peeled his clothing off, not even wanting to know what had made them so crusty they could damned near stand up and dance on their own.

He could have conjured himself clean, but he needed the steady pounding of hot water against his battered flesh. Besides, conjuring would take far more energy than he had right now.

The spicy, citrusy scent of shampoo revived him little by little. By the time he'd cracked open the bottle of body wash and lathered from head to toe for the third time, he felt almost human. Almost was pretty damned good, all things considered.

As he was toweling dry, Sebastian's ringtone screamed through the bedroom. Growling, he considered crushing the phone. Or stomping on it. Or throwing it against the wall. Or out the window. Anything to make the damned thing shut up. Lord knew muting it was no longer an option, courtesy of Mikhail and whatever it was he'd done to the damned thing. Despite a serious lack of social skills, that bastard could do some crazy shit with electronics.

The phone continued to ring. *Can't they take a damned hint?*

Checking up on him? Making sure he hadn't gone off the reservation, were they?

Well, too damned bad for them, 'cause that ship sailed. Three weeks ago, to be precise.

Or had it been much longer than that?

At least he didn't have to worry about Mikhail calling. The Demon of War wasn't exactly the babysitter type. If you weren't helping him kill something, or weren't the thing he was killing, then he didn't have time to waste on you. Dude was so cold penguins would drop over dead of hypothermia just standing in the same state.

Gideon pulled on a pair of jeans and, despite the pain using his powers would cause his already splitting head, he conjured himself a caramel macchiato—the grande the better. He took the first sip and groaned appreciation.

Bliss. Pure, undiluted bliss.

With a great amount of effort, he made his way down the grand staircase, intent on the big kitchen at the back of his Civil War era plantation home deep in the heart of Tennessee. For the first time in weeks, he actually looked around. The once majestic house he'd taken pride in, the inviting home where he used to find peace and comfort, his haven, was an absolute wreck.

Priceless period furniture had been overturned and tossed about, shattered in fits of rage and despair. One-of-a-kind oil paintings had been slashed or ripped from the walls altogether. Luxurious window coverings sagged to the floor, pooling on one side of the window. Mud and only God knew what else had been tracked over once gleaming floors and expensive carpets. The place looked as if it had been invaded by a hostile army.

But Gideon knew the sad truth. He was the only thing to have crossed that threshold in months. He'd done this. He'd wrecked the beautiful oasis he'd once called home.

Sadly, he couldn't find it in himself to care.

Gideon pulled up short three steps across the foyer. He did nothing to temper the nasty snarl he aimed at the blurry disruption of air near the front doors. Half a second later, golden blond hair, piercing blue eyes, and a powerful body took shape.

"Nobody's home," Gideon snapped as he walked

right on by the Demon of Vengeance without a second glance. "Go away," he growled over his shoulder for good measure.

"You didn't answer your phone." Undeterred, Sebastian followed him toward the kitchen. Gideon heard the Demon of Vengeance swear beneath his breath as he stepped over the splintered pile of what once had been an expensive side table. And, once again, he couldn't muster up the energy to give a damn.

Gideon ignored the pained disapproval on Sebastian's face. If he didn't like the mess, he could damned well leave. No one was keeping him here. In fact, no one had invited him in the first place.

"You haven't answered your phone for three weeks." Sebastian glanced around the room, clearly looking for a safe, relatively clean seat. Unable to find such a place, he pushed empty, and some not-so-empty, pizza boxes and takeout containers down the long table to clear room and conjured his own chair.

"Mikhail doesn't answer his phone for three months," Gideon bit out as he buried his head in the fridge to dig out a couple cartons of leftover sesame chicken and fried rice. *When did I get Chinese?* He shrugged, popped the tops open and grabbed a fork from a drawer. Didn't appear to be anything green in there that wasn't supposed to be, so he dug in. "I don't see anybody calling out the National Guard or dropping in on him uninvited," Gideon added.

The latter probably had something to do with the fact that anybody stupid enough to "drop in" on Mikhail was liable to end up decorating the top of a very long pole. But neither one of them bothered to point that out. Vlad Tepes had nothing on Mikhail.

Then again, neither one of them bothered to point out the obvious either. But they were both thinking it. Gideon could tell by the uncomfortable expression tightening Sebastian's face. Right now, Gideon was the one his brethren were all worried about. The one they were all waiting to take a swan dive off the deep end. The one they all expected to go rogue.

They also thought they'd done a good job of hiding their concerns, that he didn't know they doubted him.

He wasn't blind, nor was he an idiot.

Not that he could begrudge them their doubts. He was just as unsure of himself as they were.

"Yeah, well, I'm still on the right side of the grass. I didn't play with my food last night." He paused, giving Sebastian a mock-thoughtful frown. "At least, I don't think I did. The last half of the night's entertainment is a little blurry, so I can't guarantee anything. I didn't enslave half the human population of…well, wherever the hell I was. Again"—he shrugged noncommittally—"blurry, so no guarantees. And I didn't wake up with a bed full of strange women, not that it would matter. You know, the whole not-being-able-to-touch-anyone curse and all," he snarked bitterly. "So you can run along now like a good little demon and reassure the others."

"Well, aren't we just Sally Sunshine this afternoon?"

The look he shot Sebastian would have made a lesser demon piss himself.

Sebastian arched an eyebrow and considered him in silence for a long moment. Subdued, he asked, "What's this about?"

Gideon swallowed a mouthful of coffee and shot

him a deadened look. "What are you talking about?"

"This attitude. For a while there, it was like the old Gideon had returned. We all thought you'd found your focus, found your faith again. And then wham. Look-at-me-wrong-and-die Gideon is back. I mean, hey, we understand, dude. We do. Given the situation we've all been forced into, it's not out of the question to second-guess what we're fighting for here. It's perfectly natural to get a bit...ah, depressed. Maybe feel a little antisocial, you know."

Gideon stared at Sebastian, unable to wrap his mind around the fact that the Demon of Vengeance was getting all Psych 101 on him.

Sebastian rubbed the back of his neck. "Look, I'm just gonna throw this out there and you can do with it what you will. We've been...concerned about you for some time. It's been pretty obvious you were starting to lose your way. The last several months, the way you've been with Carly and Kyanna, well, we were beginning to think you'd gotten back on the wagon, so to speak. Now it's like you just don't give a shit about anything anymore. You gotta know we're all struggling here." Again, Sebastian rubbed at the back of his neck. "Dude, don't make me say this shit out loud, don't make me get all warm and fuzzy." His gaze pleaded with Gideon to let him off the hook.

Normally, Gideon would've had a snappy comeback. Maybe something about Sebastian never being warm. Fuzzy maybe, but never ever warm. Normally. But Gideon stayed silent. Needling his friend held no appeal.

At Gideon's lack of response, Sebastian's frown deepened. "Is this about the loophole?"

He'd confided in Sebastian once, a few months back, about the possibility of the Amulet of the Gods being able to lift his curse. He'd been drunk off his ass and half out of his mind with jealousy over Xander and Niklas both finding mates. Leave it to Sebastian to not let what was said in a drunken stupor stay in a drunken stupor.

"Loophole's closed," he snapped, letting his tone make it clear he wasn't discussing the issue. Ever. Again.

Sebastian opened his mouth, pity written all over his face.

"Closed," Gideon snarled.

"Whatever," Sebastian growled, none too pleased. "Look, since you can't just answer your phone like a normal dick, I drew the short straw and had to come find your sorry ass. We need you to intercept and guard a Halfling."

"Oh, sure, no problem," Gideon snipped between cold bites of sweet and spicy chicken, "'cause they're just falling out of the sky left and right. If this Halfling's so damned important, and you have enough time on your hands to come check up on me, why aren't you doing the search and rescue thing?"

"I'm off to Michigan as soon as I leave here. We've tracked down a descendant of the Guardian charged with protecting the Sword of Kathnesh. We're hoping I can find something that might help us trace the stolen relic, maybe recover it."

Gideon took a swig of coffee, unimpressed. "Send one of the others."

"Mikhail, Xander, and Niklas are already tied up with missions of their own. By default, that leaves you."

The Sword of Kathnesh, along with the Arc Stone, the Scrolls of Prévnar and the Chosen One, made up the four Sacred Relics. It had long ago been prophesied that whosoever controlled the four Sacred Relics would possess the means to overthrow Lucifer. Only problem with that scenario was that the demon prince, Stolas—who'd already absconded with the sword and was, even now, working on stealing the rest—intended to unleash Armageddon, as the veil between Earth and Hell depended solely upon Lucifer's life force.

That had been God's own curse. Lucifer existed, therefore the veil existed. If Lucifer perished, then the veil fell. Pretty effective torment for someone whose sole heart's desire was the one thing that could only be had at the expense of his own life.

As much as they all hated bad old Lucy, Gideon and his legion of penitent demons couldn't let it go down like that. So, regardless of the fact that they'd turned their backs on Lucifer centuries ago, regardless of the fact that Lucifer now hunted them with a vengeance, putting a price on their heads few demons could resist, they fought to keep him in power down under. Not to protect Lucifer, but to protect the human race, and—hopefully—earn forgiveness.

Gideon gave Sebastian a droll stare. "Easy enough to figure out. Guardian sucked at his job. Sword's in enemy hands, out of reach. End of discussion."

"You need to shut up and drink your coffee," Vengeance snarled.

Where's all that vaunted patience now? Well, good. Maybe if Gideon pissed him off enough Sebastian would go the hell away and leave him alone.

Gideon grunted, flipping him the bird with one hand as he tipped the coffee cup to his lips with the other.

"Back to your mission. That key you found a while back in the spine of Kyanna's book? Xander and Kyanna figured out what it goes to," Sebastian went on. Kyanna was Guardian of the Arc Stone. Five mostly reformed demons, one Guardian and one little human were all that stood between the status quo and the complete and utter enslavement and annihilation of the entire human race. No pressure or anything.

Only an idiot would bet on those odds.

"Key belongs to a strongbox Kyanna's mother had stashed away in the floorboards of the attic where they used to live. The strongbox contained several journals Kyanna's mom had kept over the years. We now have several angelic lines to follow up."

Kyanna was more than a Guardian. She was also a Keeper of Secrets, charged with the safety of a precious family heirloom. A book—or several, by the sounds of it—that, among other things, tracked the lineage, both old and relatively new, of those of angelic descent, aka Halflings. It was her duty to teach those Halflings all they needed to know to survive in a world where everyone was out to either use them for their own purposes or kill them outright. Overall, Gideon liked Kyanna. She was no-nonsense, compassionate and sharp as a tack.

Although, considering who she'd hooked up with, the poor girl had abominable taste in males.

"Then again," Sebastian continued, beating a dead horse, "if you'd bothered to listen to any of the dozen or so voicemails we left, you'd already know this shit."

Gideon set the soggy white carton aside. Apathy

21

battled curiosity. It was a toss-up as to which was winning. "And?"

"We have confirmation of a first generation Halfling. A name and location." Sebastian dropped the bombshell.

Gideon began to take interest at last. A first generation Halfling was huge. For more reasons than one. First and foremost, it meant an angel, one of those Heavenly creatures that were above sin and condemnation, had come down from the Heavens and had carnal contact with a human.

Naughty, naughty.

Second, and perhaps just as important, it meant the other team—and by other team, he meant Stolas, Prince of Hell, and all his countless minions—would be hunting this Halfling to the ends of the Earth and back again. Their intent, as Gideon and his comrades had learned via a very reliable source, was to breed this Halfling with a powerful demon to create the Chosen One, the fourth relic.

So far the score was one and one. Gideon and his brothers in arms had the Arc Stone. Stolas and his team possessed the Sword. The Chosen One and the Scrolls were still up for grabs.

Heaving a defeated sigh, seeing all too clearly where this was headed, Gideon scooped up the cartons of Chinese and settled at the table, conjuring his cup full of caramel macchiato once more. He was going to need a stiff shot of caffeine if he was going to have to deal with this crap. That, or something a hell of a lot stronger.

Sebastian braced his forearms on the table. "Her name is Maggie Michaels. We need—"

"Michaels?" Gideon interrupted, his eyebrows shooting up in shock as his head angled forward. Since angels didn't technically have last names, Halflings were rumored to use their sire's first name as their surname. Rumored, because Halflings were about as easy to find as the proverbial needle in the haystack of humanity. "Michael…as in…"

"We believe so, yes."

"Holy hell," Gideon whispered, leaning back in his chair. You could have knocked him over with a feather. Michael. At one time, one of Gideon's best friends, now his fiercest enemy.

That lying, righteous, rat bastard hypocrite.

"Michael's one of the most powerful Archangels ever created. If Michael is her father, then her bloodline has to be…*holy hell!*" Gideon breathed again, shaking his head, his breakfast of sorts turning to a rock in the pit of his sour stomach.

He shook his head again, barely able to wrap his mind around the very idea. The raw power pulsing in that Halfling's veins had to be off the charts. And he would know if he ever got near her. That had been his little gift, once upon a time, from Lucifer. The ability to sense power. Power was to Gideon as lies were to Xander. There was no way to conceal power from him, no way to disguise it. If it was there, he'd know.

"If Stolas gets his hands on her, we're screwed." Gideon ran a hand through his hair.

Dear Lord, the consequences would be catastrophic.

"Exactly." Sebastian nodded. "Which is why you need to get to her first."

"Easier said than done. I mean, once I find her,

how do you expect me to bring her back? Hell, take her anywhere? Especially if she doesn't want to go willingly? It isn't exactly like I can just shimmer her here." He held his hands up and wiggled his fingers, a wordless reminder of his no-touch clause.

"For now, we just have to get somebody there, somebody who can protect her in case Stolas's minions have found out about her too. But...these might help. Maybe." Sebastian dug in his pocket and held up a pair of identical, hammered silver cuffs, one slightly smaller than the other. They looked average, certainly nothing special. Matching, ancient engravings covered both surfaces. A spell. Dark magicks. The cuffs hummed with power.

Sebastian held them out to Gideon. "Got these from Asher. Put one on your wrist. He's pretty sure, if you can get the other one locked on her wrist, they will, for all intents and purposes, bind her to you...so long as you're both wearing the cuffs, that is. They're supposed to be like a homing beacon. You'll be able to locate her anytime, anywhere; just focus on the link between the cuffs. If you shimmer, she'll shimmer with you whether she wants to or not, no touching required. But there's a catch."

With Asher, there was always a catch, always strings attached. The guy was a regular Geppetto.

Sebastian went on. "She has to willingly accept the cuff and put it on herself. She can't be forced to put it on, but once it's on, her will is bound to yours."

"Till the first time we shimmer, and she decides she's had enough of playing tagalong and takes it off."

"No can do. See this little slot?" Sebastian turned one of the cuffs on its side. The hole, located on the slim edge, was damned near invisible. "Once they go on, they don't come off...ever...not unless you have the key." Sebastian produced a small flat, oddly shaped piece of silver. It looked nothing like a key.

He dropped the key into the palm of Gideon's extended hand. Lifting the key to the light, Gideon examined it meticulously. Just to be sure, he tested the lock. The key fit perfectly, the cuff sprang open. He put one cuff on his own wrist and, without using the key, attempted to remove the cuff. It didn't budge, no matter how hard he tried.

His curiosity was kindled. Why would the Demon of Vengeance have a pair of cuffs like these? But then Gideon changed his mind. He didn't want to know why Sebastian might feel the need to chain somebody to him. He figured this fell firmly into that *don't ask, don't tell* category.

With a shrug, he shoved the second cuff deep in his front pocket and then reached up to remove the silver chain from around his neck. He threaded the key onto the chain so it rested against the small, ancient silver cross that dangled there. He refastened the chain and dropped it beneath the collar of his shirt.

"Asher's cuffs also come with a warning," Sebastian said.

Gideon's wary gaze met Sebastian's. Help from Asher, a mercenary demon with a nasty reputation, always came with warnings as well. And a price tag. Usually a very steep price tag one was only willing to pay when one had no other choice.

That phrase, "making a deal with the devil"? Yeah, it had *not* been coined with Lucifer in mind. That was Asher, all the way.

"Asher said those cuffs work both ways, what binds one, binds the other."

Gideon leaned forward, his brow drawing tight. "You mean, if I put those on the Halfling, she could force me to do her bidding?"

"He didn't specify. You know Asher, everything's a damned riddle." Sebastian shrugged. "I'd just be careful if I were you."

Gideon grunted. He was the one in possession of the key. Wasn't like she would have the power here.

His loyalty to his brethren was the only thing keeping him from falling over the razor's edge of a treacherous cliff, however precarious his balance was. He owed them that much. So he would take this last mission. For them.

He didn't have to like it. He just had to finish this.

But once this was done, once the Halfling was secured, he was through. He'd go find this Maggie Michaels. He'd bring her back and leave her with Niklas or Xander, let one of their women take care of her. And then he'd end this pitiful excuse of an existence. He refused to return to Lucifer, whether the ruler of Hell would accept him back or not. And he feared if he stayed this course much longer that was exactly what would happen.

Oblivion—death for the soulless—was waiting for him, and he welcomed it with open arms. He refused to live another day longer than absolutely necessary, let alone another century unable to touch or be touched.

Oh, he'd go down like a warrior. He'd find the biggest, baddest nest he could, shimmer into the middle of it, and take out as many of the bastards as possible before he bit the big one. But he just refused to do this anymore.

He, more than anyone, knew you didn't have to be alone to be lonely.

Pushing a hand through his tangled hair, he heaved a defeated sigh. "Tell me where to find the Halfling."

****

Maggie took a sip from the cocktail in front of her as she listened to Gail complain about a particularly trying customer she'd had that day. An odd hum of energy buzzed through her veins. She did her best to ignore it and focus on the conversation. The small group of friends sat around a table in the corner of Angel's Fall, the popular nightclub they occasionally visited on their rare girls' nights out.

"Ugh! She sounds like the same woman who came into the bakery last week," Molly said, setting her cocktail aside. "Tall, painfully thin, short dark hair, pinched expression, fiftyish?"

Gail leaned forward, nodding. "Yes! That's her!"

"Some people," Molly grumbled, slurping on her Long Island Iced Tea.

"I know, right?" Gail agreed.

The conversation went on all around her, but Maggie struggled to follow along. Something felt…off. The fine hairs on the back of her neck all but stood at attention. Her nerves vibrated with a strange…awareness.

Sweet Mary, what is that?

Please don't be another angel. And please, please, please, don't let it be him again.

She gradually became aware she'd lost track of the conversation, jumping slightly when Cori leaned close. Her shoulder brushed Maggie's, and Cori hissed under her breath, "Mags, that tall guy over by the bar? The blond dressed all in black? He hasn't taken his sexy stare off this table for the last fifteen minutes. And, girl, I think he's been watching you!"

Maggie glanced over, a frown tugging at her brow. Who would stare at her of all people? And why?

As her gaze connected with his, she forgot how to breathe, her glass suspended halfway to her lips. She'd never seen this guy before. She sure as hell would remember if she had. He stood with an air of casual negligence, bracing one elbow against the bar, hip cocked, black biker boots crossed at the ankles. But there was an alertness in those stunning golden eyes. A watchfulness that said he'd already taken in every little detail around him, compartmentalized it, and dismissed anyone he deemed not as dangerous as himself.

In other words, everyone else in the bar.

And yet, just as Cori had noted, his glittering focus seemed fixed on Maggie.

Whipcord muscle gave definition to his tight black T-shirt and black leather pants. A pair of silver aviator sunglasses was tucked into the neck of his shirt. The lean muscles of his bare arms were encased in extensive tattoos. The guy was in his late twenties to early thirties, if she had to guess. His strong jaw and lean cheeks sported a golden five o'clock shadow, emphasizing the most alluring mouth she'd ever seen. Sensual, supple lips that curled up at the very edges. Just enough to make his grin seem a bit taunting, a little mocking and a whole lot sexy. His tawny hair was a little too long, a little too mussed, adding to his dangerous appeal.

But it was his eyes that drew her attention.

Probably because they appeared to be locked on her, following every move she made. That hard stare was pure amber. Striking. Hypnotic.

Seductive.

He was midnight fantasies, the promise of uninhibited sexual gratification and forbidden sin all rolled into one. Temptation incarnate from the top of his tawny head to the tips of his big bad boots. He could very well have been the reason the walk of shame was invented.

She forced a swallow, quickly glancing down and away. Heat flooded her checks. And that tiny vibration of awareness from earlier turned into a relentless hum in her blood.

"Is he still staring, Cori?" Maggie asked her friend, careful to keep her eyes downcast and her voice hushed.

"Yep," Cori replied, sounding a little too excited for Maggie's comfort.

"Is who staring?" Gail turned in her seat, craning her neck, as did Molly.

"Oh God! Don't look!" Maggie hissed, grabbing Gail's forearm, tugging at her. But Gail looked anyway. No, on second thought, she didn't look. She ogled.

"He is hawt!" Molly fanned herself, her wide-eyed attention glued on the guy. "And Cori's right. He's staring right at you, Maggie."

She couldn't help herself. Maggie glanced up again. He seared her with those unwavering eyes. He hadn't moved one of those luscious muscles. Now that she was finally looking at him, really looking, she'd expected him to break eye contact. That was, after all, a normal human reaction, even if only for a second. But he didn't. He just kept right on staring. He didn't even blink.

Something about him had her instincts firing, her nerve endings tingling. Grudgingly, hating every moment of this, hating the ability itself, she opened herself up, opened her senses as she focused on him, preparing herself for the worst as her friends chatted on around her, oblivious to her little *gift*.

A blankness met her probe. Emptiness. Like a hollow shell with just the glimmer of something she couldn't quite pinpoint.

Cocking her head, frowning, she focused harder. And still she came up puzzlingly empty-handed. She could sense neither good, nor evil in him. But neither was he a normal human.

He was…different. More.

But she couldn't tell what that more was.

One corner of his mouth tilted upward, and he tilted his head, as if he'd somehow sensed or felt what she was doing. She slammed her shields closed. Well, as closed as she ever could, which was to say not quite entirely. Not nearly as tight as she'd like. She dropped her focus to the glass in her hand, and she traced a bead of condensation.

Clearing her throat, she sat up straighter and adopted an uninterested expression. "Well, he is kind of…cute. But it doesn't matter. Brett and I went out on a date last Friday night, and I agreed to see him again tomorrow."

That's right, she reminded herself. *Think of Brett. Harmless, normal, very human Brett.* As far removed from that other world as a man could be.

"You only agreed to go out with Brett because he nagged you into it," Cecelia finally chimed in.

Cecelia was right. Brett, a lawyer, had worn her down, petitioning his case with dogged determination for three months. Even so, Maggie shot her a withering look. "Brett is perfectly fine."

"More like perfectly boring," Gail said, taking a drink as the other women in the group nodded and murmured agreement. "He is so not your type, Mags. You need someone with energy, someone with a…a zest for life. Someone who's gonna shove you up against the wall and steal passionate kisses. Not someone so full of himself he can't put anyone else first. Doesn't Brett irritate you? My goodness! The few times I've spoken with him, I've felt like I was in the jury box at one of his trials!"

"He's not like that," Maggie insisted. *Well, not all of the time.*

Okay! Okay, he is *like that, some of the time.*

Okay! Okay, most of the time.

"You should go over, say hi," Molly prompted. She peeped over her shoulder at the guy by the bar, then turned back to Maggie with a wide smile. "He looks like he has some experience with wall sex. Make sure you give him your number."

"I'm not going over. And I'm not giving a perfect stranger my phone number," Maggie said, staring hard at the table in front of her, willing herself not to look at him again. Willing herself to ignore the unbidden images of the sexy blond pushing her up against a wall, just as Cecelia had suggested. She wouldn't think of him like that. She wouldn't think of him at all. Even if he was the most attractive man she'd ever seen.

Ever.

Attractive men were trouble. And out of her

league.

This guy was so far out of her league he wasn't even playing the same sport.

Besides, she didn't like that she couldn't get a read on him.

"Well, if you're not going over," Cecelia said, pushing her chair back and rising from the table, a siren on a mission, "I will."

Maggie's jaw dropped on a protest, but she quickly clamped her mouth closed. After all, she'd more or less just told the group she wasn't interested. That she was seeing someone else. She didn't have any right to cry foul now that Cecelia had called dibs.

Still, she couldn't help but watch jealously as Cecelia sauntered across the bar, tossing her long blonde hair over her shoulder as she sidled up to Maggie's sexy admirer. Much as it rubbed her raw, Maggie couldn't look away while her friend spoke to the man. Cecelia then leaned close to him, revealing a generous amount of cleavage. She offered him a business card.

Only the man hadn't taken his eyes off Maggie. Not once.

An odd sense of intimacy was blooming between them, and Maggie became flustered. She'd never experienced anything like this before and didn't know what to do about it.

He subtly shifted away from Cecelia, intriguing Maggie despite herself. Seemingly with great effort, the man finally tore his gaze from Maggie long enough to smile at Cecelia. He said something, very brief and to the point. He refused Cecelia's offered business card. And then his attention was back on Maggie.

Implacable. Unwavering. Compelling.

She couldn't quite squash the tiny thrill when Cecelia turned away, a disappointed sulk on her beautiful mouth. She returned to their table alone.

"Looks like it's Maggie or nothing for Mr. Tall, Blond, and Sexy," Cecelia grumbled. She picked up her drink and took a big, irritated gulp.

Maggie's brows shot up, and her lips parted in shock, as did Gail's and Molly's. Cori, as she usually did whenever Cecelia didn't get her way, simply smirked. Theirs was a strange friendship. They knocked each other all the time, but let someone else do the knocking and blood would spill.

Maggie shook her head. Someone had shot Cecelia down? Over her? Inconceivable. Cecelia was every man's walking wet dream. No way would a healthy, red-blooded man pick Plain Jane Maggie over Blonde Bombshell Cecelia. There had to be something wrong with him.

Scraping her teeth over her bottom lip, she glanced up beneath lowered lashes. He'd shifted his weight to the other foot, and he had a bottle of beer in his hand now. But he still watched their table, watched her, causing a strange insidious warmth to spread through her body, at once making her feel both edgy with attraction, and yet protected. As if he was a sentinel standing guard over her.

Baffling.

Frowning, she struggled to focus on the conversation that had resumed around her, making what she hoped would pass for appropriate sounds when necessary. She didn't look his way again, no matter how badly she wanted to, and he never approached the table. But she could feel the weight of that amber stare like a physical caress. Once her friends decided to call it a night, while Maggie gathered up her own purse and jacket, she finally risked a glance, unable to stop herself.

He was gone.

Disappointment slid through her. She tried to tell herself it didn't matter. She was dating somebody else already. And Brett was fine.

Perfectly fine.

Right?

Yet, she couldn't quite shake the memory of that entrancing amber stare.

Chapter Two

Gideon sucked in a cool breath of night air as he faded into the shadows across the street from a swank little nightclub nestled in the heart of Portland aptly named Angel's Fall. His gaze lingered on the door as he waited for Maggie Michaels to exit the building. He'd found her at the middle school where she taught, per Sebastian's intel. He'd then followed her home, to a little bungalow style house in the suburbs. And then he'd followed her here.

He'd slipped inside to keep a better eye on her. At first, he hadn't meant for her to see him. But then he figured, *what the hell?* He was going to have to get the cuff in his pocket locked on her wrist, wasn't he? Sooner or later she was going to have to see him.

Might as well make it sooner.

Besides, it wasn't as if she appeared to be cautious of strangers. Oh no, quite the opposite, in fact. Everybody was her bloody friend, as far as he could tell. On her convoluted route to Angel's Fall, he'd watched as she'd dropped off a couple boxes of groceries at a shelter for battered women. She'd walked around the shelter for nearly an hour, touching this person or that, holding babies and playing with kids, leaving calm, smiling people in her wake.

He'd also witnessed her giving money to three different homeless men on the street. Homeless men, he might add, with whom she seemed perfectly comfortable enjoying idle conversation. It was the do-gooder angel blood in her, he supposed with a disgusted shake of his head. How the hell was he supposed to ensure the safety of someone who petted every stray and fed every homeless person she came across with no regard for her own safety?

Once she'd arrived at Angel's Fall, she'd sat at a table of women with whom she laughed and seemed to have a good time. At least, she had until she'd realized he was watching her. After that she'd been subdued, her captivating smile rarely making another appearance. He'd caught her sneaking a covert glance his way now and again. He wouldn't let himself think about those pretty, innocent eyes of hers. They would only make him want. And wanting led to bitterness, bitterness to anger, and anger unleashed the beast within. Because no matter how badly he might want her, he could never have her.

Not that he'd allow himself to want her. She was a Halfling. And not just any Halfling. She was Michael's daughter, by the love of all that was holy.

Michael's daughter!

She had the same stubborn tilt to her chin with the same tiny indentation that her father had, though her jaw line was decidedly more feminine, softer. Her eye and hair color were the same. The patrician nose was similar, but the slash of her eyebrows and the angle of her cheeks were different from Michael's, giving her a definite look all her own. Gentle. Alluring.

Confusion swirled in his gut. To be so attracted to her, to the Halfling, was wrong.

Michael's daughter! kept whispering through his

head from the moment he'd first spotted her. Just from the look of her, there was no doubt anymore. And yet, the tug of unwanted attraction was still there. Unsettling.

She'd nursed the same cocktail all night while her friends had ordered drink after drink after drink. She'd politely declined an offer to dance with some polished creep in dress slacks and a dress shirt, sans the tie, sleeves rolled up to his elbows. Gideon didn't like the guy on sight. Didn't know why, didn't care. Quite honestly, he entertained a brief fantasy that involved his fist and that guy's gleaming white teeth. All on Michael's behalf, he tried to assure himself.

Liar.

But just as quickly as it occurred to him to punch the guy out, he shot it down with a frustrated growl. That same curse that interfered with his ability to touch a woman also inhibited his ability to reach out and touch that bastard too, no matter how badly that bastard needed touching.

Then again, Gideon reflected, he hadn't fed in quite some time. Feeding was the only way he could have physical contact with a human while in this form, his palm centered over a human's chest as he sucked the soul from their body. Granted, that poor excuse for a sensation of touch wasn't quite the same and lasted a matter of minutes, but it was all he'd had for longer than he liked to think about.

Gideon reserved the privilege of being his food for those truly deserving of such a gruesome and painful death. Murderers, pedophiles, rapists, thieves. Those who would otherwise escape punishment for their crimes. He'd never preyed on the innocent. Not even now, after having finally given up the good fight, after losing his faith, would he stoop that low. That was a line his own honor wouldn't let him cross, no matter the personal cost.

At least, he usually limited his feedings to those humans filled with such evil they deserved an expedited trip to Hell. But that guy who'd asked Maggie to dance had continued to watch her even after she'd declined. The only thing that stopped Gideon from luring him into the alley behind the nightclub was the fact that the bastard had eventually turned his sights elsewhere.

As soon as Gideon saw Maggie and her friends gathering up their belongings, he'd beat feet outside, wanting to trail her without her knowledge. It'd be easier—though he wasn't sure how he was going to go about it just yet—to get that cuff on her wrist while she was alone, not surrounded by a gaggle of women. One thing he'd learned early on while under Lucifer's thumb? Gather as much intel as you could about your chosen target before you made your move. Learn their regular haunts, figure out their patterns. Surprise was often a risk you couldn't afford. And Gideon, the strategist, was never taken by surprise.

The door opened again. Maggie's group of friends began spilling outside. He scanned the pack, but he didn't see her. His unease grew as he watched the women totter into waiting cabs and disperse.

And still no Maggie.

Where the hell is she?

"Damn it," he hissed beneath his breath. He hadn't sensed any demon presence inside Angel's Fall. That didn't mean one couldn't have been there, concealing himself somehow.

Christ on a crutch.

He'd let himself become distracted. By her. He knew better.

Gideon straightened from where he leaned against the brick wall, intent on crossing the street and storming back inside after her. The air just to the side of the nightclub's doorway began to waver. Gideon darted back into the shadows. Three demons solidified. He couldn't tell what species, given they were all in human form, but it didn't matter much. Demon was demon. All that *did* matter was the fact they were standing between him and the Halfling he was supposed to be guarding.

Gideon licked his lips. Did he dare shimmer inside and risk someone seeing him? Did he risk leaving a shimmer trail?

Hell, what did a shimmer trail matter? The raw power the Halfling exuded would probably overwhelm it anyway. The moment he'd walked inside the bar, he'd known she was there. Had felt her power like a shower of electrical sparks over his skin. They would feel it too. The only thing a shimmer trail would do was speed their efforts to find her before someone else got their hands on her.

The demons were now entering the club. By their serious expressions, he'd be willing to bet they were there on a mission and not just out for a little action.

A mission named Maggie Michaels.

One of the demons paused, there on the threshold, his malevolent grin growing wide. Gideon would bet his guard stone encrusted Rolex the bastard had already sensed her.

Screw it. Centering his focus, he visualized the dark hallway that led to the restrooms. The shadows around him, the rough brick wall at his back, the filthy concrete beneath his boots, the cool night air blurred, faded away and were replaced by the scent of expensive booze, cloying perfume, sweating humans, and cheap disinfectant cleaners. Hardwood beneath his boots steadied him. Corrugated steel walls appeared on either side of him, a long dark hallway that led to restrooms on one end, and a loud, packed dance floor on the other. No one screamed or shouted in alarm when he solidified. Aside from himself, the hallway was empty.

Gideon darted to the end of the hall nearest the dance floor, and scanned the bobbing heads, scanning faces in the crowd. As tall as he was, with the sunken dance floor, it wasn't difficult to see the whole room at a glance. The group of demons stood near the front door, scanning the dance floor as well. On the plus side, they hadn't found her yet either. On the other hand, where they were standing, they were far more likely to catch her first as she'd have to pass by them in order to leave the building.

He didn't want to draw their attention, at least, not if he could help it. While he would relish the chance to wipe the floor with them, there were far too many innocents in the direct line of fire. He might have an acknowledged death wish, but that didn't mean he was willing to take a bunch of unsuspecting, innocent humans with him.

He debated his best plan of action, his mind quickly and without conscious effort calculating the best odds for success in each scenario. Bottom line, he had to go out there, weave through the crowd without letting anyone realize they weren't actually touching him, even though it looked as if they should be, and find her before those demons did. He cursed Sebastian to Hell and back for asking him to do this.

"Um, excuse me?" A soft, feminine voice drew his attention.

He froze for a split second, then turned as the hint of cinnamon and vanilla wafted closer. His eyebrows shot up, and he grinned wide. He couldn't believe his luck.

"Oh, it's you," Maggie Michaels whispered, a becoming blush flooding her cheeks beneath the pulsing neon glow of the dance floor lights.

Despite the mad swirl of color and strobe of lights, a heavy dusting of freckles along the bridge of her nose and across the upper ridges of her cheeks was clearly visible. Her eyes were a blue-green, not quite one color, not quite the other, but a beautiful combination of the two. Like tropical waters. Crystal clear and alluring.

Her lips looked soft as the petals of a flower, and just as delicate. He could so easily see himself partaking of that mouth. Over and over. Imbibing until he was completely intoxicated with the taste of her. She was not tall, stick thin runway supermodel. No cool, touch-me-not waif. She was nose level with his sternum, though given his own height, that didn't exactly make her short. And her curves were lush. Warm and inviting. And very, very womanly. His entire body seized with raw lust.

Her gaze dropped, and she cleared her throat. He realized he was staring. And that he hadn't moved an inch. And that a jolt of lust had just sucker punched him in the gut, hard, catching him by surprise.

Holy hell! He sucked in a sharp breath and dragged his gaze upward, staring blindly at the ceiling.

Michael's daughter!

The reminder didn't seem to be helping.

And the burning need in his gut seemed to be growing with every inhalation of her delicious scent.

She stepped to the side, nodding toward the front of the club. "Excuse me. I was just, um, going that way."

But as she said the last, her gaze drifted past his arm, and a frown knitted her brow. She tilted her head, staring hard at something, at someone, out there in the crowd behind him. A surge of power shot from her. Much the same as the one he'd sensed earlier when she'd stared like that at him. What was she doing? He glanced over his shoulder before peering back down at her. Her brow furrowed deeper as the power surge coming from her ceased, though he could still sense a glimmer of it resonating around her. If he could sense her power, would those other three demons also feel it? The Halfling looked alarmed, and more than a little green around the gills.

"What's wrong?" His eyes narrowed suspiciously.

Could she somehow sense the demons? Was that what the power surge was? Did her angelic blood somehow clue her in to what they were? And if so, why then couldn't she realize he was as they were—demon? Why didn't she seem to fear him?

"Ah, nothing." She shook her head and offered him a very wide, obviously fake smile. "Nothing's wrong."

He didn't need Xander the walking lie detector to tell him she was lying through her pearly whites. Xander, the Demon Slayer, had once described his curse as feeling like a thousand spiders were crawling over his skin when a lie was told, no matter how small or inconsequential. Creepy. Still not as bad as Gideon's own curse, but creepy as hell all the same.

Her panic was palpable, her focus darting over the club walls, high up, stopping when she spied the glowing exit sign on the far side of the dance floor. Her expression fell as she glanced back toward the demons that'd now fanned out and were sweeping through the dancers. Squarely between her and all the exits. She looked like a cornered rabbit.

"I hate to call a lady a liar, but I'd have to be blind, deaf, and dumb as a doorknob not to see something's bothering you."

She licked her bottom lip and then little white teeth began to gnaw on the plump pink flesh. His nostrils flared, and his brow drew together as his groin grew painfully tight in response.

"I, um…" She glanced over her shoulder. No exit there, either. "I just realized I need to go, I mean leave. I need to leave. Go home," she stammered.

She searched his face then, assessing and shrewd. He could see the wheels grinding away in that pretty little head of hers. She glanced past him once more, then quickly stepped to the side so that his large frame effectively shielded her, blocking her from anyone who might look this way from the dance floor.

"And there's somebody out there you don't want to see when you leave." He raised his voice just enough there at the end so she could take it as a statement or a question.

"Yes," she admitted, smiling at him in a relieved sort of way.

"So who are we avoiding?" he asked, deliberately making them a team, hoping to build her trust by inserting himself into her situation as a coconspirator. Turning his head, he scanned the crowd as if he didn't already know the answer.

"See that guy over by the Budweiser sign? The bald one with the denim jacket?" Gideon nodded. "And the one over by the exit sign? Blue hair and green ripped T-shirt?" She went on, her tone reluctant and embarrassed. Lifting a brow, Gideon turned his head to look at the second demon before nodding. She hesitated a moment longer before adding, "And the guy with the sunglasses and long blond hair, yellow shirt, by the front door?"

Damn, she'd pegged all three of them. He began to wonder what other little gifts her angelic blood had given her.

"Three?" He injected a note of incredulity into his tone and watched the color in her cheeks darken. "I'm thinkin' it's a good thing I decided not to ask you to dance after all. You seem to make a habit of leavin' a trail of broken hearts in your wake." He didn't know why he was messing with her like this, but he couldn't seem to help himself.

"Oh, it's not like that at all!" the Halfling blurted, then seemed to catch herself. "I mean, ah…"

"It's okay." He relented, grinning. "I'll get you out of here without them seeing you. Trust me?"

She stared up at him, long and hard, her brow furrowed. As if she was trying to read the secrets of his soul. Again, power surged around her, so strong he feared Stolas's minions would home in on her. Tilting her head, her lips slightly parted, she drew a deep breath.

"You're dangerous," she murmured. "But you

don't intend to cause me harm." Then, louder, she added, "Yes, I trust you."

"I have one little stipulation." That had been rule number two. Find what your target needed and use it as a bargaining tool. Asher wasn't the only one with a corner on that market. Tempt them with what they wanted most. But hold it just out of reach until they were willing to do anything you wanted, anything you asked to get what they needed. He'd always been one ruthless SOB, willing to fight dirty to get the job done and done well.

Smiling now, feeling like the proverbial wolf in sheepskin, he reached into his pocket and pulled out the cuff, regarding her suspicious expression with something akin to dark amusement. This was too easy. Dangling the cuff by the tip of one finger to minimize the chance for her to touch—or rather, not touch—him, he said, "You have to accept this."

Her eyebrows shot upward as she stared at his offering. "I don't understand." She shook her head, clearly confused. "You want me to accept your bracelet, in exchange for you helping me to slip by the…ah, by them."

"Yep." He let the breath he realized he'd been holding seep out slowly, unobtrusively.

"But—"

"Better hurry," he interrupted, feigning a glance over his shoulder. While he could still sense the demonic presence in the building, and he could feel they were moving around, he could also tell they were not moving closer. Yet. "They could head this way any minute."

She caught the tip of her thumbnail between her

teeth for a moment, indecision etched on her face. Gideon wiggled his finger, sending the silver cuff swaying like a pendulum before her eyes, silver glinting in the strobe lights from behind him.

"Okay." She capitulated, her expression stating that he should be checking himself into the nearest psych unit. Then something behind him caught her attention and she quickly added, "But you have to understand this—the jewelry—it doesn't mean anything. I have a boyfriend."

Gideon didn't say anything, but he couldn't help gritting his teeth. For some reason, the idea of another man claiming her didn't sit all that well with him. Another man caressing her perfect skin, molding that delectable flesh with his hands, tasting those luscious lips—

The beast living inside him, just beneath his skin, rose up and snarled. Gideon schooled his features and took a calming breath, reminding himself this was a mission. His last mission. And then? Oblivion. He had no business caring one way or the other who touched or kissed her.

Let her father worry about her. That rat bastard Michael. The being who'd taken Gideon's fall as a personal betrayal. The being who'd sworn to end Gideon no matter the cost.

The being who'd once been Gideon's best friend.

"Do you accept the cuff?" he pressed, pushing the past aside. Last mission, he reminded himself. The sooner he got this over with, the sooner he could end his suffering.

Frowning, she met his gaze as she reached for it. "Yes."

He lifted the cuff a few inches higher, eluding her grasp. "Willingly?"

Now she regarded him as if he'd flat out lost his mind. Like she was beginning to have second thoughts. She even glanced at the dance floor again, as if to gauge her chances of ditching him and slipping out on her own. But the exits were still covered.

Frowning, she reached again. "Willingly," she added, her voice an odd mix of resignation and determination.

Cocking his head, he lowered the cuff within her reach. Taking the silver in her hands, she fingered the hammered metal, running the pad of her thumb over the carvings.

"What does this say?" But as she glanced up in expectation of an answer, her attention swerved to his side. "Oh, crap. Here they come! Your turn," she blurted. "How do we get out of here?"

"Put it on," he prompted.

"They're coming!"

"Put it on," he urged.

"Oh, for the love of—" She snapped the cuff onto her wrist, then held it up and shook it so he could see she'd complied. "There. Happy now?" But her exasperation quickly turned to a frown as she examined the cuff more closely and realized there was no way to release it. "Hey, how does this come off?"

His grin grew far more wicked than it had any right to be. "It doesn't."

Her mouth fell open. Alarm flooded her pretty features. Gideon chuckled. Pulling in his power, focusing his energy, he visualized the kitchen in Sebastian's farmhouse.

47

Chapter Three

A piercing scream nearly shattered his eardrums. Gideon cringed, his gaze darting to the pale, shaking woman a few feet away.

"Well, damn! It actually worked." Bemused, he held the cuff on his own wrist up in wonder.

A flash of movement at the edge of his peripheral vision was the only warning he got. A split second later, he ducked as a toaster went sailing past his head. The small appliance no more than crashed into the cupboard behind him, clattering loudly to the floor, before the coffee pot followed. Dodging the latest missile, he moved to the side, tracking his charge.

Maggie dug through drawers and doors, yanking out whatever came to hand, throwing it at Gideon with all her might.

"What did you do to me?" she shouted. A handful of cooking utensils rained down upon his head and shoulders as he ducked behind a kitchen chair. A coffee mug, blessedly empty, soon followed, shattering on the floor beside him. "Where am I? How did you get me here?"

"Now, just calm down—"

A large butcher's blade imbedded itself in the cabinet door near his head with a resounding thud. "Don't you dare tell me to calm down! Where am I?" she yelled as she grabbed hold of a frying pan and let it fly. It clipped his shoulder. Her aim was improving.

This shit was so not what he'd signed up for.

"Sebastian!" he yelled at the top of his lungs. "You rotten bastard, get down here!" He dodged a cutting board, batting it aside with his forearm. That was going to leave a bruise. Couldn't the Demon of Vengeance hear Maggie destroying his kitchen? Where the hell was he?

Pulling his phone from his back pocket, trying semi-successfully to stay out of her line of fire, he punched in Sebastian's speed dial number. It went straight to voicemail. The bastard. He'd done this on purpose.

He tried Mikhail next. Also voicemail. He hadn't really expected anything else, but he was desperate and had to give it a try.

He thumbed in Xander's number, and he waited, tense and alert for the next projectile. A drawer was jerked out so hard it crashed to the floor, and all the while, she aimed a furious verbal tirade at his head.

"Yeah?" The crackle and hiss of plasma balls echoed over the phone line, mingling with Xander's ragged breathing.

"I have the Halfling." A spatula slapped his cheek. "Son of a—"

"You want a medal?" Xander's harsh voice rasped over the line.

Asshole. "I want somebody to come get her. We're at the farm, but Sebastian isn't here."

"I'm busy," Xander snapped. A second later, a loud explosion on Xander's end caused Gideon to jerk the phone from his ear for a moment.

"But—"

"Got a shitstorm going on here. You actually need something, or d'you just call to whine?"

"Look, where's Kyanna? I'll take the Halfling to her and—"

"No!"

"Why the hell not?"

"Every demon tied to this rebellion is going to be gunning for that Halfling. Probably any angel that catches wind of her existence too. You are *not* bringing that danger to my woman's door. No."

The line went dead.

Despite the fact that Kyanna herself was a Guardian of one of the Sacred Relics, experienced in the ways of angelic enchantments and all manner of mystical protections, Xander, the Demon Slayer, guarded her more fiercely than a mother bear with a lone cub. If Xander had hidden Kyanna away, you'd have better luck stumbling over the Crown Jewels on display at a sidewalk sale.

He knew then and there it'd be useless to call Niklas to ask for Carly's help. Niklas was every bit as protective of his own mate as Xander was his. Dammit.

Desperation clawed at him. He tried Sebastian's phone one more time.

"Yo."

"Where the hell are you?"

"On my way to Great Falls, Michigan. The last lead was a bust." The bastard sounded perturbed. Good.

Gideon snarled. "Why aren't you here?"

"Still chasing after the new Guardian. Got a fresh lead," Sebastian said.

He didn't give two shits about some new Guardian of the Sword of Kathnesh. The sword was a lost cause.

The old Guardian hadn't done his job. The new Guardian didn't even have anything to guard. Gideon already had the Halfling, for the love of Saint Peter. Capturing her had been shockingly easy, thanks to the three demons that'd shown up at the nightclub. Granted, she was currently off the rails and desperately needed subduing. Something he couldn't do, compliments of his curse. He needed help. Now. "I have the Halfling. We're at the farm. You need to come take care of her."

Crouched behind the table, Gideon raked a hand through his hair. To hell with his so-called brothers and their fickle loyalty. What had he done to deserve this? A series of plates shattered against the countertop beside him. Gideon scooted out of the way, swearing beneath his breath as shards of broken dishes rained down upon him.

"What the hell was that?" Sebastian barked. "Dude! Did you let some demon follow you to my place?"

"That was the Halfling. She's renovating your kitchen. Next we're moving to the living room. I'm sure she'd love to use your flat screen rather than my head as a target."

"Harsh, dude. Harsh. Why is she tearing my kitchen apart?"

"Because I shimmered her without warning her first and she's not too happy with me."

"So pour on some of that legendary charm of yours and save what's left of my kitchen, man."

"Kind of hard to pour on the charm," Gideon growled, "when every time I show my face, she tries smashing something into it."

Raucous laughter poured through the line.

51

"Glad to hear you find this so amusing. I wasn't kidding about that TV, you know?"

Sebastian's mirth slowly wound down. "It'd be worth it! Finally, a woman who hasn't fallen under your spell."

"Glad you're so fond of her. Here's an idea. Get your ass home and *you* take care of her."

"Can't." The sound of a plastic wrapper crinkled over the line. "I'm closing in on the professor. I think I finally pinned her down. Call Niklas or Xander."

"Tried. They don't want her in the same state as Kyanna or Carly. Worried she'll draw too much heat."

"They're probably right."

"That's helpful," Gideon snapped through gritted teeth.

"Careful." Sebastian chuckled. "You're going to give Xander a run for his money as the reigning king of sarcasm at that rate. Look, you're just going to have to deal with her for a little while longer. Take her back to your place and keep her under wraps for a bit."

"Yeah, so she can wreck my stuff?" Never mind that he'd already wrecked it.

"Tie her up," Sebastian suggested unhelpfully.

Actually...

Gideon found the idea very appealing. More appealing than it should be. For far more reasons than protecting his home from her propensity to throw things.

"Look, dude, I gotta go. I'll call when I have more information. Have fun."

Gideon opened his mouth to protest, but the phone went dead before he could utter a sound.

Gideon glanced down at the phone in his hand and,

growling, he struggled not to crush the slim device in his fist. That selfish, rotten, no-good, Garnoch-kissing bastard.

His anger at Xander and the others over abandoning him in his time of need distracted him. The sharp corner of something clipped his shoulder. Damn it, she'd drawn blood that time. Granted, the wound was shallow and would be gone in less than a few minutes, but still, she'd drawn blood.

Gideon scuttled to his left and pulled one of the ladder-backed chairs in front of him as a shield. He ground his teeth together. This was ridiculous. Women didn't throw things at him. Well, unless it was intimate articles of clothing. Or themselves. His gaze skimmed her womanly body through the slats, and he began to wonder what kind of intimate undergarments she might choose for herself. She looked like a lace kind of girl. All sugar and spice. Black lace for sure. Maybe a little more spice than sugar.

Hmm...

Shocked by the very real tremors of the first true, burning lust he'd felt in longer than he cared to consider, Gideon berated himself.

No! Don't go there. Not like you can do anything about it anyway. This is the last mission, remember? Then Oblivion. Focus!

Nettled frustration began to worm its way through his system. Frustration and no small amount of desperation. Not because he wanted her—wanted her as he hadn't wanted another woman in...well, ever...wanted her more than he dared to admit even to himself—but because she was proving to be an aggravating, royal pain in the ass. Yeah, that was what had him frustrated, he assured himself, striving to ignore the thread of desperation worming its way through his system. She was a pain in the ass. Women didn't throw cookware at him. Women loved him.

At least, they used to. Before he'd been cursed. And even after that, they'd still flirted outrageously with him, thrown themselves at him, though he was ever vigilant to never let them touch him—or not touch, as it were.

So maybe she had a right to be irate with him. He'd never shimmered a woman anywhere before. A tiny part of him suffered a sliver of guilt. Kyanna and Carly both had complained about the sensations shimmering caused. And he hadn't warned Maggie about what he intended to do at all. How had he expected her to react?

A whisk whizzed past his ear. "What the hell are you?"

Sweet Christ! How many kitchen doodads did Sebastian seriously need? She was bound to run out of ammunition sooner or later…wasn't she?

He heard another drawer rattle open. A handful of forks rained down upon his head, followed by spoons and butter knives.

All right. Enough was enough. He was a demon—a former general in Lucifer's army, no less—not some spineless Charocté. He didn't cower from anyone, especially not some tiny human female that didn't even come up to his chin.

Pushing to his full height, he scowled and pointed a finger at her. "Damn it! Stop throwing things at me," he thundered.

He might have once been a legendary seducer, tempting even the most stalwart and pious with their darkest desires, but he could also be one scary SOB when he wanted. Usually he reserved this dangerous, dark side of his temper for others of his kind, but she'd hit the limits of his patience. She was bringing his wrath down on her own head, damn it.

"Screw you." A rolling pin smacked against the center of his chest hard enough to leave another bruise. He gasped in shock. In outrage. Demons trembled in the face of his wrath. He couldn't wrap his mind around her reactions to him. Her resistance. Her rebellion.

Her pupils had dilated, and he could sense her fear, but she hadn't backed down. Not one tiny bit.

Admiration swelled inside him. Brave girl.

No! Foolish girl, he corrected. He could not afford to soften toward her. *Foolish!*

"Calm down—don't throw that!" He ducked as a hand mixer crashed into the cupboard behind him. "Give me a few minutes, I can explain."

She paused then, chest heaving, shoulder length brown hair straggling from her lopsided ponytail, beguiling eyes wild and wide, clutching another large knife ominously in her raised fist.

Dear God, she is so damned sexy!

No! Do. Not. Go. There!

"You have two minutes." She patted at her back pocket with her free hand before pulling out a slim cell phone. Her thumb hovered over a button. "Then I'm calling the police."

Oh, to hell with this. Focusing, he visualized the kitchen of his plantation. Then, glancing around at the havoc she'd created, he changed his mind, instead visualizing his den.

Heat swelled in his chest, power coalesced. His

surroundings blurred, falling away, and were soon replaced with familiar furnishings. The massive stone fireplace on the far wall, with a modern flat screen TV above it. Shelves and shelves of old books running the length of one wall. His big mahogany desk. Everything was in place in his den, clean and organized.

Hmm. His path of destruction must not have reached this room yet.

But he didn't stop there, didn't pause. He conjured ropes and darted close to her the moment Maggie solidified. Close enough to intimidate her while she was already disoriented, so close she instinctively stepped back to get away from him. Her face was chalky white, and she gasped, blinking as she tumbled onto the chair behind her. And then she was screaming again. Dazed as she was, he made short work of relieving her of the knife she'd still been clutching, as well as her cell phone, and tied her wrists and ankles to the chair, careful as always not to let his hands brush her skin.

She was already freaked out enough as it was. Imagine how she'd react when she realized his hands could ghost right through her.

Stepping back, he reached over and turned on the lamp. Soft golden light flooded the immediate area, leaving the far corners, the bookshelves and the fireplace in the shadows. And all the while, her shrill screams echoed inside the room, ringing in his ears.

Prowling around her, he stepped close to the back of her chair and bent near her ear. The scent of her, cinnamon and vanilla, made his mouth water. The heat of her skin tempted him as nothing else could. Her ponytail had come undone, and the warm brown tresses tumbled around her shoulders now. Unable to help himself, he reached out to skim the backs of his fingers over her hair, but quickly drew back at the last moment, knowing it would only torment him.

Seeing his hand against her hair, but not being able to feel the warmth, the silken texture, it was just too cruel.

"Stop screaming or I'll gag you as well. There's no one here to hear you anyway," he growled.

The scream quickly morphed into less than helpful—and physically difficult, if not completely impossible—suggestions. He shook his head, conjured a gag, and stuffed it into her mouth. He tied it behind her head, extra careful not to let his fingers come in contact with those tempting strands.

After pulling out the matching chair in front of his desk and spinning it around to straddle it, Gideon sat facing her. That brilliant, furious aquamarine glare cut him to ribbons.

He crossed his arms along the back of the chair and pinned her with a steely gaze. "Do you know who your father is?"

Confusion and panic blinked through her angry eyes, quickly stifled as she turned her stony stare to a point just beyond his shoulder.

He waited a beat, two. Yet she refused to acknowledge him.

"I asked you a question. Do you know who your father is?"

She finally turned back to him and began a heated, if muffled tirade of mumbled syllables through the gag. Her pitch and tone rose and fell on her garbled end of the conversation.

Gideon looked on, utterly fascinated, as her angry

tirade transformed into disgusted disbelief. She rolled her eyes and shook her head, all the while spewing a grumbling verbal barrage at him. Then the disbelief was gone, and once more, anger held sway and her words became a furious snarl through the gag. He waited until she wound down, then reached out and tugged the material from her mouth, letting it sag around her slender, tempting throat.

He waited, watching her in silence as his body vibrated with pure lust.

What. A. Woman.

A muscle in her jaw clenched as she glared holes clean through his hide. At last, she spoke, her voice filled with contempt. "Did that bastard send you?"

****

Stolas looked on in disgust and cursed the Fallen once more. The Halfling writhed in agony on the floor of the cell in his dungeon in a pool of her own blood. Every scream, every convulsion of her body caused the fury inside him to build until he felt the need to crush something, anything. Another Halfling dead, or as good as. Another setback in his plot to overthrow Lucifer.

Why weren't they strong enough? Why did they continue to fail him? A female's primary capacity—after a male's pleasure, of course—was to bear spawn, wasn't it? Why, then, did they keep hemorrhaging shortly after impregnation?

He snarled his disgust at the female as she began to pale, the flush of pain and fever fading to the translucence of death. The convulsions continued to rip at her body, but she didn't even try to fight them any longer. Her cries grew weaker, until she barely made the slightest whimper.

He'd given up on healing the Halflings. Subsequent pregnancies always ended the same way, so why waste the energy? If she wasn't strong enough the first time, she wouldn't be game for a second try, much less a third, thereby rendering her useless.

That he was forced to rely on these weaklings to accomplish his goal, to attain his birthright, was debasing. But he couldn't get his hands on the Chosen One without a Halfling. And so he was forced to deal with this, forced to sift through Halfling after Halfling until he found one strong enough to bear demon seed to fruition.

Turning away, fists clenched at his sides, he stalked down the long, dim, stone corridor lined on either side with cells. He stopped at the third on the left and let his gaze travel over the bedraggled creature crouching in the corner. A third generation Halfling, he'd been told when she'd first been brought to him. Long, matted hair straggled down her back and shoulders, partially concealing a narrow, pinched face. Her clothing was torn and filthy.

When she'd first been captured, her birdlike gaze had darted this way and that, intelligence lurking in its pale green depths. She'd displayed a will to live, a fighting spirit that had kindled a spark of hope in his breast. Oh yes, she'd given him hope. Perhaps, young as she was, possessed of the nature to fight as she was, she would be the one to bear the Chosen One.

But she'd proven as useless as all the rest. Even now she cowered, nearly comatose, her gaze dull as she stared at nothing. Though she'd lasted longer than the others, he didn't have much hope for this one anymore either. She'd been here almost a full four months so far and had failed to breed.

Unable to find a first generation Halfling, he was growing desperate. Even so, he was too angry over the last Halfling's failure to even contemplate mating this one again. Not now. In this state, he was just as likely to kill her as get her with spawn. Another lesson he'd learned the hard way. Halflings were a fragile lot. And they were getting harder and harder to find.

He shimmered to the sanctuary of his great hall, took a seat at the head of the long, onyx table, and summoned a Charocté from one of the shadowed corners with a flick of his wrist. The servant scurried forth and bowed in submission. It summoned a decadent feast before him, then dropped to its knees a few feet from the table, arms crossed over its chest, fists pressed to shoulders, head lowered, all but prostrate as it awaited Stolas's pleasure.

Stolas lifted the goblet to his lips, his mood too dour to savor the vintage of the blood therein. He toyed with the steak, watching the blood pool on the silver platter. The bread tasted of ash. The aged, hard cheese tasted of ash. The meat tasted of ash. Even the blood. All ashes in his mouth.

He leaned to the side, and propped his chin on his fist, as he glanced at the still kneeling Charocté. With Ronové's demise, he'd been forced to enlist another demon capable of summoning him to Earth's plane. A task easier said than done, but he couldn't leave the bowels of Hell without the ritual being performed. The curse of his lineage. The problem was it took time to amass the necessary followers, time to build an earthbound nest stable enough to perform the rituals.

Time he did not have.

He cringed every time he was forced to bring another demon into his circle. But the Fallen were picking his minions off like flies. And it rubbed him raw—powerful as he was—having to rely on others to perform certain crucial tasks.

He longed to summon the Sword of Kathnesh to him, longed to hold it in his own hand, just once, just to feel the power radiating from it. He wanted to witness the blade with his own eyes, the blade that would set him free and make him ruler of all.

But he didn't dare. Couldn't risk having the blade anywhere near him lest Lucifer suspect him of such foul treachery. Nor would he risk bringing the sword out in the open, not even for his own peace of mind. It was safely tucked away, still under his control, but just out of his reach. He would have to content himself with that.

Especially now that the Fallen had stolen the Arc Stone out from under his nose. Now he had no choice but to press his timetable forward. The pressure to find the other relics was mounting, and time was running out. The longer it took for him to collect the relics, the greater the risk of discovery. Without interference from the Fallen, he would have been able to continue his search with none the wiser.

Now? Now it felt as if his every move were being broadcast across the realms.

Just the reminder of that cursed bunch of traitors made his blood boil. He motioned toward the Charocté with two fingers and watched as it fell, writhing on the floor, its features contorting in hideous pain. He flicked his fingers this way and that, like a metronome. The servant flopped about on the floor, its mouth stretched

61

wide as its screams filled the air.

Stolas sighed. *Why is begetting one offspring so difficult?*

Blood welled in the Charocté's eyes, gushed from its mouth. A slash of Stolas's hand caused bones to snap and skin to rupture. Bored, he waved his hand again, and the Charocté erupted in flames, eventually disintegrating in ashes.

More ashes. How I despise ashes.

He'd been born of this realm. Born to fire and brimstone. Born to ashes and searing heat. But the stories his minions had brought back of Earth fueled his determination. A color called green. He wanted to see it with his own eyes. Trees with actual leaves. Waters that ran cold and smelled pleasant, not stagnant, sulfurous pools that boiled flesh from bone. And things called snow and ice. Rumored to be so cold they could freeze a living thing dead.

Just imagine the sheer decadence of that!

Nothing would stop him. He would feel snow upon his skin. He would bury his enemies beneath a mountain of it.

Chapter Four

When her captor didn't immediately reply, Maggie turned her face to the wall, determined not to give an inch. If the sperm donor thought this abduction was going to scare her into submission he had another thing coming.

"Well, that saves a bit of time then," her abductor said in his honey-smooth Southern drawl, his amber stare drilling into her, searching, she was sure, for the slightest hint of weakness. From the periphery of her vision, she watched him as he tilted his head—only a fool took her attention off her enemy.

"Do you know *what* your father is?" he pressed.

She snapped her teeth together, gritting them in a desperate bid for control. She would not shout that Michael was *not* her father. A father was someone who was there for you when you needed him. Someone to teach you to swim and ride a bike. Someone to scare away the nightmares and to hold you in his arms when it stormed. Someone who told you he loved you no matter what.

A father didn't show up out of the blue the day of your twenty-first birthday to tell you that you were different.

Not special. Not precious. Not loved.

Just different.

He didn't place his hand upon your head and

Brenda Huber

"unlock your special gifts", as he so magnanimously decreed. Well, his gifts had turned out to be curses, as far as she was concerned. What good were random visions of the future when you couldn't change them? What good was a sixth sense, the ability to identify those who meant her harm, if it didn't also include a way for her to fight them off or escape should they capture her?

Like right now.

And a father did not resort to scare tactics like this.

"Have you met him? Spoken to him?" That honeyed drawl came once more.

The sperm donor's henchman could press for answers all he wanted. She was a clam. She wouldn't talk. She bit back a mocking laugh as she heard the henchman draw a deep breath, as if he was seeking patience. Well, he'd better have an endless well of it, because she had nothing to say to Michael or any of his cronies, no matter how attractive they might be.

"You noticed those three demons at the nightclub right away, didn't you?" So he wanted to change tactics, did he? It wouldn't do him any good. She wouldn't answer. "How did you know what they were?"

I'm sure as hell not going to answer those questions either.

She wasn't about to tell him anything about herself, or her ability. An ability that hadn't been as reliable as she'd first assumed, obviously. Case in point, trusting the man who'd just abducted her and tied her to a chair, and now sat staring at her as if he'd like nothing more than to strangle her with his bare hands. She hadn't sensed any harmful intent in him when he'd stared at her across the nightclub. Nor had she sensed malevolent objectives when he'd offered her his assistance.

A tiny frown pulled at her brow. Even now, glaring at her as he was, she still couldn't sense any imminent threat from him—though he was dangerous, of that she had no doubt.

Her attention swerved to him against her will, and she studied his features head-on. Amber eyes so bright they all but glowed. Like sunshine on gold. His jaw was strong, his shoulders and tattooed arms well muscled, his lips…

Nope, not looking there.

His hair was a wild, tumbled mess. Like fingers had raked through it in the grips of passion. Over and over.

Sexy.

Nope! Nope! Nope! Doesn't matter!

But exactly what he was, she still couldn't figure out. He wasn't human. His little magic tricks had proven that. He wasn't an angel. He didn't radiate goodwill, didn't give off that warm, fuzzy feeling angels did. Not that she'd had all that many encounters to rely on, only the couple of times she'd come face-to-face with the sperm donor.

But she'd had more than her share of run-ins with demons, albeit from a distance. And he didn't feel like that either, not exactly anyway. There was no choking, cloying sensation of evil, like the greedy, malignant black of an oil slick, oozing from him. In fact, try as she might, she couldn't sense either good or evil within him. He was a void. Favoring neither, but capable of either. Any sense of danger came solely from her human instincts alone, the instinct for self-preservation and survival.

Survival. That was what this was all about, wasn't it? The sperm donor's decree that she would learn to recognize and avoid the constant threat of a world he'd forced upon her. A world that, up until her twenty-first birthday, she'd been blissfully ignorant of. So the sperm donor had wanted her to be able to recognize angels and demons, wanted her to hide herself away and avoid notice. Well, she already knew how to recognize angels and demons, thanks to his birthday curse. That wonderful sixth sense clued her in every time.

She eyed the man in front of her. Well, *almost* every time. But the sperm donor had refused to show her how to fight, told her she was too weak. Told her that her only chance for survival was to hide.

Well, hiding wasn't exactly in her nature. And it hadn't been a very effective strategy anyway. Witness her current situation.

Aside from showing her how to conceal her curse—and obviously he hadn't done a stellar job of even that—the sperm donor hadn't wanted anything else to do with her. Perfectly fine with her. She had a life, one she wasn't going to ditch every time she caught a whiff of something-evil-this-way-comes. She had a good, solid career. Great friends. A nice home. She didn't want anything to do with the sperm donor either, him or his crazy messed-up world.

Her abductor regarded her with a new intensity. "Do you know what I am?"

She tore her gaze from him, focusing on the massive oil painting behind him. Horses and hounds. A fox hunt.

She felt like that poor little fox right now. Trapped.

Helpless. With no way out.

Damn Michael to Hell and back.

"I don't know anything," she finally said, in a voice as calm as she could possibly make it. "Just let me go. I won't tell a soul about this. I promise."

"You don't know anything?"

"That's right." She looked him right in the eye and lied through her pearly whites. "Not a thing."

One corner of those delectable lips of his lifted, just slightly, just enough to reveal the hint of a dimple in his cheek. "But you know Michael?"

Gritting her teeth, she cursed her earlier slip of the tongue and returned her attention to the oil painting.

"Did your father—"

"He's not my father," she hissed, the angry words exploding from her before she could contain them.

He leaned back, his head cocked to the side as he regarded her with unmistakable surprise. One long moment passed, then another as he seemed to search for the right words.

"Let's start over, shall we? I think we got off on the wrong foot here, darlin'."

So he wanted to play nice now? She jerked her wrists, hands splayed upward, to remind him of his manners. "Do you tie up all your guests?" Frustrated when he made no move to untie her, she thumped her fists against the arms of her chair. "And I am not your *darlin'*."

Something flashed in his eyes. Just for a moment. Just a flicker of emotion, was it pain? Regret? She couldn't quite say, but it was quickly masked by a charming façade. His grin blossomed fully. The sight of it made her catch her breath. "I only tie up the ones that like to throw things." He waited a beat, and then he winked at her. Actually winked. "And the ones who ask for it, of course."

"Untie me. I promise I won't throw anything else," she said with enough sweetness to guarantee a mouthful of cavities.

"I think we'll talk first. Get to know each other a little better, what do you say?"

"A name would be a good place to start," she suggested, trying to figure out the best angle.

"Forgive me." He bowed his head in acknowledgement. "Where are my manners? I'm Gideon."

"Gideon what?"

"Just Gideon. One name's all I need."

Oh, he was pouring the charm on thick now. Not that it would do him any good. Then another thought occurred to her. Maybe she could use this to her advantage. The sperm donor may not have taught her how to fight, but that didn't mean she was helpless. She had a quick mind. She could figure a way out of this.

"You want to talk, so talk," she coaxed, softening her tone. She could pour on the charm too. "What are you?"

"I figured you knew the answer to that already." His chin dipped. "I'm a demon. The Demon of Temptation, to be exact. Well, former Demon of Temptation, at any rate."

The heat of his gaze sent a shiver of awareness skating up her spine. But his words caught her off guard. Frowning, she argued, "No, you're not."

"I am Temptation," he insisted. Clearly, she'd offended him somehow.

"I'm not disputing the temptation part," she said. He grinned then, all kinds of sexy. Maggie scowled in response and forged on. "It's the demon part I don't believe. I would feel it if you were. So what are you? Really?"

The sensual playfulness drained from his features. He was all business now. "Feel it? Feel what exactly? How?"

She chewed on the inside edge of her lip. How much should she tell him? How much would it take to get him to trust her, to let her go?

"I can feel evil, and good. I can feel when someone intends harm. It's like a...a sixth sense." She snapped her wrists against the restraints. "Though, obviously, it isn't always reliable."

"Then you know I don't intend to hurt you." Statement, not question, as he ignored her less than subtle reminder. Why wasn't he questioning her honesty? Why wasn't he doubting her claim? Or her sanity?

And then a deeper truth hit her. He was right. Unless her instincts were wrong yet again. He did not intend her any harm.

But he also claimed to be demon. Yet he didn't feel like a demon.

Why couldn't she read him like she could all the others?

She pressed, "If you don't intend to harm me, then why tie me up?"

"Because you needed to calm down long enough for me to talk to you. And because you need to stay here. With me. For your own safety. I need to know you're not going to try to sneak off on your own."

"Why? Why do I need to stay with you?"

"I've been charged with protecting you. For the time being, at least."

"Protect me? From what?" She narrowed her eyes. *What's Michael up to now?*

"Look, I'll tell you everything. But it'll help me to know what you know so I know where to start."

She blinked at him. Was this a trick?

Instincts. It all came down to her instincts. And, as with earlier at the nightclub, her instincts were telling her she could trust him, abduction and restraints notwithstanding.

"I know who, and what, Michael is," she finally allowed, grudgingly.

"And do you know what you are?"

Puzzled, she frowned at him. "Of course I do. I'm Maggie."

"I said what, not who. You are a Halfling."

"Oh, that," she said flatly. She vaguely recalled Michael mentioning that term. But she'd been too dazed by his sudden appearance and declaration to pay much attention. Add to it the stunning moment he'd laid his hands upon her head and the wall of dizzying heat that had slammed into her like a freight train and, well, scientific—or biblical—names just hadn't ranked up there on her list of details to make note of.

"So you know you're a Halfling, and that your fath—Michael," he quickly amended when her eyes narrowed once more, "is an angel. Like you, I have special…gifts. I sense power. And you're near to bursting at the seams with it. Yet you still refuse to believe I'm a demon?"

"Correct. You don't give off the same vibe as the

other demons I've come across."

"Are you trying to insult my manhood?" His words were obviously meant in a joking fashion, yet there was a definite spark of curiosity there.

"Show me then. I've seen a demon transform before, from a distance, of course." She was lying through her teeth, but he didn't need to know that. "If you're really a demon, then transform. Show me what you really are."

His expression was comical. He looked utterly horrified, and yet, much as he might try to hide it, just the slightest bit tempted.

"No." Gideon rubbed his palms up and down his thighs, as if they'd begun to sweat. He shook his head and pushed from the chair to tower over her. And yet, agitated as he was, she still sensed no threat from him. "You have no idea what you're asking for," he warned.

"Sure I do. I know you'll get bigger. And scary looking—" At least, she assumed so.

"Scary looking?" Gideon huffed out a mirthless laugh as he paced away, paced back. "You don't know the half of it. I won't change for you because I'll—" He broke off. Color suffused his cheeks. Was he embarrassed? Angry? It was a simple request. Why did he look like he was about to freak out?

He raked a hand through his already messy hair and admitted, "I can't control that other side of me. The rage takes over and there's no more logic, no more sanity. I become a killing machine. I have trouble distinguishing friend from foe…hell, half the time I don't even care. No." He shook his head again, moistened his lips and visibly forced a swallow. "I won't change. Not to satisfy your curiosity, not to convince you. Believe me, or don't. That's your problem."

"But—"

"Damn it! I said no." He'd started pacing away, then swiveled to face her. "Actually, I can do this. But this is all you get."

Holding his arm out to his side, open palm up, he gave her a grim smile. That was all the warning she got. A seething, pulsing ball of a lavalike substance erupted, hovering in the air just above his palm. Even from that distance, she could feel the searing heat of the thing. Her mouth fell open.

Gideon abruptly fisted his hand, and the ball disappeared with a hiss.

"Satisfied?"

She slowly nodded her head, her gaze still locked on his hand. When she realized she was still gaping, she snapped her mouth closed and dragged her focus back to his face.

Clearing her throat, she worked hard to sound calm and unimpressed. "Okay then."

She took another moment to compose herself. A moment to form coherent questions. "Why are you different?"

Now he looked wary, almost defensive. "What do you mean, different?"

"With other demons, I get that oily, oozy sensation. With angels, it's the warm fuzzies. With you…there's just…nothing. Like an emptiness. A void."

The look he gave her was fiercely blank. Like a wall had dropped between them. And then he looked down and away. His brow crushed on a frown.

Gideon drew a deep breath, making a visible effort

to relax. His moods were mercurial, to say the least. Once more he straddled the chair in front of her, his seductive grin back in place. Those grins were dangerous.

And they were starting to get to her.

Confused, she glanced away from his face, only to watch as long, slim fingers toyed with the heavy watch on his left wrist where it hung over the chair's back. Tiny specks of odd colored stones glinted from the watch's face. She didn't want anything to do with this world, she reminded herself forcefully. And while she may hate the only angel she'd ever met, that didn't mean she was ready to jump into bed with a demon either.

Jump into bed...

No, she hadn't meant it that way. Jumping into bed had been a figure of speech, nothing more. Certainly not some subconscious suggestion.

Whatever! Focus!

"So," he said in that purring drawl of his. "If you hate your f—Michael so much, why keep his name?"

That question hit her out of left field. "That's none of your business."

"Not only am I protecting you from others of my kind, but I'm protecting you from *his* kind as well."

That gave her pause. One of the sperm donor's warnings came back to her. *Good can be just as dangerous to you as evil. Surround yourself with humans. At all times. Use your gifts only when absolutely necessary and then leave the area immediately afterward.*

"Why would you need to protect me from angels?"

Heaving a weary sigh, Gideon raked both hands

through his hair, leaving it all but standing straight on end. "We're just going round and round chasing our tails here. So this is what we're going to do. We're going to have full disclosure between us, yeah? I'll tell you everything I know. You have questions, I'll answer them. But you have to answer whatever questions I have too. Deal?"

She gnawed on the inside of her lip.

"The only other alternative you have," he said softly, "is to spend the foreseeable future locked up in one of the rooms upstairs. Makes no difference to me, but one way or another, you aren't going anywhere. You're too valuable to risk."

Valuable? Me? What is this guy playing at?

There was more going on here than she knew about. That much was obvious. To be honest, curiosity was getting the better of her. She wanted answers now, more than she wanted to escape. She could always escape once she got what she wanted. She hoped. She could lull him into a false sense of comfort. Later. Maggie huffed out a breath, stirring the loose tendrils of hair tickling her skin. Irritated, she scraped her cheek along her raised shoulder to swipe her hair back.

He watched her movements, his features…hungry? She had no other word for the look on his face. His expressions were doing odd things to her insides. Things she'd been working hard to ignore since the moment she'd first noticed him in the nightclub. It wasn't getting any easier.

Grudgingly she nodded acceptance of his deal, quickly adding, "Untie me. If you expect me to trust you, it has to go both ways."

He stared at her, hard. Trust did not come easily to

this man—*demon*, she corrected—any more than it did to her. He leaned toward her. A long, wicked looking knife appeared in his hand in the blink of an eye. She didn't even have time to flinch. With a flick of his hand, her bindings fell to the floor. Maggie clasped her hands over her wrists. It was more the idea of the bindings she rubbed away rather than pain since the bindings had never been tight enough to cause hurt.

Gideon crossed his arms over the back of his chair and asked once more, "Why keep the name of a man you clearly hate? And, speaking of, why do you hate him so much?"

"I kept the name because it was all I had."

At his arched eyebrow, she bit the bullet and let it all out. Trust went both ways, she'd told him. Then she needed to keep her end of the bargain. "Clarisse Michaels was the name listed on my birth certificate as my mother. My father was listed as unknown. I didn't know, didn't understand until I was twenty-one that Michael was my—the sperm donor's given name, not my mother's surname. My mother changed her last name to reflect his possession." She couldn't help the sneer of disgust that crept into her voice, did nothing to hide it.

"My mother died within hours of my birth." She flexed her fingers, fisting her hands in her lap. "She stayed alive long enough to name me, long enough to leave specific instructions for my adoption, instructions that required my name never be changed. By the time I realized the truth, it was just too much trouble to change it."

"So that explains the name. What about the hate?"

That tangled jumble of emotions that surfaced

whenever she thought of the sperm donor came roaring to the surface. And so she combated it the only way she knew how. With bitterness and anger, because those were her strongest emotions, the strongest emotions she would let herself feel.

"Angels are supposed to be these benevolent, compassionate beings, right?" At Gideon's nod, she barreled on. "So if my…the sperm donor…is an angel, a being of light and love, why would he leave his…his offspring alone and defenseless? Dependent on the charity of others? Just another file in a system that's flawed and overburdened already?"

She could feel the weight of his stare upon her, but she couldn't bring herself to meet his gaze. "Where was Michael while I was dumped in one foster home after another? Where was he when—" She abruptly cut herself off. Shame filled her, flooding heat into her cheeks. She wouldn't be a victim. She was *not* a victim. And she wouldn't wallow in self-pity. There were a lot of other people out there who'd had it much worse than she.

"When what?" Gideon's voice was so gentle Maggie had to blink to keep the tears at bay.

"The last foster home I was placed with was a real treasure. There were already three other foster kids in place when I got there. The kind of kids that gave the rest of us a bad rap. Patty, the foster mom, liked to drink. A lot. And…" She had to stop, force a swallow as the memory of groping hands and fetid breath came back to haunt her. "Randy, the foster dad, he liked his girls young and too weak to fight back."

Just like that Gideon sat up straight in his chair, fury rolling from him in waves. Enough fury to level a small city. The force of it pushed her back in her own chair. Here was that scary demon feeling she'd recognized in the others. The promise of death. Slow and excruciatingly painful. The only thing that kept her from running off screaming into the night was the fact that his fury wasn't directed at her.

His voice was a deep raspy growl, barely discernible. "Did he—"

"No," she quickly assured him. Shaking her head, hugging her arms around her waist, she forced herself to finish before he got any more upset. The sight of his anger did strange things to her. It didn't make her hide in terror, fearful for her safety, as she had assumed it would. Instead, it filled her with the urge to soothe him. To run her hands over him, speak softly, and to hold him, calm him.

And it made her feel protected.

Baffling.

"No, I never gave him the chance. When I realized what was going on, what he'd done to some of the other girls, I lashed out. He wasn't expecting to meet the sharp end of a steak knife when he came to my room that night. He got twenty-six stitches, and I got taken out of the home and dropped into a placement facility."

His expression still murderous, Gideon gripped the back of the chair hard enough she was surprised it didn't splinter apart. "Those places—"

"I know what you're thinking, but you're wrong. Stonebridge Academy was the best thing that ever happened to me. At first, the adjustment was difficult. But the staff was really great, and I'd just turned seventeen. I was only there a year. They gave me a lot of tools to cope and helped me get started out on my own. I'm still in touch with a couple of the counselors, and my primary counselor still sends birthday and Christmas cards every year."

Some of the livid color had begun to drain from his face. He no longer looked as if he wanted to massacre someone, so she took that as a good sign.

"I refuse to feel bad about hating Michael, and I refuse to apologize. I don't believe for one moment he's this beneficent being. Because if he were, he would never have left me in some of those situations. He would have been there to protect me. He gave me these gifts"—she made sarcastic air quotes—"made me aware of this world of angels and demons, and then he abandoned me. Again. He wouldn't even show me how to fight, how to protect myself. Even when those demons showed up at the club, he wasn't there to keep me safe."

She fell silent for a moment as she studied the knees of her jeans. Then, slowly she lifted her gaze to his. Her brows were pulled tight in confusion, and she whispered, "But you were."

Chapter Five

Gideon studied the Halfling. For a long moment, she looked so terribly lost, so wounded and confused, that he found it almost impossible not to reach for her, not to pull her into the shelter of his arms. The only thing stopping him was the knowledge that his arms would have ghosted right through her, as intangible as mist.

He wanted to promise her she'd never be alone again, never have to fear the shadows because he would always be there to protect her. But he couldn't do that either, could he? Not when he'd already promised himself Oblivion.

With a tenacious resolve he couldn't help but admire, she squared her jaw and stared him right in the eye. "Your turn. Why am I here?"

He drew a deep breath. Where to begin? He'd only ever considered the basics of this mission. Find the Halfling. Check. Rescue the Halfling from any potential demon threat. Check. Bring the Halfling to a secure location. Check—thanks to Sebastian's nifty little cuffs.

He'd never stopped to consider for a moment that he might have to be the one to stay with the Halfling, let alone have to explain the current power play by a rebellious demon prince.

He'd also never imagined how badly he'd want this one particular woman for his own. His curse had been a nightmare before. Now?

Torment. Utter mind-blowing torture.

Oblivion, he reminded himself with more than a touch of desperation. He just had to get through this last mission. Keep the Halfling safe until one of the others could step in. And then, sweet Oblivion.

Where to start? "Long story short, you've been dropped into the middle of a demon rebellion."

"What?" Her delicate features screwed up into an expression of complete disbelief. She clearly thought he'd lost his mind.

"Long ago, four Sacred Relics were created—" he paused, frowning. That wasn't strictly true. Shaking his head, he amended, "Three—three relics were created. The fourth relic comes later." He held his hands up to fend off the questions he could see brewing. "Just bear with me here, I wasn't planning on being the one to have to explain all this to you. Okay, where was I? Yeah, so, the relics are part of the Prophesy."

At this pronouncement, she let out a disbelieving snort. "A prophecy? Really? That's the best you could come up with?"

Gideon ground his teeth together. "*I* didn't make this shit up."

"Uh-huh."

He took a deep breath.

Control. Breathe in. Breathe out.

Damn irritating woman.

"You know, believe it or don't believe it. I don't really care. But you better understand the demon prince staging this coup does. Fanatically. And whether or not you like it, whether or not *you* believe, because of that prophecy, you are now in a great deal of danger."

He had her full attention now. She remained silent for a long moment, her lips pressed tight together. Grudging cooperation flickered in her gaze, and her shoulders squaring in determination. "So what does this prophecy say?"

Finally. Progress. "Whosoever controls the four Sacred Relics will possess the power to overthrow Lucifer and assume control of Hell."

She frowned at him, obviously trying to follow along with his theory. "And that's a bad thing?"

"Very bad. The barriers between Earth and Hell are dependent upon Lucifer himself. If he dies, those barriers crumble. If they crumble, demons will overrun Earth. The human race would be annihilated."

Her eyebrows lifted, and she tilted her head slightly forward, waiting for him to go on.

"So the three relics were stolen and hidden away in Earth's realm by ancient Guardians, and subsequently protected by those Guardians' descendants until present day. The Scrolls of Prévnar, rumored to contain spells to make one immune to Lucifer's suggestions or control. The Arc Stone, which makes a demon or angel nearly impervious to harm. And The Sword of Kathnesh, rumored to be the only blade capable of taking Lucifer's head."

"And how do you fit into this rebellion?" She considered him with a great deal of suspicion now.

"I'm making a mess of this, aren't I?" he asked with a wry twist of his lips. Where were his golden tongue and all his vaunted charm now? "Almost two hundred years ago, two of Lucifer's top generals...defected, for lack of a better term. Niklas, the Seer, and Xander, the Slayer. Lucifer had promised freedom and unlimited pleasure, but he delivered only despotic tyranny and torture. They regretted the decisions they made leading up to their fall from grace and had come to loathe their existence as Lucifer's followers."

"Sounds like buyer's remorse to me."

He gave her one long, piercing stare, and then trudged on as though she'd never spoken. "They knew there were others of us with the same inclination. Myself. Sebastian, the Demon of Vengeance, and Mikhail, the Demon of War. We saw the error of our ways, but, unlike the rest, we were willing to do something about it. We escaped Hell and came to Earth. Now we protect innocent humans from others of our kind in hopes of—" He caught himself.

Redemption, he'd been about to say. In their own way, Xander and Niklas had found exactly that, he supposed. While Sebastian and Mikhail continued to relentlessly strive for vindication, for that ever-elusive forgiveness.

But redemption wasn't in the cards for him, was it? There was no hope left in him. He was through trying. The best he could wish for was an honorable death. A ceasing of his existence, for there would be nothing for him after that. Just the extinguishing of his soulless life.

"In hopes of what?" she prompted softly.

"They strive for forgiveness, to earn their place in Heaven once more," he replied, his tone flat and final.

"And what about you?" The Halfling pressed, too perceptive for his comfort.

"I want…peace," he finally said. And, as far as he was concerned, it was true. Oblivion would end his torment; hence, he would finally achieve peace.

The little furrow deepened between her eyebrows. She opened her mouth as if to speak. Would she dispute his claim of wanting peace, as she had his claim to being a demon? She seemed to take it as her life's mission to argue with him about everything, to challenge him at every turn. But she didn't push him, instead snapping her mouth closed, as though she thought better of whatever she'd been about to say.

"You still haven't told me how I fit into this," she reminded him.

"To do that, I need to tell you about the fourth relic."

Her brow puckered. But to give credit where credit was due, she remained quiet, waiting for him to finish his story. Miracles did happen.

"The fourth relic is a person. A child, to be exact."

"How can a person be a relic?"

He knew that silence had been too good to last.

Gideon shrugged helplessly. "It's the Prophesy, okay? Do you want to hear this or not?"

How could this one lone woman make him lose all his finesse? He charmed women, he didn't snap at them, didn't lose his cool. Yet something about her sucked up every last ounce of his patience and drove him to distraction.

She nodded, pressing her lips together in silent promise.

He turned his head to one side and then the other, popping his neck. Gideon dug deep for self-control. It wasn't her, he assured himself. He was giving her too much credit. He was just impatient to get on with his own plans, impatient to leave all this behind and seek peace at last.

Yeah. That was it.

"The Chosen One will be conceived of a demon and a first generation Halfling. We're assuming it means that, if spawned by evil and born under the control of that same evil, the child will be raised as a warrior, honed as a weapon of destruction. One whose sole target is Lucifer himself."

He could see the cogs turning. One plus two equaled *oh hell no*.

"And you believe that *I'm* the Halfling that's supposed to…" Her voice trailed away as the ramifications of her situation settled fully upon her. "That *I'm* going to…"

She shook her head. Her jaw lifted as mutinous anger firmed her lips and sparkled in her eyes.

"I can't be the only Halfling on Earth!" She glowered at him as though this were all his fault somehow. "You've obviously made some mistake. I sure as hell don't intend to…to mate with a demon!"

"It wouldn't have to be consensual." Gideon gave her an apologetic smile. "I don't think the fact that you might object is even the tiniest concern to Stolas."

"Stolas?"

"The demon prince leading this rebellion."

Maggie leaped to her feet. Gideon tensed, prepared to shimmer to the doorway to head her off, but she strode instead toward the fireplace and back. Dragging both hands through her hair, she continued to pace, mumbling under her breath. At length, satisfied she didn't intend to flee, Gideon relaxed and watched her stomp back and forth across his study.

She whirled on him, desperation evident in her strained tone. "I'm not the only Halfling out there, right?" She stormed right up to him, holding both hands out in supplication. "You could have made a mistake? Grabbed the wrong girl? Right? It's a possibility, isn't it?"

"There are other Halflings," Gideon conceded reluctantly. But he didn't want to get her hopes up. "They're rare, first generation rarer still. To our knowledge, you're the only first generation Halfling still alive. Aside from that, with Michael as your f...as your, ah, *sire*, the power rolling around inside you is much greater than your average Halfling. Stolas has already stolen the Sword of Kathnesh and killed its Guardian. We have the Arc Stone. That leaves the scrolls and the Chosen One up for grabs. Whether or not you are the only first generation Halfling out there, we aren't willing to risk Stolas getting his hands on you. We need to keep you safe. Keep you off his radar."

"Oh, my God," she whispered, sliding downward until she landed on the chair she'd vacated earlier. Haunted eyes turned on him, pleading. "You keep saying I'm so powerful. Really, I'm not. There's nothing special about me. So I can sense the presence of angels and demons, and I have a useless vision now and again. That's really not so much, is it?"

His eyes narrowed as he canted his head. "You have visions?"

She nodded numbly. "Sometimes. Of the future. Brief flashes, really. But what good are they? I can't ever change what happens. I've tried."

"Some things are meant to be," he stated as calmly as he could, though his mind was racing. Visions? What had she seen? What had she yet to see? As Halflings were exceedingly rare, he couldn't say what was normal or not normal for a Halfling in the way of what, or how many, powers they might possess. Or how they might manifest. He himself had once been precognitive, knowing things before they happened. And he knew just how frustrating that could be at times.

What other gifts did she possess that had yet to awaken?

From the shaken expression on her face, now didn't appear to be the optimal time to explain anything further or press her about her "curse", as she clearly viewed it.

Gideon watched her in silence as she assimilated all he'd told her.

"Can I…can I have a glass of water?" she whispered, her voice hoarse.

Without a word, not giving it a second thought, he conjured a glass of water on the desk beside her. The Halfling bolted upward like a frightened cat, toppling the chair as she hopped sideways with a screech of alarm.

"Sorry. Sorry," he said, holding up his hands. "It's okay. Just water."

"H-how did you do that?"

"It's one of our…ah, gifts. Sort of like, picture something and poof, there it is." That was oversimplifying, but she didn't exactly look like she was up to technical explanations. "We can vanish them almost the same way," he added, hoping to eliminate any further stress later, should he forget to warn her about something disappearing.

"Handy," she said as she righted her seat and sat down once more. But she didn't pick up the glass, just stared at it, and him, as if one or the other were a snake about to strike.

Then again, maybe she did need at least a basic explanation. Something, at least, to make her stop viewing the glass, and him, like he'd just performed some type of dark magic. Any minute now, he expected her to leap from her chair again, holding her fingers up in the sign of a cross as she backed toward the nearest cloves of garlic. "Handy, yes. But it comes with certain drawbacks."

Finally able to drag her attention from the glass of water, she eyed him with wary suspicion. "Such as?"

"Conjuring weakens us. Something small like that glass of water is just a blip. A drop in the bucket, if you will. Barely noticeable. Something bigger—like say, a house or a car—would weaken us much more drastically. Sure, we recover. But how weak we get, and how long it takes to recover, depends on the nature and size of what we conjure. If we're already weakened, like after we've turned demonic and back again, or wounded, well, it can actually cause physical pain in some cases."

"I see. I think." But she didn't sound as if she understood. She looked distracted. And dazed.

"Look, all things considered, will you give me your word you won't run off? If for no other reason than for your own safety? At least for the time being?" He thought about reminding her about the cuff, telling her that he'd only bring her back anyway. But it didn't look as if it would take much to push her over the edge.

She nodded, eyes wide and somewhat glassy.

She needed someone to hold her, but he couldn't help her out with that, so he offered her the only thing he could. "I bet you could use a little time to yourself."

She drew a shuddering breath. "Please."

"If you'll follow me, I can show you to your room."

"My room?" Finally a spark of life came back. "I can't stay here."

She'd just agreed to stay. *Gah!* He could pull out his hair.

"You don't have much choice, unless you want to meet Stolas and his minions, up close and very personal."

She forced a swallow and then drew a deep breath. "I'll stay here for now, for tonight," she conceded. "But I have a job. I have to be back in Portland Monday morning. I have classes to teach."

Frustration rolled through him. "Did you not listen to anything I just said?"

"I did. But I also have responsibilities, obligations—"

"Screw your obligations," Gideon snapped. "If we found you, it was only a matter of time before they did. Hell, they were only half a step behind me as it was. Who do you think those three demons in the nightclub were looking for? What do you think they would have done with you once they got their hands on you? What do you think was going to happen here? You've been warned, so now you can go on your merry way? Hide in plain sight as you were? Put your head in a hole and pretend all Hell isn't breaking loose around you?"

"No! Okay? No. But I have to figure this out. My life, my responsibilities might not mean squat to you, but they're mine. And they mean something to me. I can't just duck out without a word, without an explanation. My job is important to me. People depend on me."

Crap on a cracker, the woman was aggravating. He was trying to save her life here, and she was worried about her double damned summer school classes.

"Look, *darlin'*," he ground out, holding on to his patience like a dying man clutched at his rosary. "I'm not taking you back to Portland. I might as well tie you up with a bow and deliver you straight to Stolas's doorstep, save him the trouble of sending someone else after you."

"One more time," she bit out, "I am not your *'darlin''*." Temper sparked as she stood up. Regal and cool as a queen, she demanded, "Show me to a room. I need to think, need to figure this out, and I can't do that with you nagging at me. But you'd better understand, this is only temporary." That being said, she stomped over and jerked the door open, then stood there, chin up, back ramrod straight as she waited expectantly for him to get up.

Nagging? Nagging!

He was surprised steam wasn't rolling from his ears by now, fire spewing from his nostrils.

Gideon had half a mind to just shimmer her there. Partly to just get rid of her faster, partly just to piss her off. But he didn't relish the tantrum that was sure to follow. With a growl, he shoved to his feet and strode past her.

"This way, your highness," he grumbled.

Taking the steps two at a time, all shreds of chivalry stretched to the limit, he didn't care if she fell behind. At the top of the steps, he turned right and strode to the end of the long hall, placing her as far from his own bedroom as possible.

But at the door, he paused and his conscience started to eat at him. She hadn't asked for any of this, he reminded himself, hadn't asked to have Michael as her father. Hadn't asked to become a pawn in a deadly game of good versus evil.

Drawing a calming breath, he opened the door and stepped inside. Moth-chewed dust cloths covered the old furniture. Cobwebs and grime coated everything. The windows were too filthy to see through, the drapes sagging and riddled with holes. No one had occupied this room in over a hundred years. There wasn't even a bathroom.

It was then that he truly realized how badly he'd let the house go. When he'd first taken up residence, he'd brought everything back to its original grandeur. But that had been long ago. Years of demon hunting, decades of failed attempts to thwart his curse, had not been kind, to him or to his home. Looking at the place now, through fresh eyes, he could see that years of neglect and disuse to many—most, if he were honest—of the rooms had taken their toll.

For a moment, resentment fluttered in his breast. None of it should matter one bit. The Halfling was the only thing standing between him and his escape into Oblivion.

Just as quickly, he snuffed that resentment out. That wasn't fair. It wasn't the Halfling's fault. It was the mission. Not fair to hold her personally responsible, yet that was what he'd been doing. Yes, she was…difficult to deal with. But wouldn't he be the same in similar circumstances?

He could conjure the room clean, could conjure an adjoining bath, but it would sap his strength, and right now he was on his own. The only protection she had. He didn't know what kind of threat they were facing, and weakening himself for something so inconsequential seemed like a stupid move. Not when there were other alternatives available.

Oh, hell.

Who was he trying to fool here anyway? He might not be able to hold her in his arms as he wanted, or make love to her like he had all the time in the world and two hundred plus years of lust to burn, but the idea of her sleeping in his bed was erotic as hell.

It would be as close as he would ever come to having her for himself.

What else did he have to look forward to, besides Oblivion? At least he could experience what it was like to have his scent all over her. He may not be able to personally put it there, but his sheets, his pillow, his room would surely mark her.

And there he was, like a royal dumbass, torturing himself all over again with things he'd never have.

He strode back down the hallway toward her.

"This way," he mumbled as he passed her, proud of his controlled tone.

She stopped in her tracks and turned to follow him once again. He was only thankful she hadn't made some snide comment about getting lost in his own house. If she had, he probably would have left her in the dingy bedroom, wouldn't even have made the effort to clean it up. As it was, he led her into his own room, kicking himself every step of the way. This was such a bad idea on so many levels.

As soon as he opened the door, he was faced with the shambles of his own bedroom and realized he had no choice. Clean this bedroom or clean the other. Given the vast state of neglect in the guest room, his room would be far less work. At least that was what he tried to convince himself of. That it was more a question of effort and expended energy rather than some sick need to know it was *his* bedroom she would be living in, *his* shower she would be naked in. *His* bed she would sleep in. *His* scent all over her. He quickly conjured the room and adjoining bathroom spotless, replacing the bedding, towels and toiletries while he was at it.

He'd been reduced from feared demon hunter to housekeeper.

Welcome to Hotel Gideon.

"The bathroom's in there," he said, pointing to the door on the far wall. "Make yourself at home. I'll be downstairs in the study if you need anything."

"Thank you," she said stiffly, standing in the middle of the room, looking forlorn. Unable to offer her the kind of comfort he wanted to, he stepped out into the hallway and closed the door behind him.

Gideon stood there for a long moment, his head tilted back and shoulders pressed against the door. He recalled how she looked, standing there in the middle of his bedroom. The rightness of it—of having her there, surrounded by his things—staggered him. That damned word, *his*, kept whispering through his mind. Need coiled tight in his gut, longing nearly crushed his chest.

But he couldn't have her.

Lust turned to resentment, resentment to anger.

Rage began to swell. His hands shook with it. His palms stung with the urge to form plasma balls and burn the place down. His skin stretched taut. His muscles began to burn and ache as the beast inside clawed for freedom. She would never be his.

And then he heard it. A muffled sob. Gideon turned and tipped his forehead to the door, pressed his palm to the cold hard wood and closed his eyes once more. His entire body tightened with a different kind of need. A need he'd had precious little experience with. The need to comfort. The beast inside settled back on its haunches with a bewildered growl. No longer did it want to come out, no longer did it thirst for blood.

Instead, it trembled with…worry? Uncertainty? He could hardly fathom it.

He heard the bed give the slightest squeak as it accepted her meager weight. Her cries were a little louder now, but still muffled, as though smothered in a pillow. But he could hear them through the feathers and through the wood. He felt them in the black hole where his soul used to be. And he couldn't do a damn thing about it. Couldn't hold her as he wanted, couldn't soothe her with the touch of his hand, or the press of his lips. The sound of those muffled cries undid him.

Unable to take another second of those soft, heartbreaking sounds, he shimmered himself to the sanctuary of his den once more.

Chapter Six

One minute Maggie was sitting on the edge of the big bed, clutching a pillow as she bawled her heart out, her world falling apart around her ears. Damn Michael. The next instant, she was standing in the middle of Gideon's den, feeling as if she'd just been dropped without warning from a cliff. Gasping, lightheaded, fighting down a wave of nausea, she staggered back a step.

Gideon stood a few steps away. He whirled to face her, shock registering on his handsome features. Before she realized she was still clutching the pillow, before she realized what was happening, she threw the pillow at his head with all her might.

"Stop doing that!" Maggie yelled.

The pillow caught him square in the face, and then fell to the floor. He didn't even make any effort to catch it. She watched him glance down at his wrist, at a cuff identical to the one he'd tricked her into putting on before telling her there was no way to remove it. He looked back up at her with a distinctive look of alarm. But that alarm swiftly shifted. Determination and concentration etched his face.

Without warning, the room swirled and dissolved, and her stomach dropped once more. Another room wavered into focus. Maggie screamed and reached out for a high backed kitchen chair as her knees threatened to give way. She caught a fleeting glimpse of what looked like a kitchen, but before she could find purchase on the hardwood floor, before her fingers could grasp something solid for support, that vision wavered and was gone, replaced once again by Gideon's den.

"No more," she begged hoarsely. Gasping, arms wrapped tight around her middle, head bowed, Maggie fell to her knees as a merciless wave of dizziness swept through her. "Please, no more."

Silence met her request, but they stayed in the same room, so she could only hope he'd heard her and decided to comply. When she finally risked glancing up, the sight of Gideon took her by surprise. He stood immobile, his arms stretched out to her, as if to pick her up, yet he didn't touch her. Instead, he stared down at her as if she were some foreign creature he didn't know how to handle. Utter anguish lined his expression.

Seeming to recall himself, he drew his arms back. Only then did something click into place with sudden clarity. In the entire time she'd been with him—granted not all that long in the grander scheme of things—he'd never, not one single time, ever touched her. When he'd given her the bracelet, he'd deliberately held it in a way so their fingers wouldn't risk brushing. Even when he'd tied her to the chair, he'd not touched her skin with his. Not once.

Why not?

"Are you all right?" he asked, his voice wooden, distracted.

"No, I'm not all right," Maggie snapped as she pushed shakily to her feet. The room around her swayed. Quick as a flash, Gideon picked up the chair by the desk and dropped it beside her. She fell onto the chair, dead weight. She frowned. Most anyone else would have taken her by the arm and led her to the chair. Yet he'd avoided contact once more.

"You're white as a sheet. You're not gonna pass out, are you?"

"Well, if I did, it'd certainly serve you right."

"Put your head between your knees or something," he suggested.

If looks could kill, she'd be digging a hole in the backyard large enough to accommodate his six-foot-plus frame. And she was angry enough that she didn't think she'd even need help dragging his dead body.

"I don't need to put my head between my knees. What I need is for you to stop…zapping me from one place to another without warning."

"Shimmering."

"Excuse me?"

"It's called shimmering."

"I don't care what it's called. If you do it to me again without warning me first, I swear I won't be responsible for my actions."

Gideon sat on the corner of his desk and crossed his arms, his expression pensive. "I'm sorry about that. Honestly. I didn't know…didn't realize…" He fell silent. His brow puckered. She didn't have the strength right now to play twenty questions, so she was grateful when he offered explanation without prompting. "The cuff I gave you"—he held his own up, lamplight glinting off the hammered silver on his wrist—"is bonded to the one I wear. I didn't realize that you'd shimmer *every* time I do. Even if I don't want you to," he added reluctantly. "So I guess from now on where I go, you go."

But his expression hadn't calmed by a long shot. A look of such dread crossed his face, fleeting but there all the same, that it made her decidedly nervous.

What wasn't he telling her?

She'd been accused more than once of being too suspicious. Well, her suspicious nature had served her well all these years, particularly once Michael had so beneficently bestowed his "gifts" upon her. And right now, her little suspicion detector was rattling like a Geiger counter at Chernobyl.

She thrust her wrist out to him. "Then take it off," she demanded.

He shook his head, his sensuous lips set in a mulish line. "I'm sorry, darlin'. I can't do that."

"Okay. First. My name is Maggie. Not darlin'." Addressing her by some random endearment wouldn't soften her. Especially not when he used such a snide, patronizing tone. And so help him if he dared call her *baby*. She wouldn't be responsible. She leaned back in her chair, crossing her own arms. "And second, why can't you take the bracelet off?"

"Would you willingly put it back on when I told you to?"

"Not on your life," she answered without thinking. As soon as the words left her mouth, she wanted to kick herself. She should have lied right through her damned teeth.

He dipped his head, as if she'd just proven some point for him. "I may need to remove you from a potentially dangerous situation. I won't always have time to stop and discuss the options with you or get your permission first." When she opened her mouth to argue, he quickly cut her off. "You're just going to have to trust me on that. The subject is closed."

She glared at him. "Then take off the one on your wrist."

He seemed to weigh that option for a moment. A muscle jumped in his jaw. "No. I won't do that either. First, I'm not going to take it off and just leave it lying around for you to pick up and run off with." She gritted her teeth, for that was exactly what she'd been hoping would happen. "Second, there's no saying it won't work the same if it's in my pocket rather than on my wrist anyway. And just in case it doesn't, I won't always have time to stop and put it on in the middle of fight. So both cuffs stay as they are."

"Then you can't shimmer anymore."

He shook his head. "Not an option."

Damn frustrating man/demon. "Do you know what it feels like, as a human, to shimmer?"

He hesitated. A guilty expression flickered across his handsome face. "I heard Carly tell Niklas once that it felt like a roller coaster drop."

"Who's Carly?"

"Niklas's wife."

She frowned, angling her head. "I thought you said Niklas was a demon. The Seer, isn't he?"

"He is."

"And yet…" She paused, her gaze dropping to the floor as she tried to reason it all out. She frowned as she looked back up at him. "He has a human wife?"

Gideon looked decidedly uncomfortable. "It's complicated."

"I'll bet." She eyed him, rolling all this information around in her head. She studied the bracelet on her wrist a moment, as a new idea began to form. They looked identical. Didn't it stand to reason that they might then have the same power? Granted, she couldn't shimmer him anywhere. But if she didn't want to be shimmered, could she prevent him from shimmering? "Well, she's right. It feels like falling off a cliff without any warning."

"Some people like that sensation."

"Yeah? Well, not me."

Gideon scrubbed a long-fingered hand over his jaw and mouth.

"Does Niklas shimmer his wife very often?"

He frowned at her. "Yes. Quite often, in fact. And Xander shimmers Ky as well. Though she doesn't ever complain about it," he added pointedly.

"And who is Ky?"

A strange look passed over his face. He'd obviously opened up a can of worms he didn't want to have to explain. "Kyanna. She's Xander's wife."

"Another demon/human pairing?"

Gideon nodded, looking like he'd rather be sitting in a dentist's chair about to have every last one of his teeth pulled. Sans anesthetic.

"Let me guess," she said, sarcasm dripping from every word. "It's complicated."

With a wry twist of his lips, Gideon shrugged.

"So they all have these bracelets then. Don't they ever take theirs off? Maybe if you asked one of them, they might know how to get around the…"

Now he looked really uncomfortable.

She wasn't about to let him off the hook this time. "What?"

"They don't have bracelets…cuffs," he corrected

99

with a shake of his head. Oh, yeah. Definitely uncomfortable. "They don't need them."

"Why not?"

His face turned to stone. "This discussion is over."

"Like hell it is."

"Over," he reiterated. "Now, unless you want me to shimmer you to my—your room, I suggest you get there on your own two feet."

Touchy, touchy.

Then she realized what he'd said. *My.* As in *my room.* She'd thought she'd detected the faint scent of him—masculine spice and citrus and sandalwood—in the bedroom, on the pillow. But then the scent of him tantalized her here as well, and she'd just chalked it up to his house—his scent.

So, he'd given her his room.

Why?

Questions to mull over later. Right now she had a theory she wanted to test out.

"Shimmer me there."

"I thought you said you didn't like shimmering." Now look who was drowning with suspicion.

"I don't. But I want to know if it's any easier if I'm expecting it."

He looked irritated enough to chew nails. And not the kind on the tips of his fingers.

"Are you ready now?" he asked with exaggerated patience.

Taking a deep breath, concentrating very hard on staying glued to the chair she was currently sitting in, Maggie nodded. She felt a quick tug, but resisted with all her will, clenching both hands on the edge on the seat. A slight frown flickered over Gideon's features, but then the room fell away as before. She experienced the same dropping sensation, though, admittedly, it wasn't nearly as bad as before. Either she was getting used to it or being mentally prepared for it actually did help.

When the falling sensation stopped, and Gideon's bedroom came into focus, Maggie grinned. Gideon looked perplexed.

She was still sitting in the chair.

****

"Master," the Charocté called quietly from the corner, head bowed, fists pressed to shoulders. "The Animagi is here to see you."

"Admit him," Stolas barked. Dimiezlo had fast become one of his most loyal and trusted subjects, earning him perhaps a bit more leeway when interrupting Stolas's time.

The demon walked through the massive archway into the great hall, his gait wobbling awkwardly as his cloven hooves came down on the gleaming black marble. Dimiezlo's forked tongue slithered from his mouth. His furry arms crossed over his equally furry chest, fists pressed to his shoulders as he bowed his bald, horned head. His goat-like legs prevented him from kneeling, but he remained respectfully silent until Stolas gave him leave to speak.

"Master, we have word of a first generation Halfling," Dimiezlo said once Stolas bade him speak. "But she is already with the Fallen. Temptation has her."

Stolas sat up straight in his seat. Dimiezlo had learned to spit the bad out with the good right away. It tended not to ignite Stolas's temper quite so quickly or so fiercely when he wasn't given false hope only to have it crushed later. Though still angry, he was much more reasonable when the facts were all laid out quickly.

The Halfling in the cell below had begun hemorrhaging not half an hour past. The news of a first generation Halfling was just what he needed to brighten his day, regardless of who currently had possession of her. There was still hope. Besides, he had something in the works now, an alliance that might well render the Fallen irrelevant.

"First generation, confirmed?"

"Yes, master." Dimiezlo's forked tongue slithered around the words. "My sources report the Slayer's mate's mother was a Keeper. She'd made contact prior to her death."

A Keeper of Secrets? Well now, that was interesting. He'd thought they were only myth. Of course, the mere existence of Halflings attested to the fact that angels did indeed have secrets to be kept. Why then shouldn't there be Keepers? Wouldn't it be interesting to get his hands on one of those!

"Do we know the Halfling's line?"

At last Dimiezlo lifted his head, his black eyes gleaming like the floor beneath his feet. "Michael."

Any action Stolas might have taken over the lapse in respect was negated by the staggering revelation. He leaned back in his chair as the wind left his lungs in a whoosh.

Michael. *An Archangel. And one of the most powerful Archangels at that. By all that's unholy!*

The power that Halfling possessed would be staggering.

He'd wager all he possessed—and the very success of his plot to overthrow his grandfather—that she'd breed without complication. And not only would she breed well, but the Halfling could be employed as a valuable weapon, herself.

"You will do whatever it takes to obtain her. Promise whatever you have to, pay any fee, but keep it quiet. Utilize any and all resources available. You will obtain her, am I understood?"

Bowing his head, thwapping fists to shoulders, Dimiezlo vanished.

A first generation Halfling…of Michael's line.

Stolas would be invincible.

Chapter Seven

"No," Gideon repeated for what felt like the thousandth time.

"But I *have* to go home."

He had to give the woman points for dogged determination. The last rays of sun were streaking the sky, and she'd used every available opportunity since she'd awoken that morning to needle him on the subject. She hadn't let up one bit. If anything, his continued resistance only seemed to fuel her resolve.

The school this. Her responsibilities that. Her students. The charities she helped. Her damned houseplants. Nag. Nag. Nag.

Sweet Heaven, couldn't the woman understand he was saving her life by keeping her there? Why the hell couldn't she just say thank you and then be quiet?

"Please, Gideon," she said softly, those big blue-green eyes of hers begging. This was a new tactic, and it made him instantly wary. Up until now, she'd tried commanding, arguing, ordering, reasoning. Even shrewd bargaining. This new beseeching tone made him uneasy.

She stood in the door to his study, her hands clasped tightly before her. Dear Lord, she looked so damned good. Better every time he saw her, Heaven help him. The red cashmere sweater he'd conjured for her this morning caressed her sweet curves, as did the faded blue jeans. To his chagrin, he found he rather enjoyed providing for her. Clothing, food, whatever she desired.

Well, everything but what she wanted most. To go home.

He closed the book he'd been flipping through with a snap and turned his back to her, his gaze blindly scanning the bookshelf in front of him. "Subject closed," he reminded her over his shoulder. He reached up to replace the book on the shelf and then grabbed another, not paying the least bit of attention to the title.

The whisper of her boots crossing the area rug caused his body to slowly tighten. Muscle. By. Muscle.

In all fairness, maybe she hadn't spent *every* moment nagging him. In truth, they'd actually passed the time, for the most part, in relative peace. As long as he worked hard to ignore the painful tightening in his loins every time she was near, which had been nearly every moment of the day as he'd taken his responsibilities of guarding her to heart.

That, and he still didn't trust her not to bolt.

So he'd worked to keep them both distracted as much as possible. She was turning out to be an apt pupil with a quick mind when it came to chess. And she liked to paint. Though she professed to be nothing more than an amateur, painting solely for her own enjoyment, she was actually very good. They'd even read for a while in silence, different books in different corners of the room, but they'd been in the same room. So that counted. And they'd talked. She'd broached the subject, more than once, about him teaching her how to defend herself. He'd shot her down, of course. She wouldn't stand a chance against an angel, let alone a demon. It would be cruel of him to set her up for that kind of failure. They'd watched TV. They'd played cards.

And he was running out of ideas of how to keep her entertained.

Her footsteps were perilously close now. He could smell her, the scent of her shampoo, and that vanilla and cinnamon scent that seemed to seep from her very pores. And the hint of...him, his scent. His plan had worked all too well. Backfiring on him like he should have known it would. Damn it, just the smell of her made him painfully hard.

"Gideon." She paused a few steps away. "Please, look at me."

Drawing a deep breath, bracing himself, he turned to face her, clutching the book in front of him like a shield, though she couldn't actually touch him. For some reason, a reason beyond his understanding, he didn't want her to realize it. If she didn't realize she couldn't touch him then in some stupid, completely unrealistic way, maybe he could pretend he was normal.

Those eyes of hers, those damned beautiful, entrancing eyes, peered up at him as she caught the edge of her lower lip between her teeth. All thoughts of normal versus pretend slipped from his mind like dust in the wind. Against his will, he found himself looking at her mouth. Studying it. Craving a taste. Oh how he wanted to drink her in. Devour her. Wanted it so badly his hands trembled and his mouth went dry. His whole body burned with wanting her.

"I know you don't want to discuss this. I'm sorry, but I can't let this go. Can we at least compromise? Please?"

He nodded, distracted by the glistening moisture on

her lush lower lip. Would she taste like she smelled? Of vanilla and cinnamon? Would sampling her bring comfort? Would it ease the ache? Or would it only enflame him? Make him desperate for more? Insatiable?

"Gideon?" she whispered.

The air seemed thicker, harder to breathe. Vanilla and cinnamon. Like cookies. He'd always been a sucker for cookies. He was drowning in those ocean-colored eyes. And he couldn't think of a better way to go.

She seemed as mesmerized as he was. Another few inches and that pert little nose would brush against his. And that sprinkle of adorable freckles. He was so close he could count them. Every. Single. One. He wanted to kiss each one, trace them with his fingertips. And then he wanted to skate his hands over those lush, womanly curves. The warmth of her drew him like a magnet. Her eyelids drooped until just a hint of alluring color could be seen through her thick lashes. Her sweet, shallow breaths whispered across his lips. His arms ached with the need to hold her. His hands itched to touch her delicate skin, and he reached out for her.

Have to touch her…

Touch! Can't touch!

Gideon yanked his hands back, jerked his head up, and staggered back a step. *Damn it!*

That had been close. Too close.

"Compromise?" He echoed the first word that came to mind, shoving a shaking hand through his hair.

She blinked, clearly confused. She'd been under the same spell. He didn't know whether to laugh with joy that she wanted him too or curse his luck. But then, she seemed to recall her purpose. Her face filled with cautious hope.

Christ, what did I just say? Did I agree to something?

A slight frown pulled at his brow as he scrambled to replay the last few seconds of their conversation. No. He hadn't agreed to anything. But he hadn't rejected her out of hand either, as he usually did. And now she thought, obviously, that he was willing to listen, to entertain her proposal.

Damn it all to perdition.

She rushed on before he could interrupt, "Just give me one day. One day, that's all. I swear! Take me back so I can make arrangements. I'll tell my supervisor something's come up, a distant family member got sick or something, and I have to take an extended leave of absence. Let me just get things squared away. Then I'll stay here, or wherever you want me to stay. For a while, at least. And no more poking at you about going back. I promise."

She waited a beat, licking her lips again. He followed the movement, and he couldn't find his voice.

She must have taken his silence as a sign he was wavering. Giving him a tiny, encouraging smile, she pressed, "Please, Gideon, my job is all I have. My whole life. If I don't go back, if I just skip classes without any word to anyone, I'll get fired. I won't be able to get another job as a teacher. I need to contact my supervisor. I have to let her know what's going on. Not the angels and demons stuff," she hurried to assure him. "But I have to tell her something. And I need to let the substitute know about lesson plans and…please, Gideon. Please?"

"It's not safe for you to go to the school. They'll

look for you there."

"Then give me my phone back. I'll call her."

Guilt swamped him. "I can't."

"Why not?"

He'd searched through her phone yesterday afternoon when she'd been occupied with her canvas and paints. Looking for anything that might stand out, anything that might tell him if she'd had more contact with Michael than she'd let on. He hadn't been snooping, at least, that's what he'd tried to convince himself.

He hadn't found anything leading to Michael. But he had recovered several texts from someone named Brett. He'd read those texts shamelessly. All in the interest of protecting her, of course. And when he'd realized Brett had been expecting her for a date, well, his temper had gotten the better of him. The phone had drifted from his hand in tiny, crushed pieces before he'd even realized what he'd done.

"The phone's gone," he said flatly.

"Gone? Why?"

He scrambled to come up with a viable explanation. Something other than the truth. That he'd been jealous.

"They might be able to track you through your phone."

There. That sounded reasonable. Never mind that it sounded like something he'd picked up off some TV crime show. Hell, yeah. That was a damned good possibility.

This news annoyed her. He could tell by the brief tightening of her lips. But she let it slide, thinking fast on her feet.

"Then let me use your phone," she stated firmly. "I won't have to go to school at all. You can take me to my house so I can pick up some things. I won't take long. I promise." She blinked up at him. "Please?"

He was going to cave. He could feel it, resist though he tried. This was a bad idea. Very bad.

"Stolas's minions will be watching your house too. They won't care who gets hurt," he warned her.

"I'll be fast, I promise. You can protect me, right? You can go everywhere I go. I won't be out of your sight. Not for a minute. And there are the bracelets. If things get too hot, if someone—something—shows up, you can shimmer me away. I'm safe with you here, right? I'll be safe with you there too."

"There are ward stones surrounding this property, and spells, like there were at Sebastian's farm. They prevent—or hinder, at least—other demons and most angels from shimmering inside the house and repel them from the property."

"We'll be careful. I'll do everything you tell me." She smiled, all innocence. Lifting her hand, she held it out, palm up in invitation. "You can even hold my hand so you know I won't be too far away if we come under attack."

Gideon recoiled from her hand, swiftly retreating behind his desk.

Her brows drew together on a sharp frown. Slowly, she lowered her hand, watching him now with unsettling awareness.

"Ten minutes," he blurted. If he gave her what she wanted, maybe she'd be too happy to ask the questions he could see already forming on her tempting lips.

"Two hours," she bargained instantly.

He narrowed his eyes. "One hour. No more."

"Deal," she chirped, grinning like that had been her goal all along. It probably had been. Frustrating woman. "I can call the school first thing in the morning. I won't tell my supervisor where I am," she added when he opened his mouth to object. "We could go to my house tonight, grab a few things and be out of there quickly. They won't even know we were there."

He heaved a defeated sigh. "You can use my phone tonight. Leave a message. The less you speak with anyone, the fewer questions you'll have to answer. We'll go to your place tomorrow."

Whirling around, she hurried to the door as if worried he might change his mind if she lingered.

But at the door, she paused, turning back. "Thank you, Gideon," she said. And then she stepped out into the foyer and disappeared from sight. The sound of her footsteps faded as she ascended the grand staircase.

Like a brick upside the head, Gideon realized what had happened. He'd just been played. She'd come in all soft and pleading. So very different from how she'd behaved before. He should have been on his guard. Hell, he *had* been. And she'd still gotten around him. She'd identified what he'd wanted most, for her not to ask about his obvious aversion to touching, and used it to distract him, used it to get her way.

An admiring breath hissed from him as he sprawled onto the padded chair behind his desk. He braced one elbow on the armrest and balanced his chin on his thumb. Rubbing the edge of his finger thoughtfully back and forth over his lips, Gideon stared at the empty doorway.

He arched an eyebrow. The edges of his lips

gradually lifted.

The little minx had no idea what she was up against.

****

Maggie's internal clock woke her around six in the morning. Yawning, she rolled over and stretched, appreciating the languid rush of blood through her muscles. She'd tossed and turned most of the night, haunted by the scent of Gideon. It seeped from the pillow, and the bed itself. From the very air around her.

Her captor. The man who'd saved her—*no*, she corrected herself, *the demon*—the *demon* who'd saved her. She couldn't stop thinking about him.

But determination rode her. She'd given it a lot of thought and made up her mind last night after she'd gotten off the phone with her supervisor. She'd even wheedled a second call out of Gideon, explaining that she needed to contact Gail otherwise her friends would worry and eventually get the police involved. He'd grudgingly agreed.

Staying with Gideon, perhaps, could turn out to be a blessing in disguise. While the last thing she wanted to do was immerse herself any further into this other world, she'd be a fool to go on pretending that it didn't exist. And an even bigger fool for not taking advantage of the situation. She wanted to survive, didn't she? More than that, she wanted to live. A full, rich, rewarding life. Not a life spent looking over her shoulder, jumping at shadows.

And so, she would convince Gideon to teach her how to fight. Somehow. She'd get him to teach her about those spells and special stones he'd referred to last night too. She'd learn how to protect herself so she never had to rely on someone else again. So she'd never be taken by surprise again.

Starting today.

After tossing back the covers, she rose and crossed to the bathroom. She brushed her teeth, changed into a pair of running shorts, a sports bra and a T-shirt, and pulled her hair back into a ponytail. Sitting on the edge of the bed to tie her running shoes, she caught sight of something peeking out from the edge of the dust ruffle. Maggie got down on her knees and pulled a book from beneath the bed.

A Studied Compilation of Ancient Mayan Myths and Rituals.

It was an old book. Worn. As if someone had been using it regularly as a point of reference. Several pages were dog-eared. Curious to see what a man—*demon*—like Gideon might find so interesting, Maggie flipped the book open to the first marked page. Balancing the book in one hand, she crossed the room and pushed the button on the TreadClimber. As the machine started up, she paused. Glancing from the book in her hands to the TreadClimber and back, Maggie recalled all the art supplies in the main dining room. And she suffered a pang of guilt.

He'd asked her what she liked to do. She'd mentioned that she liked to paint. Then, mindful of that last ten pounds she never quite managed to lose no matter how much she worked out or starved herself, she also told him that she often went to the gym in the morning before she went to work. Later that very morning, Gideon had directed her to the dining room, now empty but for an easel, a pile of canvases of varying sizes lined the walls, and a small work table holding a vast array of paints and brushes. The freshly repaired curtains had been thrown wide to let in a flood of sunshine. Later that night, when she'd returned to her—*his*—room, she'd discovered the corner of the massive bedroom filled with a hodgepodge of exercise equipment, and a stack of exercise wear and running shoes on the foot of the bed.

While it was true he'd been deliberately avoiding her questions—deny it all he wanted, she wasn't an idiot—he'd gone out of his way to make sure she had every comfort. And here she was, blatantly invading his privacy. She nibbled her lip and debated, for all of half a second, over putting the book back where she'd found it.

Squaring her shoulders, telling herself it was just a harmless book, she propped it in the media holder. After climbing onto the machine, she began reading that first dog-eared page.

The Amulet of the Gods.

Nearly two hours later, showered and dressed, she headed down the hall in search of her host. *The Amulet of the Gods.* If the book had been any indication, Gideon appeared to be obsessed with the thing. Notes lined the pages, some sort of code, or words written in a language she'd never seen before, she couldn't quite tell. Shoved haphazardly throughout the book had been numerous scraps of papers, written in the same elusive text. Elegant script had transcribed page after page of information. There were also sketches. Amateur and untutored, but quite detailed all the same. And always of the same theme. Centered around the same piece of ancient jewelry. It looked like a heavy piece, gold inlaid with rough-cut rubies. Presumably the amulet itself.

The question was, why was Gideon so focused on this one talisman?

She came to the end of the hallway and stopped in front of the door she'd seen Gideon go into last night. She didn't know for sure she'd find him here, had no reason to believe this was where he'd been staying, other than her own instinct. Easing the door open, she peered into the shadows. The drapes were drawn, but not tightly. Slivers of light forced their way in through moth-eaten drapes, determined to chase away the gloom.

Soft snoring came from the huge, antique-looking four-poster bed on the far wall.

Unable to resist, she tiptoed across the room. Halfway to the bed, she paused and glanced around, frowning. The only thing not covered in massive, dingy dust cloths was the bed. Everything else wore a layer of grime and cobwebs. He'd given up his room for her. And now he was sleeping here. In this neglected mess. Because of her.

Feeling herself softening toward this puzzle of a man/demon despite her earlier resolve to look out for number one, she crept closer to the bed.

Gideon lay sprawled on his stomach, one knee drawn up to his side. A pillow was clutched tight beneath one arm. Another was bunched beneath his head. The very corner of a sheet was twisted around his hips—very low on his very naked hips—and partially covered one leg. The rest of his mouthwatering, golden-skinned body was bare. Naked all but for that hammered silver cuff and a thin chain around his neck.

His arms bore extensive tattoos, but the light was too dim to get a decent look at them. The dim light and the dark tattoos, however, couldn't hide the ridges of his powerful, bunched muscles.

Nor did they hide the hideous scars slashing their way over his shoulder blades.

It took her a long moment of study to finally realize what they were, those scars. They were from where his wings had been removed. Viciously, brutally, by the looks of them. She clutched her throat, resisting the urge to cry in sympathy.

Oh, my poor Gideon.

Forcing her gaze away from the stark evidence of his origin lest she give in to the urge to cry after all, she surveyed the rest of his body. She'd like to pretend that she looked at him with the frank appreciation of an artist. But she couldn't lie to herself. Whatever she felt, it had nothing to do with an artist's eye. What she felt was a purely feminine attraction for a very fine masculine form. Defined muscles roped his broad back, dipping down to a trim waist and the upper curve of firm buttocks. A light, golden dusting of hair covered his powerful bare legs. Even his feet were sexy. Was there an inch of this man she wouldn't mind nibbling on?

Her greedy gaze skimmed over him once again, head to toe.

Nope. Not one single inch.

Maggie stepped up to the side of the bed. Sunlight struggled through cloud cover and, for a few minutes, it seemed to be winning. The light broke free, illuminating his face for a few moments. Dark lashes rested upon his lean cheekbones. A hint of blond stubble covered his strong jaw. His wildly mussed hair shone bright in the light, a lock of it falling across his forehead.

He looked so peaceful. Like the angel he must have once been. Her heart fluttered in her chest.

With the light as it was, she could see the rough patch of pink skin on his side. A fairly recent wound. A huge one. A wound that would have likely killed a human. One that had left the golden perfection of his skin puckered and marred with pearl-pink scar tissue. Carefully, praying he wasn't ticklish, she reached out to touch the rippled scar.

As her fingers connected with his warm flesh, she froze. Just like that, the world around her dimmed and slid out of focus.

Oh God, no. Not another one. Not now.

The vision sucked her out of place and time. Fast flashes. Vivid, unmistakable images. Lights and shadows. It was like a movie in fast forward, and she a trapped viewer. A reluctant voyeur. She could sometimes discern where the vision took place, based on the surroundings she caught glimpses of, but she never knew when it would happen, only that it would. Events she could not avoid no matter what she did to prevent it.

A future she could not change.

She saw herself. And she saw Gideon. He had her pressed up against a wall. She couldn't tell where, didn't recognize the wallpaper. Then again, she had trouble tearing her vision from the naked couple writhing in reckless abandon. Gideon held one of her wrists clamped above her head. Her face was tipped up, her eyes closed, her mouth open as she gasped in ecstasy. He devoured her neck.

His free hand was clamped on her bottom, firm and

unyielding, possessive, gripping tight. The muscles of his arms and back were taut. Fine beads of perspiration glistened on his skin. And on hers. Maggie had wrapped her legs around his lean waist, locked her ankles over his tight buttocks. His back flexed and bunched as those lean hips pumped in a primal, unstoppable, brutal rhythm.

Just as quickly as the vision hit her, it disappeared. She was slammed back into the here and now. Maggie stumbled back a step, panting softly. Her body ached, trembling with need. Her blood sang in her veins.

Never before had she experienced a vision like that. Ever. Not one so sensual, so corporeal. Normally it was like watching a movie with familiar faces. Very 2D. Sometimes even 3D with action going on all around her. But this vision had been anything but. She swore she'd actually felt his teeth rake over her skin. She could still feel the slight sting on her flesh. She'd felt him pressing into her, felt his heat fill her. Felt him moving inside her, stretching her, stroking her. She shivered at the delicious phantom sensations.

Her mind raced, swirling with so many thoughts she was a bit lightheaded. But one thought kept coming back to her, over and over. In that vision, she'd been mindless with passion, oblivious to all else. Angels could have descended en masse from Heaven. Demons could have risen from Hell in droves. Armageddon could have happened all around her, and she wouldn't have known.

Wouldn't have cared.

She'd never experienced that, a complete and utter loss of control, loss of awareness.

The very idea scared the living hell out of her.

Temptation

Try as she might, she couldn't escape the vision. Couldn't put it from her as she did other visions, couldn't store it away until she could sort it all out later. Her body was strung out. Her emotions were tangled.

Without thought, she reached out once more and whispered her trembling fingers across his brow. His hair felt like silk against her skin. Feeling brave now, or maybe it was the vision that drove her beyond all good sense, she gently eased her fingers along his jaw, savoring the rasp of his sandpaper stubble. What would it feel like to have that stubble scrape along the side of her neck? Along the curve of her breast? Her sensitive nipples?

She'd be finding out, soon enough. Her visions never lied.

Forcing a swallow, she jerked her hand back. Touching him only made her body ache for more. She had to clear her head. Had to think this one through. He'd come so close to kissing her in the study. And she'd come so close to letting him. In that moment, she had never wanted anything more. Not even her freedom.

But then he'd pulled back. Just like he always did. Why was he so careful never to touch her? Not even an accidental brush of his fingers?

According to her vision, he'd get over that aversion. With a vengeance.

He shifted in his sleep, and she jolted back. Clarity swept over her. She should be waking him up. Should be hurrying him along so they could get back to Portland. She wanted to go home, needed to see familiar things around her. Pack some of her own things to bring back with her for the short time she intended to

119

stay with Gideon.

But she couldn't shake the unsettling vision of them together.

Biting her lip, she stepped back, turned and silently slipped from the room.

Space. Time. Distance. She needed to get out of here. She needed to think things through. Vaguely, she realized she was panicking. Nearly hyperventilating. She couldn't rationalize. Couldn't breathe.

She needed air.

Her feet flew down the grand staircase, and Maggie hit the door running.

****

Stolas stepped outside one of the cells in his dungeon and closed the door behind him. With a sweep of his hand, the lock engaged. Sweat covered his body, and blood coated his hands. While he didn't need to physically touch those he tortured for information, sometimes it proved a pleasant diversion.

His thoughts turned to his bedroom and the demoness he currently had chained to his bed. A luxury. A rarity. Female demons were, perhaps, even harder to find than those cursed Halflings. But, oh, the fight in this one was more than worth the price it had cost him to procure her.

He'd no more than begun to pull in his energy to shimmer there when a servant scurried around the corner at the end of the hall and bowed to him.

"Master, I beg your forgiveness, but Dimiezlo is back."

Stolas gritted his teeth. He didn't like disruptions in his plans, but Dimiezlo might have captured the Halfling.

"Have him meet me in the great hall."

The servant vanished.

Taking a moment to conjure himself presentable, Stolas shimmered to the great hall. Dimiezlo was already waiting. Stolas motioned for him to speak.

"Master," Dimiezlo hissed. "We do not have the Halfling yet, but I have commissioned Mortikaï to capture her."

"Mortikaï!" Stolas bellowed. Mortikaï was Captain of the Guard, warden of Lucifer's personal prisoners.

"Mortikaï's hatred for the Demon of Temptation is far greater than his loyalty to the Dark Prince. He's on his way to the Halfling's house even as we speak."

Stolas rocked back on his heels. Having one so close to Lucifer aware of the plot was beyond dangerous. And yet, in a way, brilliant. Provided Mortikaï could be trusted. And in all honesty, what demon could really be trusted?

Still. Mortikaï could prove a valuable ally.

"Keep me apprised. And Dimiczlo? If this goes badly, you will suffer."

Chapter Eight

"Maggie?" Gideon strode down the hallway, a frown tugging his brow. Where the hell was she?

He'd checked his—*her* bedroom, the kitchen, the den, and the dining room where he'd set up her easel. Even though he strode down the hall, calling her name to no avail, he was dead certain the house was empty. Damn frustrating woman. He should have known better than to trust her. He should have locked her in his—*her* room.

He could have sworn when he'd woken up a little bit ago, he could actually smell vanilla and cinnamon in the room. Hell, the Halfling was driving him to distraction. He'd probably just imagined it. Conjured the scent in his dreams, just like he'd dreamed of touching her. Dreamed of her touching him. Dreamed of making love to her. The ghost sensation of her fingers gliding over his flesh taunted him.

He'd lived with his curse so long now one would think he would have gotten used to not being able to touch anyone anymore. And he had, with most everyone else. Sure, there was still the urge for physical contact, and the inevitable sadness and resentment when he couldn't. But with Maggie it was different. With her, the need was somehow magnified. A burning demand. One that grew exponentially with every passing hour in her presence. And the fury at being thwarted was nearly too much for him to contain.

But you can touch her, a sneaky little voice in the back of his head echoed. *You know how...*

Just as quickly, he squashed it.

Or tried to, but that voice wouldn't be denied. Not this time. It taunted him, offering him that which he wanted most. Maybe because his need was so great?

Hungry desperation was driving him to consider something he'd never let himself even think about before.

He physically couldn't touch her—that was true. Not while he was in *human* form. But he could touch her while he was in demon form. A fact not many beings knew about. Demon form was the only way he could physically touch anyone. And that was his darkest curse of all. The mindless rage, the primordial drive for destruction and carnage while in demon form made him a menace to anyone—everyone—who got close to him. Friend or foe.

In demon form, he'd be more likely to kill her than caress her.

No. He would not touch her. He couldn't put her in that kind of danger.

Mindful of her aversion to shimmering, grinding his teeth, he headed for the door. If he didn't find her within the next five minutes, he would shimmer, thereby forcing her to his side, to hell with her preferences.

The front veranda was empty. Every step farther from the house ratcheted his anger up another notch. He stopped where the long gravel drive split into a circle around a large fountain in the front yard. The fountain was dry. Vines had snaked up and around the fountain,

Brenda Huber

and now clung, withered and brown, to the aged and crumbling stone. His gaze skimmed the long tree-lined lane before he turned and strode around the side of the house and headed toward the overgrown backyard.

He was just about to shimmer when he caught a flash of bright color in the distance. There she was, seated upon the decaying steps of the neglected gazebo. She hugged her knees, staring pensively at the slow-moving river. Much as he hated to admit it, relief swept over him. Anger and irritation seeped away. She hadn't run after all.

She looked up as he approached, maintaining eye contact for only moment before turning her gaze away. She focused on the river once more, as if all the answers to the universe's questions were streaming by and she didn't dare glance away again for fear she might miss something important. But she was too late. He'd already caught the fleeting look of panic in her eyes.

She looked…haunted? No, perhaps *hunted* was a more apt term. Definitely cornered.

He sat beside her, bracing his forearms across his knees. The silence stretched on between them. Without taking his gaze from the muddy brown water, he quietly asked, "Wanna talk about it?"

She jolted and turned to him. "About what?"

He gave her a measured stare. Oh, yeah. That was panic he'd just heard in her voice. A whole lot of panic. "About whatever it is that's got you so spooked."

Her lips parted, then pressed shut, only to part once more. She looked like a fish gulping for air.

Whipping her head back to face the river, she croaked, "I'm fine. Nothing to talk about."

124

Yeah? And I've got a helluva deal on a dirt-cheap bridge.

But he held his tongue and let the silence stretch once more.

Eventually, he heaved a sigh. "Aside from going back to your old life and burying your head in denial, what is it you want most?"

She turned to study him now. Was the color in her cheeks just a bit darker? Had her breath just caught? Was she glancing at his mouth?

Or was he just imagining it? Seeing what he wanted, rather than what was really there?

She moistened her lips and cleared her throat. "Honestly?"

He nodded.

"I want—" She paused, drawing a deep breath. "I want to be able to fight. I want to know how to defend myself. I don't want to have to rely on somebody else to keep me safe. And I don't want my only defense to be running away and hiding. I don't want to be helpless. I don't want to be at the mercy of someone else's whims anymore," she added softly.

Gideon regarded her. He wanted to insist that she need not worry. As long as he was alive, he would always keep her safe.

As soon as that thought crossed his mind, he frowned. Number one, she wasn't his to keep. Not only was she a fiercely independent woman, but she would also be passionate. A woman like her needed a male who could touch her. A male who could stoke her passions and satisfy her in ways that Gideon could only dream about.

And number two, if he stuck to the plan, his life

expectancy would be woefully short.

Oblivion, remember?

Standing, he paced away, paced back, paced away once more as he struggled with every instinct inside him screaming to keep her hidden away and safe, as far from danger as possible. And so, he would do the only thing he could for her. Give her the only thing he was capable of giving to ensure she would be protected long after he was gone.

There was only one answer.

Turning, he regarded her, feeling as if the weight of the world was sitting on his chest.

"I'm going to make a phone call, and then we're going to go to your place"—he pointed a warning finger at her—"for no more than one hour. You're going to pack only what you absolutely need. And then we're going to come back here."

He drew a deep breath, praying he wasn't making the worst mistake of her life. "And when we get back, I'm going to teach you what you need to know to survive. Not how to hide," he amended, holding up his hand when she made to object. "I will teach you how to fight. I'll teach you what you need to know about ward stones and guard stones and angels and demons...the truth about angels and demons. And I'll get Kyanna to teach you the rest. The spells and incantations, and whatever else it is that she can."

A hint of tears glistened before she blinked them away. His heart lurched inside his tight chest. Her tremulous smile hit him like a sucker punch to the gut, leveling him as nothing else ever had.

"But," he quickly added, his tone ruthless, unbending, "in return, you will stay here at the plantation willingly, for as long as I see fit." The thought of her continuing to live here after he was gone, safe and protected, gave him comfort in some strange way. "You will promise you won't try to leave without me for any reason. When we're training, and especially when we go to your place to get your things—any time we leave the plantation for that matter—you'll do as you're told. Exactly as you're told. No arguments."

"Yes, I promise," she chirped. He eyed her with a great deal of suspicion. She beamed back at him, which only made him more wary.

He recalled her troubled expression when he'd found her earlier. "And no more secrets. You don't keep anything from me. Deal?"

Maggie bobbed her head, her smile growing blinding. His groin tightened in response. She was moving, closing the distance between them. Panic scored him. He'd seen that kind of body language before, usually whenever Carly flung herself into Niklas's waiting arms. If Maggie touched him or, more importantly, *didn't* touch him—she'd know. Know what a freak he was, even among his own kind. She'd know the truth of his curse.

He threw his hands up between them—as if that could physically stop her—and took three giant steps backward in retreat. Maggie skidded to a halt, her expression sliding swiftly from overjoyed gratitude to startled rejection. She was quick to school her features, but he'd seen it, nonetheless, and her emotions sliced him like a poisoned athamé.

"I'll make that call now," he muttered, pivoting on his heel and all but running away. He may just as well have had his tail tucked firmly between his legs. Never

127

had his curse tormented him more.

Once he was inside the kitchen, safely alone, he leaned against the counter and dropped his head back on his shoulders. She was bound to find out, sooner or later. Why was he prolonging the inevitable?

Because he didn't want her to look at him like all the others did. With pity. Even Carly, Lord love her, would slip once in a while and look at him with sympathy when she thought he wasn't paying attention. God, he was sick of this. Yeah, he was dangerous. Feared by his enemies and, even to a point, among his own brethren. And yet, powerful as he was, even he was pitied.

So make the call and you'll be that much closer to ending this mission, asshole.

Still, he hesitated. Ending this mission meant never seeing Maggie again. And that didn't sit well. Gideon shook his head and steeled his resolve. He'd made her a promise. And himself. Teach her. End his misery. That was all that mattered. Still, her face haunted him. He almost wished… But no.

If he couldn't have her, couldn't touch her and keep her for his own, then he'd do everything in his power to make sure she had the tools to survive.

The sound of a door closing softly somewhere in the house brought him back to the task at hand. Traces of vanilla and cinnamon lingered in the kitchen, giving him the strength to do what needed to be done.

Fishing his phone from his pocket, he thumbed in Xander's speed dial number.

"No," was Xander's brisk greeting.

Asshole.

"You don't even know what I was going to ask."

"It involves the Halfling, doesn't it?"

"Yeah, but—"

"Then, no."

Okay then. Since Xander wasn't going to be reasonable—big surprise there—it was time to pull out the big guns. "I'd sure hate for Kyanna to find out you aren't letting her do her job."

A beat of furious silence met his threat.

"You wouldn't," Xander snarled.

"In a heartbeat. Out of respect, I'm coming to you first. But don't think for one second I won't go around you if I have to. Maggie needs training only Kyanna can give her." Gideon pushed ruthlessly. "Are you willing to risk letting a first-generation Halfling fall into Stolas's hands because you're being an overprotective prick? What do you think your little mate will have to say about that?"

Hoarse, foul curses stabbed Gideon's ear.

More silence stretched, but Gideon knew he had Xander over a barrel. Xander loved his woman beyond all else, beyond reason. But he'd made the mistake of promising her never to interfere with her jobs as a Guardian. Nor with her determination to protect the Halflings listed in the books her family had passed down, generation to generation. And he'd made that mistake with an audience. What's more, Xander would never break a promise to his woman.

Gideon wasn't above using that promise to get what he wanted.

"We're going to Maggie's place in a little while to gather some of her things. When we get back, I'll begin her training. Be here first thing tomorrow morning." Gideon let a grim smile twist his lips as he disconnected the call, cutting Xander's blunt opinion of Gideon's dirty play short.

Shoving the phone back in his pocket, he went in search of the thorn in his side. Following the scent of vanilla and cinnamon, he ascended the stairs, only to pause in confusion. The scent trail—and the soft sounds of movement—were coming from the room he'd slept in last night, not from his—*her* room, as he'd assumed. Quietly, Gideon strode to the doorway, pausing to lean against the doorjamb. Crossing his arms over his chest, he stood, watching her in silence.

She'd stripped the sheets from the bed, the shabby curtains from the windows, and the dust cloths from the rest of the furniture. She'd thrown the windows wide open, and a strong breeze of fresh air swept through the room. She was currently standing on a chair, stretching on tiptoe, using a broom with a towel wrapped around the end to clear cobwebs from the corner.

Industrious little thing.

Despite his resolve to keep things impersonal and his determination to stick to the plan, he couldn't stifle the spurt of warmth seeping through his chest somewhere in the vicinity of his heart. She was cleaning his room, seeing to his comfort. Her courage and her spirit had called to him. Her beauty, the scent of her, the curve of her smile, her lush body, hell even the freckles on her face, drove him insane with lust. But this kindness despite their brief and oftentimes tense acquaintance touched him. No, touched wasn't strong enough. It slayed him.

Why?

He had no friggin' clue.

What he did know, with blinding clarity, was that if

he could have had any woman for his own, any woman in the world, he would have chosen this one. He knew it as he'd never known another truth. He would have chosen Maggie.

And he could never have her.

The anger crept up on him, insidious. Debilitating. The rage inside him began to stir, and the beast reared its ugly head.

Nostrils flared, teeth gritted, Gideon clamped down hard and fast on the monster, shoving wants and desires down deep, burying them beneath a mountain of indifference. He pushed from the doorway and strode into the room.

"What are you doing?" Ice crystals dripped from his tone.

She bobbled the broom, throwing her arms out to balance herself, and she gasped aloud. "Oh, my goodness. You startled me."

"I asked you a question. What do you think you're doing?"

She glanced around, as if the evidence should be obvious. "I know you gave up your room for me." She climbed down from the chair and set the broom aside, brushing dust from her hands. "So, I thought…" Her voice trailed off as she stared at the severe frown on his face.

She cleared her throat, lifted her chin, squared her shoulders, and pushed on. "I thought, since you agreed to teach me to defend myself…and well, with the paints and the exercise equipment…and you gave up your room for me…" She heaved a frustrated sigh. "I was just trying to show my appreciation. This was all I could think of."

"Don't worry about it," he said, deadpan.

"But this room is filthy!" She took a step in his direction, only to pull up short, as if she'd thought better of approaching him. "You can't stay here in this—"

Gideon gave a very dramatic, totally unnecessary flourish of his hand and conjured the room spotless. New curtains framed the now gleaming windows. Fresh bedding covered the perfectly made bed. Dulled framed landscapes now gleamed as if the paint were still drying. Chipped and broken furniture stood perfectly repaired and ready to be used. Neither a speck of dust, nor a cobweb was to be seen.

He arched a sarcastic brow. "Happy?"

Her breath caught as she swiftly spun in a circle, taking in his mad housekeeping skills. Slowly, she turned back to face him. "If you could do that, why were you sleeping in this room with it the way it was?"

"Are you ready to go?"

Her lips tightened in a flat line, and her eyes narrowed. After a moment of deep breathing, she said in a very polite, very clipped tone, "I just need to wash up a bit."

He gave another dramatic, sarcastic flourish, conjuring her clean.

"Ready now, darlin'?"

Temper flared to life, sparkling in her eyes. Before she could explode, Gideon pulled in his power, focusing on the mental picture of her little bungalow in the suburbs. The bedroom fell away, and the grass of her backyard solidified beneath his feet.

He watched as she materialized nearby, wobbling on unsteady legs. Her face had lost every last drop of color. Squelching the urge to reach for her, to steady her, to apologize, he marched past her and headed toward the house.

"One hour and not a second more," he bit out, not letting himself so much as glance her way. "Better hop to it."

"Jackass," she hissed beneath her breath and stomped after him.

Despite his determination not to bend, a slow, appreciative grin curved the edges of his mouth.

That's my girl.

Chapter Nine

The moment Gideon cleared the doorway, he knew something was wrong. He came to an abrupt stop, but it was too late. Maggie, hot on his heels, was already inside.

"Gideon, wait," she cried. "Something here is wrong! I can feel it."

A dark chuckle echoed through the living room. "So the Halfling has powers of her own? Perhaps I'll have to spend a bit of time with her before turning her over to Stolas."

Mortikaï.

The memory of a crushed, blackened ball of gold and fractured jewels came to mind. That amulet would have made it possible for him to touch the woman beside him. He could have kept Maggie, could have taken her as his mate. Could have spent an eternity in her arms. Mortikaï had stolen more from Gideon than he'd realized.

Rage slammed through him before he even knew it was coming. Gideon launched himself across the room, morphing into his demonic form on the fly without giving it a second thought. He plowed into Mortikaï with bone crushing force.

A shrill scream rent the air, but Temptation was too focused on killing the demon he battled to wonder where the cry had come from. Huge fists pummeled him. Razor sharp claws tore through his flesh. Temptation barely felt the blows. Unleashed fury drove him. He wanted this bastard's blood flowing between his fingers. Temptation wanted to tear him into tiny pieces. He wanted his head on a spike.

Walls cracked, windows shattered, furniture splintered and crumbled beneath his fury as he threw the demon across the room and dove after him, rolling about, teeth gnashing, claws slashing, elbows and knees flying.

Temptation felt a brief sting as his enemy made a grab for his throat. He missed tearing out Temptation's jugular, but a glint of silver flashed in the demon's bloody fist. A plasma ball exploded near Temptation's shoulder as another demon appeared in the corner.

Dodging the flames, Temptation shot to his feet, driving a fist spine deep into his foe's stomach. Another plasma ball splattered across Temptation's back. With a fierce roar, he turned to confront his attacker. He vaulted across the room, gripped the newcomer's head between his massive hands, and squeezed, crushing it like a cantaloupe.

After igniting a plasma ball, he dropped it on his fallen foe to finish the job. Spinning back, he caught a brief glimpse of his nemesis's vile smile as his foe held something small, something shiny, and sparkling silver up in his bloody fist. And then his target disappeared in shimmering waves of air.

Uncomprehending of what message his enemy had been trying to send, Temptation lunged forward, roaring for the bastard to come back. Just a hint of a shimmer trail lingered. The bastard wouldn't get away from him that easy.

But a tiny whimper snagged his attention. Still caught in the grips of bloodlust, Temptation whirled about, searching for another adversary, for something else that needed killing. Wild, Temptation stalked across the room, kicking the broken hunks of furniture out of his way.

A small female crouched in the corner, her eyes wide and terrified. Something feral rose up inside him. He could scent her fear, and he fed on it, tracking it the way a wild animal scented its prey.

The female rose, her whole body trembling violently as she braced her back against the wall. She cautiously lifted her hands, palms out, between them and spoke. At first he couldn't understand her, couldn't understand the strange language, the words foreign and difficult to process.

Hunger for destruction drove him closer. The female's soul pulsed with an energy he'd rarely, if ever, seen before. It bathed her like a golden sunrise. Feeding from her would give him energy untold. He stared at her, at first greedily drinking in the pulsing power he was soon to take, but then, by slow degrees, he became aware of her physically. And hunger of another kind rose. Her body would pleasure his first, as he hadn't been pleasured in time untold.

Temptation closed the distance between them, reaching for her. But the moment his large hand closed over the fragile bones of her wrist, the strangest sensation washed over him. It was as if he'd been bathed in white light. Magical. Soothing. Peaceful. A foreign kind of calm enveloped him. He drew a deep breath. Sweet. Vanilla. Cinnamon.

Familiar. *Why?*

Frowning, he struggled to make the connection as his body warred with itself. Feed from her. Hold on to her like something precious. Take her beneath him and pleasure himself ruthlessly upon her flesh. Protect her.

Temptation drew another deep breath. Breathing her in. With every breath, those urges to protect became more powerful, the urge to destroy muted, placated.

He reached out curiously and ran the back of his knuckles along the smooth skin of her cheek. Soft. His brow knitted as he caught a lock of hair between his thumb and fingers. He rubbed it, marveling at the smooth texture.

She nervously moistened her lower lip with the tip of a delicate tongue. His feral, narrow-eyed gaze snapped to her mouth. With cautious movements, he gently ran the pad of his thumb along the glistening pink flesh, testing texture and warmth. The acrid scent of her fear abated. He slowly met her gaze. The color, not quite blue, not quite green, caught him. Trapping him. Calming him further. The flutter of her pulse tickled the pads of his fingers, and he gentled his grip on her wrist in response.

A disturbance of energy and power behind him snapped his attention around.

"Gideon!" A deep male voice cracked through the room. "Step back from the Halfling."

Temptation whipped his head back, and he blinked at the female. She began to twist and tug frantically at her wrist, first whimpering, and then agonized moaning deep in her throat as her big eyes welled with tears. She spoke to him again in that language he couldn't understand. Her delicate wrist snapped like a twig beneath his grip, and she cried out.

"Temptation! Release her!"

His head jerked around. He didn't like that tone. Not one bit.

Who was this demon who dared to challenge him for this prize?

Sharp little nails clawed at his forearm. The female flailed, trying desperately to get away. Irritated, he tossed the female aside, turning to fully face his challenger, dismissing the pained whoosh of breath as the female crashed into something and fell to the floor with a dull thud.

"Mikhail," his challenger barked. "Get the Halfling back to the farm."

Temptation's head snapped to the side, only now aware of another demon in the room. A tall bastard, bald, scarred, and ugly as sin. Temptation snarled as the second demon approached the female. She belonged to him.

The big, scarred demon bristled with aggression.

"Not now, Mikhail," the first demon said quietly. "He's too far gone. Just take care of the Halfling."

"He is beyond reason, Seer," the big demon warned.

"I know," the challenger said, his voice resigned. "Just get her out of here."

Temptation watched the byplay between the two, not really caring what they were saying. Were they here to fight, or talk? Because he wasn't interested in talking. Only in blood. Their blood.

"I'm sorry about this, Gideon." The challenger lunged toward Temptation, wrapping massive arms around him. They crashed to the floor. Roaring, Temptation turned his full attention on the challenger.

That was all the time it took for the second demon to snatch up his prize. Then the second demon shimmered, taking the unconscious female with him.

Fury rolled through him as the soothing, strangely familiar scent of vanilla and cinnamon faded.

A meaty fist clipped Temptation in the jaw. "Snap out of it, Gideon." Another blow caught him in the temple. "We need you now, you bloody bastard. Calm down!"

Temptation swung wildly, connecting with the challenger's ribs, driving a satisfying whoosh of air from his lungs as bone snapped.

"Damn it, Gideon. I didn't want to have to do it this way." The challenger held up something in his fist. Small, metallic. Temptation sniffed the air, wary now.

A powerful electrical charge zapped into his chest, bringing him to his knees. Another jolt streamed into the side of his neck, even more powerful than the first, and his huge body convulsed as wave after wave of electrical currents slammed through him. Darkness claimed him before his head hit the floor.

****

Gideon woke with a start as ice cold water splashed onto his face. His gaze whipped around the room, and he realized he was lying on the floor. He took in the fireplace, the hunting lodge décor, and realized he was at Sebastian's farm. He couldn't remember how he'd gotten there. But that was nothing new. He'd often woken up in a different place after going demonic. The trick was trying to remember what he'd done while in demonic form. Sometimes, he never remembered.

Those times were, more often than not, a blessing.

"He's coming to," he heard Carly call out.

139

Niklas's face came into his line of sight.

"Good to have you back, buddy."

"What happened?" The room spun, but he shook his head. Whatever it was, it had been something fiercely important. "Where's Maggie?"

Niklas and Carly exchanged worried glances.

Gideon turned to the tall demon leaning over the sofa a few feet away. His bald head was tipped forward in concentration, and his broad back blocked most of the woman from Gideon's sight. But he'd know those legs anywhere.

Gideon rushed across the room. Maggie lay on the couch, unconscious, barely breathing. Blood smeared the side of her face. One arm lay across her stomach, her wrist swollen, black and blue, and bent at an impossible angle. A large, bloody tear in her shirt revealed a still healing, pink splash of skin.

Only by sheer dint of will did Gideon refrain from going demonic and possessively shoving Mikhail's large hands away from where they hovered over her chest. Mikhail was healing her, he reminded himself. But it didn't help much. The idea of any male touching her for any reason turned his vision red with jealousy.

Anxious, Gideon looked to Mikhail's face. Mikhail's expression was grim, focused. A muscle clenched in his jaw. A bead of perspiration rolled down the side of his face, pooling in the deep scars.

"What the hell happened to her?" Gideon demanded, whirling to confront Niklas.

Niklas reached over and, grasping Carly's elbow, tugged her behind him. Shielding her from Gideon's wrath, no doubt.

"Do you remember going to Maggie's house?"

Niklas asked in a soft voice.

Frowning, Gideon slowly nodded. He remembered shimmering there. Maggie had called him a jackass. The muscle in his cheek jumped at the memory. But then he frowned. Something had felt wrong once they'd gone inside the house. Maggie had felt it too.

Mortikaï.

The battle.

His stomach dropped as scene after scene flashed through his mind, distorted and shadowed. But he remembered most of it. Enough to know true horror. His entire body went rigid as he stared down at Maggie.

I did that. I hurt her. Oh sweet Christ!

His worst fears had come to pass. He dropped helplessly to his knees beside Mikhail. Gideon lifted a hand to smooth her tangled hair from her brow, only to stop at the last moment, when he remembered he couldn't touch her anyway. Why did he constantly forget himself with her? Why, when he had no problem remembering with Carly or Kyanna, did he constantly torture himself trying in vain to touch the one, the *only* woman he wanted above all else? Then again, maybe that was exactly why.

He'd never wanted anyone the way he wanted Maggie.

But he *had* touched her, he remembered now. Her soft lush lips under his thumb. Torment.

And the fragile bones of her wrist, snapping in his beefy fist. Torture.

Clenching those cursed fists in his hands, he turned his anguished eyes to Mikhail. "How bad?"

"Concussion. Broken ribs. Collapsed lung. Ruptured spleen. Internal bleeding. Lost a lot of blood,"

141

Mikhail hissed between clenched teeth, his attention never leaving his patient.

Gideon could feel the waves of power rolling off Mikhail as he worked tirelessly to heal her.

"Will she be all right?"

Mikhail gave one curt nod but refused to comment further. Time passed so slowly. Five minutes, five decades, Gideon couldn't tell. At last, Mikhail sucked in a labored breath, and drew his hands from Maggie's chest. His expression tight, his lips pinched together, his own chest hitching, Mikhail reached for her wrist. With a ruthless snap, he reset the bone, and then clenched both hands around the broken joint. Light and warmth seeped from his hands into her flesh. Bruises began to fade.

Gideon flinched, but he refused to leave her side. He'd done this. He'd inflicted these grievous injuries upon his delicate, breakable Halfling. He had no right to seek easement from her suffering. Mikhail released her wrist. He sat back for a moment and drew another deep breath. Gideon thought he spied bruises forming over Mikhail's own wrist, but the demon gave a twitch of the sleeve of his leather jacket, and the shadow was swiftly covered. Another bracing breath and Mikhail reached up once more, moving his hands over her, seeking out and healing injury after injury.

Once Maggie was resting comfortably, once Gideon felt as if he'd been tortured by the most skilled the Spanish Inquisition had to offer, Mikhail sat back on his haunches. Gideon stared at Mikhail. Gratitude was too feeble an emotion for what he felt right now for his comrade.

And he understood far more about Mikhail than he

had before, even after all this time. He'd never been this close before while Mikhail had used his powers to heal another. Mikhail had never allowed it. In the same room, yes. But never this close. And now Gideon understood why.

Mikhail hadn't just healed Maggie's wounds. He had taken those wounds into himself, absorbed them, absorbed the pain while drawing it from his patient. The depth of the sacrifice Mikhail made to help others was staggering. No wonder he disappeared for such lengths of time whenever he healed someone with severe injuries. He was likely recovering from the physical trauma to his own body. And Gideon had no way to thank him, no way to make amends.

Mikhail sat back finally, his hands resting in his lap, exhaustion—and pain, Gideon could see now— lining his features. Somewhere behind them, he could hear Carly and Niklas speaking in hushed tones, but he couldn't focus on their words. Only on the pale woman lying so still on the couch before him.

Maggie slowly opened her eyes.

"Rest, little one," Mikhail said, his voice strained. "You are safe now."

Maggie blinked. She took in Mikhail's scarred visage and then Gideon's wretched, miserable countenance. She looked back to Mikhail.

"You healed me," she said, her gaze steady. "I could feel you…touching me…from the inside out."

"I am sorry, it could not be helped," Mikhail whispered. As if he'd done something to be ashamed of.

The room fell silent as all attention turned to the hushed exchange between Maggie and Mikhail.

Maggie reached out a trembling hand, doing what no one had ever dared to do. She laid a gentle hand against Mikhail's scarred cheek and looked deeply into his eyes. "I do not know your name."

Gideon held utterly still, awash in an unexpected wave of tranquility. Power pulsed around Maggie, stronger than he'd ever noticed before.

"Mikhail," the demon beside him replied, a confounded expression on his face.

"Mikhail." She repeated his name. That strange peace filling the air intensified. Gideon glanced around to see if anyone else sensed this enthralling power seeping from Maggie. Niklas and Carly, as well as Mikhail himself, seemed...mesmerized. "Thank you, my friend. You are a gift I will cherish."

Slowly, she released Mikhail. He pushed to his feet, blinking as if in a daze. He stared down at her, long and hard. At length, he nodded curtly, and then disappeared in a shimmer trail. Maggie turned to Gideon. She reached out, only to draw her hand back at the last moment.

Self-loathing filled him. Whereas she'd been ready to throw herself into his arms before, now she obviously couldn't stand the thought of touching him.

"This wasn't your fault, Gideon." A fleeting grimace twisted her lips as she tried to push herself up, only to fall back. "Don't...please, Gideon, don't blame yourself."

"Lie still." Gideon circumspectly blanked his expression and pushed to his feet. "Get some rest. Don't undo all Mikhail's hard work."

Turning, studiously avoiding eye contact with Niklas and Carly, Gideon walked out of the room.

Chapter Ten

Gideon stood at the sink, his arms splayed, his palms braced on the counter, his head bowed.

How badly he wanted to shimmer away, anywhere but here. And he very nearly had, only catching himself at the last second, remembering that Maggie would go with him. And she sure as hell wasn't ready for that. Not after what he'd just put her through.

"Let me," Carly whispered near the doorway to the kitchen. The quiet rumble of Niklas's reply and Carly's soft murmur of reassurance pricked at his frayed nerves. A few moments later, the muted sound of footsteps crossed the linoleum.

Carly came to a stop close beside him. An icy sensation wafted over the skin on the back of his hand. He flinched and stared down at where their hands should have connected. Torment though it was, he savored the feel of ghostly cold, misty sensation on his skin where she held her hand, carefully suspended, over his.

"Oh Gideon," she whispered.

"Don't. Just don't," he said, whirling away from her, his hand ghosting through hers as he moved. "I could have killed her. Don't pity the monster, darlin'. I don't deserve it."

He was a damned fool. How could he think, for one moment, that Maggie was safe around him? As

145

long as he didn't change. As long as he kept the monster inside leashed.

But he'd been stupid to pretend. He knew better. You didn't leash the monster, you placated it. Tiptoed around it. Did everything in your power to keep it happy. Because just one slip, one mistake, and the monster came out of hiding and bit you in the ass.

He sensed Niklas's presence in the doorway. Didn't blame him one bit for hovering protectively over his woman. After all, one never knew when the monster might snap.

"Niklas," he said, turning to his friend. "I know it's dangerous, but you have to let Maggie stay with you and Carly." God, did he sound as desperate as he thought he did?

"Her place isn't with us," Carly said as Niklas crossed to stand beside her. She nestled into the shelter of Niklas's arms as if she'd been born for no other reason.

He watched as Niklas dropped a kiss to the top of her head. Icy blue eyes turned his way. "Carly's right. The best place for Maggie is with you."

"How can you say that?" Gideon exploded. Raking two hands through his hair, he gestured wildly toward Sebastian's living room as their betrayal knifed at him. "Didn't you see what I did to her? She's lucky to be alive! If Mikhail hadn't been able to—" He choked on the words, unable to even think about what might have happened without Mikhail's healing touch.

Niklas stiffened. Indecision etched his face; his doubt had returned. But Carly patted her hand comfortingly over Niklas's forearms where they crossed over her stomach. And Niklas visibly relaxed.

Why couldn't he have had that, just once, with Maggie?

"Maggie is going to be fine, Gideon." Carly smiled at him the way a woman did when she was convinced she was right and there was nothing you can say or do to change her mind. "But she needs you now. And you need her."

"She needs me like she needs another hole in the head," he scoffed, his anger building. Why couldn't they see how dangerous he was to her?

"You care about her," Carly said softly.

Giving up on reasoning with her, he turned a pleading gaze on Niklas. "I care about Carly too. Are you willing to leave her in my care?"

"I have before," Niklas pointed out. The bastard was just all kinds of unhelpful today.

Growling low in his throat, Gideon gripped the back of a kitchen chair. He picked it up and slammed it down. "That was different."

"How?" Niklas countered.

"I'm not half in love with Carly," Gideon blurted before he realized what he was saying. Niklas's lips parted and his eyebrows went up. Carly's smile widened and her eyes sparkled.

Damn it!

"No, I'd say you're more than halfway in love with Maggie, Gideon," Carly said. "I'd say you're all the way there."

"Christ on a crutch, Carly! Don't! Just don't go there," Gideon pleaded. He conjured a cup of coffee only to set it aside without taking a sip. He paced to the door leading outside but couldn't leave.

Angry, he stomped back, then strode to the living

147

room as if drawn by a magnet just to make sure she was still there, still breathing, still alive. She lay on the sofa, right where he'd left her, her chest gently rising and falling. He wanted to crawl out of his skin. Wanted to claw it from his body. Wanted to pull his hair from his head. Why couldn't they understand?

He came to a stop beside the sink once more, dimly aware that Carly had followed, Niklas close on her heels. He sure as hell didn't trust himself around Carly, let alone Maggie. Niklas damned well shouldn't either.

"Gideon, stop beating yourself up over this. It was an accident. I'm sure Maggie feels the same. You already heard her say so," Carly reminded him.

"Please, Niklas." Gideon beseeched his friend. "Take her with you. Away from me. Keep her safe. Please."

He reached for the key around his neck when it looked as if Niklas was waffling. He'd solve the problem for them. He'd take the damned cuff off and leave. He'd go straight to a nest and end this once and for all. Then they'd be forced to watch over Maggie. And she'd be safe from him.

His fingers scraped over bare flesh. Gideon grasped both hands at his throat, patting desperately where his necklace should have been.

"What the hell!" he exclaimed. "It's gone!"

"What's the matter?" Carly reached out in alarm to grab his arm, her hand ghosting right through him. "What's gone?"

"The key! The key to the cuffs binding us together. Without the key, the cuffs won't come off. Without the key, I can't shimmer without taking Maggie with me whether she wants to go or not. Without the key, I can't—"

Without the key, he couldn't seek Oblivion. Who knew what would happen if he died while still bound to her by the cuffs. Would she die too?

Would she be dragged to Oblivion right along with him?

His blood ran cold just at the thought.

"Where could it have—" The memory of silver glinting in Mortikaï's fist flashed through his mind.

Sweet Jesus. Mortikaï has the key!

Maggie would never be safe now.

Panic made it difficult to breathe. Adrenaline spurted through his system. His easy out was gone. His torment would never end.

Carly regarded him through shrewd eyes. "This is about more than the cuffs binding you together, isn't it? And more than your fear of hurting her again."

Gideon stepped back, rounded the table, putting more space between him and the couple. More space between him and reality. His back was to the living room as he faced them, as if he could shield Maggie from Carly's words. Shield her from the awful truth. He was a freak that could never touch her. But he'd fallen in love with her and would probably kill anyone else that tried to touch her. God, he was a sick joke.

"Sugar, you don't know what you're talking about," he said, striving to inject scorn into his tone.

"That's exactly it," Carly argued, undaunted. "This is about your curse, isn't it?"

Something in him snapped.

"Could you imagine living every day with Niklas, and not being able to touch him?" Gideon finally let the dam break, not caring that his words were intentionally

149

cruel. "Being close enough to smell him, feel his heat, hear his heartbeat, and never be able to feel his skin? Never be able to hold him, or kiss him, or make love to him? It's like that for me, every second that I'm with her. How could you rub that salt in my wounds? How could you expect me to continue to live with that kind of torment?"

Carly took a step toward him, her hand going to her throat as understanding dawned. "Oh, Gideon. I didn't mean to—I'm so sorry."

Great, now it looked as if she were going to burst into tears. He was just batting zero for a thousand here.

"We'll figure out something." Shaking her head, Carly set her features in determination, even as she grew more distraught. "We'll break the curse, somehow. We'll find a way around it. We have to be able to do something. You mustn't give up. We can—"

"Shhh," Niklas said softly, drawing her back into his arms to comfort her. His gaze locked on Gideon; he pressed a gentle kiss to the side of his woman's forehead. "We've been searching for almost two hundred years, Carly. Mikhail, Sebastian, Xander, and I. For a while we thought there might be a chalice in Tibet…but it was just a legend with no substance. There's no way to counter the curse."

Gideon blinked in surprise at Niklas. He remembered Mikhail spending time in Tibet, but thought he'd been doing penance. He recalled the way the big warrior had come back looking so defeated. Mikhail had avoided Gideon for months after that. Gideon had never been able to figure out why. Had Mikhail blamed himself somehow? Felt he'd let his brother down?

This wasn't their fault, none of it was. No one deserved the blame here but him.

That his brothers had been searching on his behalf…that they'd been so careful not to let him know, so vigilant not to get his hopes up… He was humbled.

"We will break this curse, Gideon," Carly stated again, her tone brooking no argument. "Don't you give up, Gideon. Do you hear me? Don't you quit on us. I won't let you choose Oblivion. So just get that idea out of your head right now."

"What are you talking about, Carly?" Niklas asked.

"Damn it," she huffed, anger pinkening her cheeks. "I'm sorry, Gideon. I didn't mean to—"

"I never told you that," Gideon hissed. How had she figured it out?

"I know you," Carly whispered. "You're like a brother to me. I. Know. You."

Gideon stared at her a long moment. Touched and betrayed. Filled with love and torn asunder. He couldn't deal with the emotions flooding him anymore. Spinning away, intent on getting the hell as far away as he could without shimmering, he drew up short.

Maggie stood in the doorway, clutching the frame for support. Her face was pale and set in a scowl as she regarded him.

"What is she talking about, Gideon? What curse?"

Shooting an angry glance over his shoulder, he felt his world crashing around him. Carly stared back, clearly puzzled.

"She doesn't know?" Carly shook her head. "How can she not know?"

"Because I've been careful to never touch her."

Misery flickered across Carly's features. "Oh

Gideon. I'm so sorry."

"Don't." Gideon held his arm up and pointed at Carly. "Don't you apologize again. And don't you feel sorry for me anymore. No more pity. I can't take it."

"Gideon, what's going on? What curse is she talking about? And what did you mean? Why have you been so careful not to touch me? I thought it was me. I thought you just didn't…" Her voice trailed away, and her face filled with confusion and doubt.

Gideon clenched his teeth, feeling as if all the air had been sucked out of the room. He stared hard at her face, committing to memory the last time she would look at him without the pity that was sure to come.

When he remained silent, Niklas finally spoke up. "No one can touch Gideon, Maggie. Shortly before we rebelled against his reign, Lucifer cursed Gideon to never again know physical touch…except for when he's in demon form. And then…well, you saw what happens when he's in demon form. He doesn't recognize friend from foe."

Maggie was frowning now. She looked back and forth between the three of them in obvious disbelief. "You're trying to tell me no one can touch him? That no one has touched him in how long?" Shaking her head, she crossed her arms, as if offended somehow.

"Two hundred years. No one can touch him, Maggie," Carly assured her gently. "Whenever I try, my hand goes right through him. Like he's a ghost. Or I am. I'm not sure which."

"You're wrong," Maggie insisted, shaking her head.

"Jesus, Maggie, I swear you argue just for the sake of arguing," Gideon snapped, frustrated and humiliated beyond endurance. "Carly and Niklas are telling the truth. No one can touch me, and I can't touch anyone else. Not without being in demon form."

Frowning now, still shaking her head, Maggie wouldn't let it go. "Why are you trying to convince me of this nonsense?"

"Because it's true."

"No, it's not."

"Damn it. Just let it go, Maggie. I'm not—"

Gideon froze as she marched across the room, preparing himself for that nightmare moment when she would reach out and her hand would pass right through him.

Maggie lifted her arm and cupped his cheek, just as she had Mikhail's earlier. Flesh to solid flesh.

Chapter Eleven

Stunned silence filled the room.

"There," she said, clearly exasperated. "You see?"

The shock of feeling her skin—her solid, warm flesh—actually touching him nearly sent Gideon into shock. His head swam. His heart raced so hard, he feared he might pass out and wake up to realize this was all nothing more than a dream. She was really, truly touching him. Not ghosting a hand through him.

Touching me!

Afraid to believe. Afraid to hope. Thoughts of keys and Oblivion were forgotten in his stunned state. His hands shook as he reached for her. He gripped her shoulders. Firm. Substantial. There.

Oh my God!

He couldn't catch his breath. Couldn't think. He was going to hyperventilate. She lifted her other hand so she was holding his face, frowning up at him. He was vaguely aware of Carly's soft gasp, of Niklas's surprised exclamation.

But the only thing that mattered was the woman he could finally lay hands on. He gazed at her in wide-eyed amazement. In sheer abandoned awe.

"I can touch you!" he whispered.

Without giving it a second thought, Gideon swooped her up in a bone-jarring embrace and seized her lips with his. Gentle was the last thing on his mind.

He still couldn't believe he was actually touching her, could scarce wrap his mind around the fact. But then she began to respond, going soft and willing in his arms, and his body took over, not caring whether or not his mind believed.

The texture of her lips was soft, supple, and warm. She wound her arms around his neck and pressed her breasts against his chest. It wasn't nearly close enough, so Gideon crushed her tighter to him. Her belly cradled his painfully hard shaft. She parted her thighs willingly when he pushed his knee between them.

He couldn't stop moving his hands, greedy for every last sensation, fearful that this might be the only chance he had to feel. Every sensation, every texture, he marveled over. The delicate skin of her neck, the friction of his fingers rubbing over the cotton of her T-shirt. The way the softness of her worn blue jeans molded to her waist and hips. The taut muscles of her pert little ass fit perfectly in his hands.

Growling low in his throat, he flexed his fingers, rubbing his hands over her in bliss before firming his grip and hiking her up higher to fit his erection more snugly in the cradle of her thighs.

A soft giggle, a male chuckle sounded from somewhere behind him. He couldn't have cared less. Maggie was in his arms at last. He was holding her. He was touching her. He was kissing her. And she was kissing him right back with wild abandon. The house could have burned down around his ears, and he wouldn't have been able to stop what he was doing.

A whisper of sound, and then Niklas's energy disappeared. He didn't need to look behind him to know that Carly and Niklas were both gone. He'd thank them later for their discretion. Much later. Right now, kissing and touching were the only things on his radar. He tore his mouth from Maggie's, desperate to sample every inch of her before this moment was snatched from him. His lips and tongue lavished attention across the bottom of her jaw and down the side of her neck. Desperate, he gripped the collar of her T-shirt and pulled it out of the way. He then proceeded to nibble and nip his way across her collarbone.

Delectable. He couldn't get enough. One hand went to the hem of her shirt, tugging it up insistently. He'd never been so eager for anything in his long, long life. He wanted to feel and taste her. Wanted to lay claim to her. Wanted to bring her to peak after peak, until she screamed his name in abandon, mindless and addicted to his touch, as he was addicted to touching her already.

He cupped her generous breast, and he devoured his way back up the side of her throat. He groaned in appreciation. So damned perfect he could have wept for joy.

The sound seemed to startle her, and she began to stiffen in his arms. At first, he ignored it, sure with a little extra persuasion she'd come around. And so he pressed his hips more firmly against her, rubbing his erection into the vee of her thighs. A tiny moan escaped her, and he grinned against her skin.

But when he tried to capture her lips again, she turned away, pushing at his shoulders now.

For a man—for a demon—denied physical contact, denied carnal contact, for what felt like an eternity, stopping now required nearly more control than he was capable of. Chest heaving, heart racing, he pulled back, but only slightly. He couldn't bear to let her go. The fear that he wouldn't be able to touch her again was too terrifying.

"What? What!"

"Slow down," she gasped. "Just…I need a second here."

She wiggled until he set her back on her feet. But he refused to relinquish her waist. Somebody would have to kill him before he let go completely.

She glanced around the room. "Where did they…"

"Gone. It's just us now, Maggie." His chest heaved as he fought to slow his breathing.

"Gideon, I have to understand this," she said, pushing gently at him, but he refused to be dislodged.

Shaking her head, she relented and rested her hands upon his chest. The feel of those small hands, the warmth, the weight of them sent pleasure coursing through his veins. His lips throbbed from kissing her. He'd never felt such a wondrous thing.

"You really couldn't touch anyone before this, could you?" Disbelief warred with baffled confusion.

"No."

"So, I'm the first woman you've been able to…to touch?"

He licked his lips, his gaze sliding eagerly to her mouth. "Yes."

"In two hundred years?"

"Yes."

Her brow puckered. Reaching up, he smoothed the pad of his thumb across the creases, the way he'd seen Xander do to Kyanna a hundred times. Her skin was smooth here as well, soft. Pleasant was too weak of a word to describe the feeling, but he couldn't think well enough just now to come up with a better one.

Shaking her head to dislodge his hand, she pushed harder until she finally succeeded in breaking his hold.

The moment he lost contact, anxiety swamped him. As a man drowning might, he gulped for air. His vision blurred. Instinct made him reach out, made him grab for her. The moment their hands connected, and his didn't ghost right through hers, he was able to take another breath.

"I'm sorry," he breathed, still caught up in the shock. "I...I just can't let you go right now. I can't stop touching you. I need...I have to—"

"It's okay," she assured him, giving his hand a squeeze. Careful not to break the connection of their hands, she took a careful step back. That space was uncomfortable for him to maintain, but he forced himself to stand still and not follow her.

Her chin dipped, and a frown tugged her lips down. Gideon reached for her face, then out of habit, he hesitated. But that hesitation lasted only a moment before he tenderly cupped her cheek in his hand and lifted her face to his. It took major effort on his part not to get lost in the creamy perfection of her skin. He searched her face.

"What's wrong?"

"I understand now," she began slowly, her voice hesitant. Uncertain. "I really do. I understand why you were the way you were before. And I can appreciate what you must be feeling right now." She paused, cleared her throat, and pressed on. But as she did so, her gaze slid sideways, as if what she was about to say embarrassed her. "But I think we both need to slow down. Think this through before things go too far. A lot's happened tonight. And we both need to, um, decompress."

Her words hit him like a punch to the gut. A slap to the face. Despite his need to touch her, he could feel her pulling away, at least mentally. A part of him, in that moment, was angry with her for putting distance between them, for relegating him back to the land of the cursed. Another part of him took up her argument. She had been through a lot. She'd watched him turn into the monster. And that monster had damned near killed her. She was probably afraid of him. Probably scared to push him.

Letting go of her hand was one of the hardest things he'd ever done in his life. But he did it. For her. Putting more space between them.

"You're right. You should get some rest."

She stared up at him, frowning, shaking her head. She reached for him once more, but this time he was the one to stiffen and pull away.

"But you said we'd train today—"

"I think you've had enough *training* for one day. After all, not many have seen a demon battle up close and personal and lived to tell the tale."

"Gideon—"

"No more today," he insisted, cutting her off. He was drained. He couldn't imagine what she must be feeling. She didn't have to worry that he would back out on his promise or change his mind. What happened today only proved she needed to know how to defend herself.

"I'll take you upstairs. You need to rest, and I don't know if shimmering you back to the plantation is safe for you yet or not with how badly you were...injured.

So, for the time being, we'll hang out here. Sebastian has ward stones in place, and Kyanna has reinforced them with spells. You're as safe here as you would be at the plantation, all things considered."

"What do you mean, all things considered?"

"Well, as safe as you can be with a monster just down the hall." He chuckled, but his voice, and his laugh, held no humor.

Before she could comment further, he dropped his old, familiar shields back in place and skirted around her, vigilant not to even let their hands so much as brush. Not touching her, now that he knew he could, was damned near killing him. He thought he'd been tortured before—that was nothing compared to this. The taste of forbidden fruit had been so sweet. And now that it was out of his reach once more, it was all the more temptation.

"This way," he called over his shoulder as he led her through the living room, past Sebastian's den, toward the staircase on the far wall. He strode up the stairs and down the long hallway, past the room Niklas usually used whenever he stayed at the farm, past Xander's room. He came to a stop beside the door at the end of the hall.

"You can sleep here," he said, reaching out to turn the doorknob.

She glanced through the doorway, then arched her brow at him after taking in the décor. "This is your room, isn't it?"

He nodded.

"I can sleep someplace else. You shouldn't have to give up your bed yet again for me."

The thought of her sleeping in someone else's bed

nearly sent him into a rage. *His* sheets would cover her. *His* scent would linger on her skin. No one else's. Even if he couldn't put it there personally.

"You'll sleep here," he commanded before turning to stalk away.

"Wait," she called and grabbed his wrist. The sensation of her touch made him gasp, and she immediately—to his dismay—let go. "Look, I, ah…I just wanted to say thank you. For earlier."

"For what? For not checking your house, for not taking basic precautions before I let you go back? For almost getting you killed? Or for nearly killing you myself?"

Her lips tightened for a moment. "For agreeing to train me. For being willing to teach me what I need to know to survive."

"Yeah, I'm doing a real bang-up job there. Damned near as good as your father, huh?"

"Gideon!" She reached out to touch him, only to pull back at the last minute when he stiffened once more. He snorted in self-disgust, furious with both of them now, and turned to walk away once more.

"Damn it! Stop!"

Gideon halted in his tracks once again, torturing himself with the hope that she might touch him, just one more time. He slowly turned to face her.

"I just don't like the whole last-woman-on-earth thing, you know?"

Frowning, he shook his head. "I have no idea what you're talking about.

She looked as if she'd like to find a hole to crawl into. "You've saved me—"

Now he did snort derisively. "I didn't save you. I

nearly killed you. Mikhail saved you."

"Oh, will you shut up!" Clearly frustrated, she raked her hands through her hair. "You have saved me, before. That night at the club? From those three demons? And if Niklas and Mikhail hadn't shown up at my place, I truly believe you would have calmed down and changed back. You were so close already, before they came." He made a sound of disbelief, but she ignored him and trudged on. "I just wanted to let you know that I understand, and I won't push."

It was her turn to walk away. But he caught the glint of perceived rejection, the sad frown, and his hand shot out of its own volition. He grabbed her.

"You understand what exactly?"

"Oh God, why are you making me say this!" Maggie was angry now. She made a fist of her hand and gave it a good tug, but she couldn't break his hold. "I get it, all right. You're not interested, now that the shock and the heat of the moment have had time to wear off. Believe me, I'm not all that hot to be swept off my feet just because I'm the last girl standing, so to speak. I mean, how flattering is that?" She lowered her voice to mimic him. She even affected a mocking southern drawl. "'Hey, darlin', you're the only girl I've been able to touch since before the time of the dinosaur. Wanna get lucky?'"

"You think I'm older than dinosaurs?"

"Compared to me, you're a fossil," she said. A spark of anger flickered in her beautiful eyes. Anger and unmistakable hurt. "You know, just once, I'd like to factor. Me. Just for myself. Just once I'd like to actually be important to someone. Not because my job and my reputation would complement someone's idea of what they believe their life should be like.

"And not because of who my father was. Not because of my bloodlines or some stupid visions I might or might not have. Not because of some damned *destiny* that sucks, by the way. I mean, come on. Boil it all down and look what I've got. I've basically been relegated to be a brood mare for some demon bent on conquering the world. Oh, please, sign me up," she snapped.

Shaking her head, she turned to walk away, apparently forgetting he was still in possession of her wrist. He jerked her back. She collided with his chest and gasped aloud.

"Is that what you think?" he demanded, incredulous. "That I see you like that, and nothing more? Or that I'm only interested in you because I can touch someone now?"

"It's what I know."

"Then you don't know a damned thing."

She stood toe-to-toe with him, her chest brushing his as her angry breaths heaved in and out. "I know the only reason you came after me in the first place was because of that ridiculous prophecy. I know every time I reach out to touch you, you freeze. Whenever I'm close to you, you're always clenching your fists, and you get stiff as a two-by-four whenever—"

"My ability to touch you doesn't have a damned thing to do with it. I've wanted you from the moment I first laid eyes on you," Gideon growled, his control snapping like dried twigs and rapidly going up in flames. "I stiffen up to keep from grabbing you up in my arms and holding you so tight I'd probably break you. I clench my fists to keep from reaching for you.

Not your powers or visions, not your damned bloodlines. Christ on a crutch! If anything, your bloodlines, your father, and the damned prophecy are prime reasons why I should stay as far the hell away from you as possible!"

He dragged in a breath, too irate to comprehend that she was staring up at him in open-mouthed shock.

"And I force myself to be still to keep myself from seizing you and dragging you to the ground beneath me," he added. "To keep myself from tearing your clothes off and devouring every inch of you. Because once I do, once I lose control, there's no going back. I'll claim you as my female. As my mate. In every way possible. And no matter how badly I want you, no matter how much I might cherish you, I will always be a threat to you. I'll always be dangerous because a part of me will always be Temptation."

He paused, giving her a less than gentle shake. "Do you get it now? If I claim you, despite the fact that I'd be putting you at risk on every front, I will never, never be able to let you go, never be able to stay away from you. I won't be able to help myself."

His chest was heaving now, the air in the hallway made thin by the tension between the two of them. He stared down into her startled blue-green eyes, and then lower to her softly parted lips.

Gideon was riding the razor's edge now, close to tipping over that treacherous point of no return. He could feel every pulse of his heart, the rushing of his blood through his veins. He'd never felt so alive. And everything inside him was yearning for her. He'd never been this ready, this eager to lose control. Normally that realization would have been enough to make him nervous, but right now there wasn't an ounce of rage in his system.

Nothing but pure, raw desire.

She placed her free hand upon his chest. "Would that be such a bad thing?"

Gideon sucked in a sharp breath. That moment, the invitation in her eyes, the weight of her hand upon his chest would forever be burned into his memory. "Woman, you have no idea the beast you tempt."

Becoming color flooded her cheeks. She glanced down and to the side for a moment before she looked back up at him. She opened her mouth to say something, but suddenly, her gaze swerved back, just to the side of his head. Her mouth fell open and her eyes went wide.

When she looked back at him, she had the strangest expression on her face. And then she gasped softly, one of those *aha* looks suddenly lighting her face. Was she having one of the visions she'd told him about? Frowning, he glanced over his shoulder, over hers. There was nothing there but bare wall.

"What?" he asked. "What are you looking at?"

She slowly turned to him, and a bemused smile lit her features. And then she began to laugh. The tinkling sound washed over him in waves, soothing his soul, pouring fuel on the flames of his need, confusing the living hell out of him.

"Wallpaper."

Chapter Twelve

In that moment, it all became clear to Maggie. Life was about choices. She'd been so tied up in the choices that other people made, in the chaos that other people created, that she'd forgotten her choices mattered just as much. She was standing at a crossroads, the wallpaper a sign. The very same wallpaper from her vision.

And although, once she'd had a vision about a specific event, she'd never been able to change the outcome, surely she could change this one. If she wanted to.

If she *really* wanted to…

Would she choose the path that led to her going into that bedroom all alone and miserable? Or would she choose the path that led to a stolen moment of passion and hunger right here in this hallway, no matter where that path might end?

This was her moment.

This was her choice, vision be damned.

Maggie stared up into Gideon's golden eyes. She might need him.

But he needed her as well.

Pushing aside her insecurities, pushing aside the little voice that told her she wasn't good enough—that she'd never been good enough for anyone else, why would she be good enough for him?—Maggie went up on tiptoe and reached for him. Reached for what she never imagined could be hers. She cupped the back of Gideon's neck with her free hand, dragged his head down and pressed her lips to his.

For a split second he froze again. He peered down at her as if he still couldn't believe his senses. And then he exploded into motion all around her. One second his lips were unresponsive against hers, his hand clamped on her wrist like a vise, his other arm rigid at his side. The next instant, his lips were devouring hers, his tongue plunging greedily into her mouth, swirling over hers, demanding and voracious. His arms crushed her so tightly she could barely breathe.

The unforgiving ridge of his arousal pressed against her, demanding and merciless, and he rocked his hips, his lean body shuddering all around her. She moaned as an answering rush of melting warmth hit her, low and deep. Tunneling her fingers in his hair, she kissed him back, pouring every ounce of desire coursing through her into her response.

Gideon groaned into her mouth, the sound of it, the vibration against the delicate skin of her lips and tongue erotic beyond imagining. Changing the angle of his kiss, he deepened the intimate contact, dragging her under wave after wave of mindless passion as he pushed her back, pressing her up against the wall, pinning her, caging her. She fully understood there would be no escape. That realization made her giddy. His hand swept down her side to squeeze her hip before slipping back up beneath the hem of her T-shirt. The heat of his calloused skin upon her bare flesh was delicious. She trembled beneath his touch.

His thigh pressed between hers, intimate and

unyielding. His fingers tangled in her hair, dragging her head back. Gideon tore his lips from hers and stared down at her for a moment, just for a slim second, as if to reassure himself this was really what she wanted. That she hadn't changed her mind.

She hadn't.

He swooped down, and he seized the sensitive skin just beneath her ear. She shuddered. His mouth, so hot, so hungry, sucked and nipped, playing there, driving her crazy. Eventually, he slid down over her throat to torment the flesh where neck met shoulder. Maggie was helpless, could only whimper for more. He skimmed along the bare skin on her abdomen, and Maggie shivered in response. The rough pads of his fingertips spread over her ribs, skating up until he cupped her breast. With ruthless, aggressive motions, he rubbed his palm against her breast until her nipple budded beneath the friction.

A low, primal growl rumbled through his chest and into her. His movements were rough as Gideon jerked his hands free. Before she realized what he intended, he grasped the collar of her T-shirt and ripped it right down the middle. Her pretty, lacy bra suffered the same fate before he dragged the tattered fabric down her arms, pulling her away from the wall long enough to toss the material aside.

Gideon leaned back for a moment, his hungry gaze drinking her in. "So beautiful," he whispered reverently, and she knew he wasn't speaking to her. Not deliberately, anyway. It had been an unguarded thought that had slipped from his lips and meant all the more to her for it.

But she was just as ravenous to feel his flesh. She

reached for his shirt, but before she could grip the material, it disappeared.

She blinked in confusion. "Did you do that?"

He nodded, his dazzled gaze never leaving her breasts as his muscular chest rose and fell on an impossibly deep, shuddering breath.

"Why didn't you just make my clothes disappear like that too?" Maggie asked breathlessly. "Why'd you rip them off?"

He finally looked at her, ensnaring her with those sparkling eyes. The grin that spread across his lips was so wicked, her throat all but closed.

"That was for me, Maggie."

He moved into her swiftly then, shoving her urgently against the wall. The cool, textured wallpaper grounded her as his chest, smooth as silk, hard as granite, and blazing hot, pressed against her front. His lips slammed over hers as his calloused hands gripped her hips in a punishing hold. Her head swam as she lost touch with everything but Gidcon and the way he kissed her, not only with his mouth, but with his entire body.

He took possession of her bottom, squeezing, flexing, squeezing. Without warning, he dropped to his knees before her. Deft fingers flicked the button on her jeans free. He jerked the zipper open and dragged them down her legs. Gideon balanced her with a hand on her hip while she stepped free.

On his knees, he slowly pushed both splayed hands up over her belly, over her rib cage, to cradle her breasts. He used his lips and tongue and teeth to lavish attention on first one, then the other. Maggie was grateful for the wall, using it to brace herself when her legs threatened to give way. Especially when he began feathering kisses down her stomach, his target more than apparent.

Using just his fingertips, he traced the lace pattern on her panties. She couldn't keep up with his mercurial changes. In one moment, he was impatient, rough, and greedy. In the next, it was as if he was trying to make up for an eternity of deprivation by touching and exploring her as much as physically possible. By the time he was finished tormenting her, her breasts felt full and achy, her sex was wet and throbbing, and every muscle in her body quivered.

Looking up at her, smiling seductively, he slowly twisted his thumbs in the lace covering her hips and slowly—*oh, dear Lord in Heaven!*—so slowly dragged it down, down, down, off. Gideon sat back on his haunches and stared up at her, worshipful awe etched in every line of his face, his body posed as one at an altar.

Suddenly and unaccountably embarrassed at being displayed like this, Maggie made to cover herself. But he was having none of it. He captured her wrists with a chiding shake of his head and pulled them to the sides, pressing her hands flat against the wall, silently commanding her to leave them there.

Then he skimmed those sandpaper-rough fingertips along the sensitive skin where hip and thigh connected, making a rumbling sound deep in his throat. Strong hands splayed at the tops of her thighs and firmly, purposefully smoothed down until they gripped her knees. With single-minded purpose, Gideon pushed her thighs apart.

His breath left him in an audible whoosh, as if he'd been sucker punched. As if he'd just stumbled upon the greatest discovery of mankind. And when his hands began a feather light ascent up the ultrasensitive flesh of her inner thighs, he groaned aloud. His brows drew together as if he were being tortured.

The first stroke of his fingertips over her trembling, drenched flesh was soft, testing. Reverent. "Exquisite," he whispered, again to himself.

Her head fell back against the wall, her eyes drifting closed on a tremulous sigh. With each successive stroke, her need for him grew by leaps and bounds. He grew bolder in his explorations, circling her, feathering over her, slicking through the wet silk of her cleft, but never quite penetrating her.

Moaning, Maggie lost track of her surroundings. Unmindful of the fact that they were in the hallway and that anyone could stumble upon them, she could only focus on Gideon and what his talented hands were doing to her. Her body shook, her hips following the rhythm of his dancing fingers. His strokes slowed, until one fingertip hesitated, poised at her entrance. Waiting.

Panting, desperate for him to ease the ache he'd so skillfully orchestrated, confused as to why he'd stopped, Maggie dragged her eyes open. He was staring up at her expectantly, watching her with acute focus, his expression a tormented mixture of pain and wonder, lust and reverence. She couldn't tell which of them wanted this more.

He'd made the rest of his clothing disappear. The sight of him kneeling before her, completely naked, fully aroused, caused a fresh wave of liquid warmth to swirl through her womb. His golden hair was tousled from her hands. His lips were slightly swollen from her kisses. His broad shoulders bore tiny scratch marks from her nails, marks she hadn't even realized she'd caused. The sight of those marks, her marks, upon his flesh sent an indelible shot of possessiveness streaking through her.

His muscular chest and ridged abdomen were free of body hair but peppered with scars of various shapes and sizes. Both arms were covered with detailed tattoos, shoulders to wrists. A confusing mixture of images, foreign runes and blocks of scripture, pictures of holy relics and bloody carnage.

His hips were narrow, his powerful thighs spread wide. And from the thatch of springy golden hair between his legs jutted his erection, thick and proud, the girth alone enough to give her pause.

His fingers twitched, there at her entrance, and her gaze snapped back to his. Once she locked on his, as if he'd been waiting his entire existence for just that exact moment, he slowly slid his finger deep inside her. As he did so, his thumb brushed along the tiny bundle of nerves he'd already caressed to a frenzied awareness. Her mouth fell open on a gasp. Her eyes all but rolled back in her head as he slowly began to move, stroking her deep, first with one finger, then two.

Her body went absolutely still in expectation when she felt the hot brush of his breath over her quivering, damp flesh. And when his tongue flicked over her and his mouth settled upon her womanhood, her entire body jolted. She cried out.

Gideon wedged his broad shoulders between her thighs and wound his free arm up between her legs to grip her bottom, holding her in place for his feasting. And feast he did. He rode out the jolt of her body, the frenzied jerk of her hips, suckling her, teasing and lapping at her, pumping three fingers inside her now.

"Gideon! Oh, God, Gideon!" she cried out, moaning aloud as she clutched blindly, desperately at the wall, at his shoulders, at thin air, for support.

Sensations rocketed through her, wild and uncontainable. Her body trembled with pleasure, arching, stretching for more. Wave after wave of bliss caught her up, shattering her, sending her drifting on the clouds.

But Gideon was relentless, and nowhere near finished with her. She'd no more than come down from one orgasm before he ruthlessly drove her up the peak of another. His satisfied growl against the soft skin of her inner thigh when she came a third time—or had it simply been an extension of the second, dragged on and on for his pleasure—took her knees out from under her. She couldn't help it. She simply collapsed.

He moved, fast as lightning, sweeping her up, pinning her between the wall and his rock-solid chest. His breath skated over her ear, burning her.

"Don't think for a second I'm done making you come on my mouth. I intend to gorge on you, over and over and over." His chest heaved as he panted raggedly in her ear. "I'm starved for the taste of you. I'll never get enough." He nipped her earlobe, a sharp little sting as if to punctuate his warning before suckling the pain away.

She was too satiated to argue, too limp to move. Here and now she fully understood the phrase, *putty in his hands*.

Gideon captured her lips, dragging her back from the edge of languid satiation, plunging her into needy awareness. Competent hands lifted her higher against the wall, till her feet left the floor. He used his body to hold her in place while his hands skimmed down her sides. He gripped her knees, pushing them up, guiding them high around his waist. Maggie locked her ankles over his taut buttocks. His motions were rough once more. Her drenched cleft skated along the rigid length of his erection, and he snarled, his fingers digging in, bruising her.

"Have to get inside you," he growled.

She whimpered. Her arms felt like rubber, but she twined them around his neck, winding her fingers in the warm silk of his hair as he kissed her senseless once more. She could feel the thick head of his shaft pushing at her entrance, stretching her though she was more than ready. She could feel every beat of his heart pulsing in his member, connecting them somehow on an elemental level. A new, corresponding ache formed in her womb, deeper, more painful and more demanding than before, and instinct told her the only way to ease that ache was to get him inside her, all the way inside, as fast as possible.

She squeezed her thighs tighter around him and rocked her hips in frenzied demand. She tugged his hair sharply when he didn't immediately shove hard inside her. Maggie sank her teeth into his lower lip. She didn't recognize this wanton, demanding female she'd become, had never had her body slip beyond her control like this before. Had never had such a physically carnal encounter in her life. It was as if she'd been awakened.

Gideon had brought this out of her. Only Gideon.

And only Gideon could satisfy her now.

A dark, guttural curse burst from him. He pried her fingers from his hair, manacled her wrist, slammed it against the wall above her head, and held it there. He jerked his head back, his golden eyes sizzling with hunger as he stared her down. Slowly, so she'd be sure to see it, she knew, he licked the thin ribbon of red at the edge of his lower lip where she'd drawn blood. She was shocked by her own behavior…and more turned on than she'd ever been in her life.

Reaching beneath her, he gripped her bottom, angling her, holding her in place as he fastened his mouth over hers again. Gideon slammed inside her, to the hilt, capturing her scream, swallowing it.

And then he started to move. Long, deep thrusts that bound them together, body and soul. He tore his mouth away and pressed his cheek to hers. His hot breath was ragged in her ear.

"You're mine now, Maggie," he growled, his voice raspy and thick. "I claim you as my mate, and I'll *never* release you from my keeping."

She couldn't reply, caught up as she was in the sensations of his body laying siege to hers. But a sense of rightness, a sense of finality slammed through her.

Gideon buried his face in the side of her neck. One hand was clamped on her bottom, firm and unyielding, possessive, gripping painfully tight, the other still held her wrist. The muscles of his arms and back were taut beneath the exploring fingers of her free hand. Fine beads of perspiration glistened on his skin. Her own flesh felt damp with it. Her legs were still wrapped tight around his lean waist, her ankles still locked over his taut buttocks. His back flexed and bunched as his lean hips pumped in an ever increasing, primal rhythm until flesh slapped flesh.

As he pushed them mercilessly toward that

glimmering peak, a fleeting thought shot unerringly through her mind.

Some things are supposed to happen, just the way they happened.

Gideon released her wrist, released her bottom, and wrapped both arms around her waist, squeezing her tight. His thrusts increased, frantic, pounding, pleasure almost to the point of pain. Her own orgasm had begun to coil tight, waiting for that final second to spring free.

And then Gideon issued a feral snarl against her flesh, driving himself impossibly deep. His teeth clamped onto her shoulder, setting off a chain reaction. All around her, his body went hard as tempered steel. Her own body quaked and shuddered, exploding in a kaleidoscope of colors and sensations. Her orgasm slammed into her the moment she felt him jerk and pulse deep inside her as a deluge of hot seed gushed from him. She screamed his name, gasped for air, and screamed again.

Chapter Thirteen

Chest heaving, Gideon dropped his forehead to Maggie's. There were no words for what he'd just experienced. His body still shook with the aftermath of their union. He kept his arms wrapped tight around her, afraid if he let go, even for a moment, she might slip away from him.

Buried deep inside her, his still-hard cock continued to throb and spasm. His hips followed of their own accord, flexing, driving his shaft deeper still. In his arms, Maggie's limp body tensed. She made a small whimpering sound in the back of her throat.

Oh God, did I hurt her?

He prayed not. Especially now, when it seemed as if his body had taken over his will, for he truly didn't know if he could release her. Already, he could feel his arms tightening around her, seemingly of their own accord, caging her to him, trapping her. His hips began to roll, grinding himself into her against his will.

If he'd hurt her, he told himself, he'd stop…somehow. He would. He didn't know where he would get the strength to leave her, but he would do it. For her.

"Oh," she gasped softly.

Gideon touched his forehead to hers and forced his eyelids open. Her face was flushed. Her lips were softly parted and swollen from his kisses. Just that brief glimpse of her face was enough to send fresh waves of fiery need coursing through him. His shaft jerked in response.

"Did I hurt you?" he asked, his lips hovering close to hers.

She shook her head, bumping her nose against his. "No," she whispered, her voice hoarse.

At last, she looked up at him. Those beautiful eyes glittered like the rarest, most precious of gems. They captured him as nothing else could.

Clawing at the meager shreds of his control, he forced his hips to stop moving.

It nearly killed him.

Her brow wrinkled, and she cried out softly.

"I hurt you." By all that was holy, he'd pull out and let her go. In just a second. It would probably make him stark raving mad, but he'd do it. He'd—

"No!" she cried when he began to slide out of her. Her nails dug into his shoulders, her legs tightened around his waist, her heels dug into his ass. "Oh my God, Gideon, don't stop. Whatever you do, don't stop now!"

A rush of pleasure, hot and all-consuming, surged through him, making his chest swell. A wide, wicked grin broke loose. He reflexively tightened his arms around her, and he began rotating his hips once more. She purred—actually purred—like a cat that had fallen in a river of cream. Maggie arched her back, rubbing her breasts against him. Luxurious bliss.

It was more than he could take. He slammed inside her with a brutal thrust of his hips. Her shoulders cracked back against the wall. Her sharp gasp of breath, her tiny moan were the sweetest sounds he'd ever heard, next to her earlier cries of pleasure, of course. He'd be hearing those sounds from her again, even if it took all night.

Gritting his teeth, he angled his head until they were cheek to cheek once more. Gideon forced himself to pause, praying she wouldn't move. Even the tiniest flexing of her inner muscles would put him straight over the edge and he wanted more than just rough wall sex. He wanted her in his bed. All. Night. Long. In every way imaginable.

"Hold on to me, Maggie," he growled in her ear. "I'm takin' you home. And once we get there, I won't stop again. I swear it to you."

She murmured incoherently, but she tightened her arms around his shoulders and her legs around his waist, so he took that as consent. Gideon gathered his focus, pulled in his power, and shimmered them to his bedroom at the plantation.

Strong as he was, his legs trembled as he solidified with her still locked in his arms, naked but for the identical hammered silver cuffs, and still intimately joined. Two unsteady steps got them to the bed. And every tiny movement caused minute shifts in the tight channel encasing his cock. The sensations rippling up his shaft nearly drove him out of his mind. He'd wanted to draw this second time out, as he hadn't been able to the first time. He'd wanted to wallow in the sensations. He'd wanted to savor every nibble and kiss, every caress and every taste of her.

As he lowered them to the bed, she deliberately clenched him and wiggled her hips. His stunned gaze shot to hers, and she smiled a smile that put Eve to shame.

"So, are you going to show me this beast I've been tempting?" she asked brazenly, flexing her inner muscles yet again. She flicked the tip of her tongue across her lower lip.

Gideon stared down at her. If he lived millennia more, he'd never forget every second, every detail of their joining, nor would he forget that look upon her precious face in that moment.

His restraint snapped. Oh, he still intended to spend hours and years and centuries exploring her, bringing her to peak over and over, pleasuring her out of her mind. Until she couldn't tell where she started, and he ended. Until she couldn't stand the thought of him not being inside her.

He still had every intention of making love to her slowly, tenderly.

She rocked her hips up impatiently against him, seating him balls deep inside her searing heat.

Slow and tender would have to come later, he decided. He gave up fighting for control and gave in to the wild desire driving him.

****

The shadows moved around her. She worked to keep her breathing slow and even. Silent. Randy was here. Somewhere in the dark with her. Her skin crawled. Maggie knew what he wanted. The other girls had warned her. Even if they hadn't, she could feel his intent. His sick, twisted hunger. It made her want to retch, made her want to shiver and scrape the creepy crawly feeling away. But she couldn't give herself away. He'd hear her, and he'd know that wasn't her in the bed. As it was, the bunched-up mound of pillows huddled under the covers on that narrow, hard bed would only buy her minutes at best.

Maggie pulled in a silent, deep breath, bracing herself for what she had to do. Even from this distance, she could smell him, the stale sweat and sticky fetid odor of old booze. Too much old booze. Hatred burned through her, fortifying her.

She flexed her fingers, readjusting her grip on the wooden handle of the cheap steak knife she'd stolen from the kitchen. It wasn't much, but it was all she could get her hands on that she didn't figure they'd notice as missing right away. It was nearing midnight, but it had to be close to eighty degrees inside the tiny room in the back of the trashy trailer house. A trickle of sweat ran between her shoulder blades—her palms were slick with it—but it had nothing to do with the heat wave sweeping through the Midwest and everything to do with anxiety.

The muffled, uneven treads of his footsteps moving across the threadbare carpet sent goose pimples rippling across her flesh. If she screamed, would her foster mother hear?

Of course, she would. The walls of the trailer were paper-thin. The real question was, would she come to investigate? And if she did, would she see what Randy intended, how evil he was? Or would she blame Maggie?

Would she turn a blind eye and pretend nothing was going on, as she had with the other girls?

The blankets were ripped from the bed in fury. "You little bitch," Randy hissed, his large, potbellied form thundering past the small window. "Where are you, Margaret Mary?"

Maggie clutched the knife tighter as he lurched

closer.

"There you are," he slurred, wiping a forearm beneath his nose. "Like to play games, do ya? Well, just you wait. I got a helluva a game for you and me to—"

His words ended on a pained howl. A gush of hot, wet fluid soaked her hand, ran along her forearm, splashed her T-shirt.

Maggie bolted upright on a huge gasp, fighting her way free of the restraining arm thrown over her waist, struggling frantically away from the hot, naked, male body lying next to hers in the bed. She twisted, thrashing, elbows flying. A whoosh of air blew her hair into her face as a hard, lean body wrapped itself around her and subdued her, trapping her in iron bands.

"Shhh," a deep, sleepy voice murmured in her ear. A bristly cheek pressed to hers. A big body rocked her gently. "Shhh, Maggie. Shhh. It's okay. It's okay, love. Shhh."

"Gideon?" she whispered, half afraid Randy was still here, hiding in a corner somewhere.

"It's me, Maggie. I'm here. Shhh."

He held her as she shook; the tremors always came after the terror. Then he held her as she sat, silent and ashamed, in the soft light of early dawn.

"Talk to me," he finally said, lying back, pulling her down onto his chest.

She shook her head, burying her face in the warmth of his neck. He shrugged his shoulder up, using the crook of his finger beneath her chin to force her to face him, waiting until she looked at him.

"No more secrets, remember?"

She felt her temper stir. She wanted to cuss him out, to rail at him, to tell him to mind his own business.

She wanted to push him away to a safe distance, physically as well as emotionally. But he'd held her, soothing her after the dream. And she remembered the night of unimaginable intimacy they'd shared after Gideon had shimmered them back to the plantation.

She couldn't do it. She couldn't shut him out, not now. Not anymore. He'd possessed her body, time and time again last night. And, somehow, when she wasn't paying attention, he'd staked his claim on her heart too.

A fact that left her every bit as horrified as it did giddy.

"It's always the same," she began, her voice not nearly as steady as she would have liked. "I don't have the dream very often, but when I do, it's always the same."

He waited patiently, a slight crease between his brows. Her palm rested just over his heart, and she counted each beat, letting them soothe her. One hand smoothed up and down her naked back, the other traced the delicate carvings on the silver cuff she wore.

"The night Randy…came to my room. I hid in the shadows in the corner." Gideon's big body tensed beneath hers, but he remained silent. His silence was the only reason she was able to continue. "I stuffed pillows under the sheets to look like I was still in bed. I could hear his footsteps. I could smell him. Stale sweat and old liquor." She worked hard to quell the shudder but didn't quite succeed. "I had the knife. It was so hot that summer, and that trailer held heat like an oven. I was sweating. I was so afraid I was going to drop that knife…" Her voice trailed off, and she shook her head, trembling at the memory. "I always wake up as soon as I stab him. As soon as I feel his blood gush over my

183

hand."

She made to push up and away from him, but he caged her, refusing to let her go free.

"I can't—" She shook her head, fighting down the hysteria. "I don't want to talk about it anymore."

"You don't have to. Come here," he rumbled, cuddling her closer. Then his voice took on a new edge, one that made her shiver. "You don't ever have to be afraid of that bastard anymore. I swear to you. He'll never hurt you again. I'll never let anyone hurt you ever again."

God, what was it about him that centered her? He was like a rock, something solid and unmovable that she could hold tight to and never lose her way.

Even as she thought that, she chided herself for being a fool. She counted on herself. Others counted on her. She didn't rely on someone else, and certainly never for her own emotional well-being. But, dear Lord, how he tempted her. Oh, how she wanted to believe him.

"I know." Anxious to dispel the pall that hung in the air around them, she leaned up and whispered, "Kiss me, Gideon. Make me forget."

She didn't have to ask again. Tenderly, Gideon reached up and laced his fingers through her hair, drawing her face down to his. His lips brushed hers, once, twice, and then his tongue slipped past her teeth. In one smooth motion, Gideon rolled, sweeping her beneath him.

His thigh slipped between hers, his hands began to explore. He'd spent every moment of last night touching her, learning the taste and texture and scent of every inch of her body. As if committing them to memory in case he woke in the morning to find his curse had returned.

As such, she was sure he knew her body better than he knew his own. She certainly knew his. She'd refused to be denied and had explored him as well. The only place he wouldn't let her touch was his back, and the unspeakable scars where, as she'd correctly surmised, his wings had been torn from his body.

She'd asked if, after all this time, they still hurt. He'd refused to answer, simply changing the subject by kissing her senseless. Even now, as her fingertips brushed over his shoulders, sliding dangerously close to those scars, he was quick to capture her wrists and force them above her head as he moved his mouth to feast on the column of her neck.

Slowly, leisurely, he began working his way down her body, leaving a trail of fire in his wake. He lavished attention on her breasts before kissing his way down each of her ribs. He grinned wickedly against her skin, knowing full well what he was doing to her. Maggie tunneled her hands through his hair, savoring the way it twined softly around her fingers. Gideon paused to dip his tongue in her navel, making her shiver deliciously. He edged lower, and Maggie caught her breath in anticipation.

The moment his lips touched her lower abdomen, Gideon froze. His entire body went rigid. Frowning, she glanced down, peering at him in confusion. He'd reared his head back. His wide-open eyes stared hard at her stomach, a look of stunned shock etched on his face. But it was the audible swallow that stirred her concern.

"Gideon?" she asked, pushing up to her elbows.

He didn't move, didn't budge an inch. Just

185

continued to lie there, staring at her stomach. She wasn't even sure he was breathing.

"Gideon!" she insisted. He was really beginning to worry her now. What the hell was going on? Had he just now remembered something? Had he had some kind of vision?

At last, he began to move. Slow, cautious, he sat up, leaning back on his haunches. With exquisite care, he reached a trembling hand toward her. She wanted to move away from him, wanted to put her clothes on and run and hide. But unspeakable, nameless fear held her still.

Gideon flattened his hand gently against her lower abdomen. He sat there for a long moment, unmoving, simply touching her, the look in his eyes distant as if he was focusing very hard on something outside himself.

And then his gaze connected with hers for a heartbeat. In that one glance, she caught fleeting glimpses of tangled emotion. Panic. Fear. Disbelief. Shock.

Without warning, the room fell away in a swirl of color. Gideon's den solidified around her as she landed with a thud, naked, on the worn carpet.

"Gideon! What the hell?"

"Oh Christ on a crutch! Oh hell." He gasped, rushing over to her and helping her to her feet. "I forgot," he stammered, clearly shaken to the core. She'd never seen him so flustered. "I didn't think about—"

He conjured clothing for both of them. As soon as she was steady on her feet, he released her and backed away like she was a bomb with the timer quickly winding down.

"What's going on?" she demanded as he began pacing around the room.

"Stupid! Stupid!" Gideon swore, long and loud. He stopped every so often to glance her way and rake both splayed hands through his hair. He'd throw his arms in the air or slap a hand to his forehead, only to resume pacing, mumbling beneath his breath. She couldn't reconcile this frenzied, flustered Gideon with the otherwise soothing and unshakable Gideon she'd come to trust and lo—*care about* in such a short time.

"Gideon," she tried again, but she couldn't get his attention. "Gideon!"

Frustrated, she glanced around the room, her attention snagging on the pillow lying in the corner—the one she'd thrown at his head the last time he'd shimmered her there with no warning.

Snatching it up, she waited until he turned her way in his pacing, then launched it into his face. "Gideon! So help me, if you don't start talking to me, and you damned well better start making some sense, the next thing I throw at your head is going to be something very heavy and very, very hard!"

Finally, she got his attention. He rushed to her, grabbing up her hands, only to drop them and back away as if he feared touching her. If he didn't explain himself really fast, she was going to lose it.

"I'm so sorry! I wasn't thinking," he gushed. He was so rattled, and it was scaring the living hell out of her.

"You already said that," she reminded him.

"No, not about the shimmering. Well, yes, about that too. But not that." He shook his head, looking like he was about to take up pacing once more. Or throw up.

His face was pale, too pale, his eyes all but bugging out of his head.

"Gideon," she snapped, striding forward to grab his shoulders before he could resume circling the room, giving him a rough shake.

"Oh God, Maggie, I screwed up." His wild-eyed gaze met hers. Suddenly, she was the one who felt panicked, she just didn't understand why. "I was so caught up in... And I could touch you! You! Not just anyone. But I wanted so badly for it to be you. And it was, and I could touch you. And it went to my head. You went to my head. Not that it was your fault. Because it wasn't. That's on me. I didn't *think*. Wasn't thinking. I didn't use protection, didn't even stop to think. Not once last night. All night! Every time we...I didn't use protection. I was so caught up—"

At last, his words, his behavior, the way he'd touched her stomach earlier began to make sense. A wave of dizziness washed over her, and she took a staggering step back, her mind racing.

"No," she whispered, her hand going to her abdomen. No, that was ridiculous. To just assume...

It was impossible. Too soon to know anything, at the very least.

"It's okay," she whispered. Clearing her throat, she shook her head and offered him what she hoped was a reassuring smile. Someone had to be calm and reasonable here. And it didn't look like that was going to be him. Besides, she was just as responsible for this mess as he was. "It's okay. We'll just have to be more careful from now on. Besides, the likelihood of...of...well, *that* happening has got to be pretty...ah, slim. I mean, it was only last night. There's no way to tell so soon if… Why are you shaking your head at me like that?"

"Maggie," he said, approaching her now with firm, sure steps. Gone was the panic, gone the hysteria. And in its place was a deadly, serious calm that terrified her far worse than she could ever imagine. His hands caught her shoulders with an urgency she'd rarely seen in him.

"Maggie, you *are* pregnant."

She shook her head, trying to pull away. A snort of laughter, so out of place, slipped out. God, she was losing her mind. Clapping a hand over her mouth before she laughed out loud, she struggled to breathe. Great. Now she was the one going hysterical.

"No," she finally managed to get out, delayed but firm. "No. Don't be ridiculous, Gideon. That's impossible! It's been less than twenty-four hours. There's no way to—"

"Maggie!" He cut her off, lowering one hand to cup over her abdomen, his touch so very gentle. She could feel a spark of something kindle low and deep. A flutter of power. As if something—something separate from her but something inside her—were reaching for him. "I can feel him, Maggie. I can feel his power. Power, individual and separate, from yours. I'm not mistaken."

She opened her mouth to argue, but nothing came out.

"You're pregnant, Maggie." His gaze held hers. Determined now. Protective. Unflinching. And very, very possessive. "You're carrying my baby."

She stared up at Gideon, unable to process his words. They just kept buzzing around in her head. No.

The buzzing was in her ears. Her throat was suddenly, inexplicably dry as a desert. She forced a swallow, vaguely aware she was swaying on her feet like a drunkard. But that wasn't right, because she was floating. The room began to spin.

And then everything went blessedly black.

Chapter Fourteen

Gideon stifled a curse as he swept Maggie up in his arms. He shimmered them back to his bedroom and gently lowered her to the bed. A quick check of her pulse revealed its flutter entirely too fast to be healthy. That couldn't be good.

Oh, dear God, please no!

What if there was something wrong with the baby? It wasn't as if he could just take her to the emergency room. Heaven only knew what a doctor would find. What if the babe wasn't compatible with Maggie's body? What if carrying his child ended up killing her?

Another panic attack hit him like a tidal wave. Nothing had ever been mentioned about what happened to the Halfling upon the Chosen One's birth. Would she...*could* she even survive?

It was in that instant that the magnitude of the situation fully hit him. In seeking her out, in bringing her under his protection—in losing control of his overwhelming desire for her—he'd unwittingly created the fourth relic.

He'd created the Chosen One.

What do I do?

He began to hyperventilate. No, he couldn't panic. Maggie needed him. Gideon clawed his way back from the edge. He would do her no good if he continued down this road. He had to figure this out.

First things first. He needed to make sure she was physically all right. Maggie and the baby were top priority. He swiped his phone from the nightstand and thumbed in Mikhail's number.

The Demon of War answered on the first ring. Gideon was so shocked it took him a moment longer than necessary to remember how to speak.

Mikhail filled the silence. "Is she with you at the plantation?"

"Yes," Gideon said, frowning. How had he known this was about—

The phone line went dead. Gideon held the device away from his face, staring at it incredulously. Before he could hit redial, he heard massive feet pounding up the grand staircase and then thundering down the hall. Gideon went instantly into a defensive crouch when the door burst open. He relaxed infinitesimally, straightening, and extinguishing the plasma ball in his hand the moment Mikhail cleared the doorway.

Mikhail took in his surroundings in a split second. He'd never had cause to be in Gideon's bedroom before, hence the reason he hadn't shimmered straight there. Demons never shimmered to someplace they'd never been before. The potential of solidifying halfway in the middle of a wall, or three steps past the end of a cliff, was something to avoid at all costs. Mikhail rushed to the bed, and Gideon could only look on in disbelief. He'd not seen the Demon of War look so…concerned.

Hell, he'd not seen Mikhail look *anything* before. Mikhail didn't do emotion.

Although Mikhail had defected from Lucifer's rule with Gideon and the others, he'd always held himself carefully apart. He'd gone about this business of seeking forgiveness in his own way, on his own terms, never relying on the others for help unless it was absolutely necessary. Even then, he'd been known to Lone Ranger it to the point of suicidal inclination on more than a few occasions. Gideon had never wondered about that before, having been caught up in battling his own demons. After all, they all had their own crosses to bear.

Now, however, certain things were starting to click into place. Like the way Mikhail had known something was wrong with Maggie without Gideon having to utter a word. Or the way he'd flown to her side and instantly placed his healing hands over her abdomen without anyone telling him what had happened. Sometimes, Mikhail just seemed to know things.

"How long has she been unconscious?" Mikhail asked, interrupting his musings.

Gideon was still trying to wrap his mind around the fact that Mikhail actually experienced emotions, and wondering over what other powers Mikhail might possess, so he didn't immediately respond.

"How long?" Mikhail barked with customary impatience.

"Only a minute or two." Gideon hurried to the other side of the bed to get out of Mikhail's way and watched. Concern for Maggie overrode his confusion over Mikhail's uncharacteristic behavior. But only just.

Mikhail sat on the side of the bed at Maggie's hip. He immediately placed both hands over her abdomen once again, dropped his chin to his chest and closed his eyes. He sat like that for immeasurable minutes. Gideon didn't say a word, though everything in him balked at having another male so close to her, putting his hands upon her.

It took every ounce of his self-restraint to keep from wringing his hands like a helpless old woman. "Can't you fix her?"

"It's not a wound. She's not broken," Mikhail bit out. "It's a babe growing within her. A healthy babe. There's nothing to fix."

Gideon hadn't meant *fixing* the babe. He'd meant fixing whatever it was that had made Maggie turn white as a sheet and pass out. He remembered the wild flutter of her pulse. Was it her blood pressure? Sometimes expectant mothers had problems with blood pressure, didn't they? Her pulse had been erratic.

But the angry hiss Mikhail emitted when Gideon opened his mouth to explain silenced him. Gideon bit his tongue. Best to let Mikhail concentrate. He glanced down, dismayed to realize he was clenching his hands together in front of him. He jerked his hands apart and fisted them at his sides as he stood still, his focus darting between Maggie and the scarred warrior.

At length, War straightened, though his gaze never left Maggie's face. The air left Gideon's lungs in a sibilant hiss. Mikhail was looking upon Maggie with unmistakable awe.

Gideon didn't know what to say, or how to react.

Mikhail reached up, his large hands hovering at either side of her head. He frowned in severe concentration.

Slowly, Maggie blinked blearily between the two demons.

Mikhail stared down at Maggie. He wasn't smiling now. He didn't offer any words of comfort and kept his expression guarded. Yet Maggie seemed to take solace from his presence. Rage rose up inside Gideon, snarling for the chance to rip Mikhail's throat out. That was *his* woman. *His* babe. Mikhail had no business...doing whatever it was he was doing to make her feel better. That was Gideon's job.

Just as quickly, Gideon slapped the monster back in its cage. No way was he letting that thing come out with Maggie in the room. Not ever again. It had damned near killed her the last time. And now that she was pregnant?

Oh, hell no.

Without a word, Mikhail conjured a glass of water. He slipped a gentle hand behind Maggie's shoulders and helped her sit up. Gideon remembered another time when he'd been the one to conjure a glass of water for her. She hadn't touched it.

Maggie took this glass from Mikhail with a grateful smile and swallowed several sips before passing it back. Mikhail accepted the vessel, vanishing it in the blink of an eye while Gideon seethed with jealousy. Over a glass of water.

"Feeling better?" Mikhail asked.

Another first. Usually, the moment Mikhail healed a human, he pulled a Houdini. He sure as hell never stuck around to make small talk. Bedside manners were about as important to War as the dirt on the bottoms of his size thirteen combat boots.

"Yes, I think so. Um, did Gideon...ah, call you?"

"Yes."

"So you know...what he thinks?" Why did the fact that she systematically continued to deny she could be pregnant with his child stab at him so painfully? She waited until Mikhail nodded before going on. "Can you explain to him he's jumping the gun? There's no possible way I'm—"

"You are with child," Mikhail said firmly.

Maggie lost what little color she'd regained. Gideon reflexively jumped closer to the bed. She wasn't going to pass out again, was she?

"H-how can you tell?"

Mikhail laid his hands upon her abdomen once more, closing his eyes, as if in communion with the being already growing inside her womb.

"I sense his essence."

"His *essence*?" Now it was Gideon's turn to shake his head in disbelief. "You mean…does he have a soul?"

Mikhail nodded solemnly. Maggie shot Gideon a baffled look. "What do you mean, *does he have a soul?*"

"He's part demon," Gideon said by way of explanation.

"It's also part human," Maggie argued, then shook her head. "*If* I were pregnant—which I'm *not*. I can't possibly be."

"You are. And the babe is also part angel," Mikhail added, quite unnecessarily, in Gideon's estimation.

That reminder brought a long moment of contemplative silence.

The Chosen One.

Mikhail rose. He reached out, placing a hand gently on the top of her head for another moment. Gideon bristled, watching as becoming, healthy color flooded Maggie's cheeks.

Slowly, Mikhail withdrew his hand, his own face

pinched and much paler than before, the scars slashing down the side of his grim visage standing out in stark relief. He turned to face Gideon, arching an eyebrow. "I am the closest thing she has to a doctor. Get used to it. Green doesn't look good on you."

Maggie reached up and grasped Mikhail's hand. The demon started, blinking down at her. Gideon couldn't help the scowl, didn't even try to hide it.

"Thank you for coming to check on me," she said. "And thank you for making me feel better."

And she *did* feel better, Gideon reflected sourly. She appeared the soul of tranquility now.

Mikhail inclined his head in acknowledgement. Gideon didn't miss the brief tightening of Mikhail's hand over hers before the demon released her.

"When you need me, I shall come again. Rest now."

When, not *if*, Gideon observed. And then Mikhail shimmered away.

Gideon stood staring at the shifting air beside the bed for a moment, scowling. Had that been a threat aimed at him? Some illicit promise to her?

She shifted on the bed, swinging her legs over the side so she could sit up, snapping Gideon's attention to her once more. Unsettled, Gideon worked to push the unwanted suspicion and jealousy away. He strode around the bed, perching beside her.

"Looks like we have a lot to talk about," he said, reaching for her hand.

Seeming to anticipate his move, she clasped her hands tightly in her lap, smoothly avoiding his touch. Gideon stiffened at the rejection, grinding his teeth.

"Look, you might not have wanted a kid—"

"I never said I didn't want kids," she said, cutting him off. "I'd love to have kids. Someday. A couple of them."

"Just not now, huh? Not mine."

"You're the one who had the meltdown," she pointed out, painfully polite as she crossed her arms.

"Yeah, well, you passed out."

He knew he was being petty but couldn't seem to stop himself. He could see her withdrawing and couldn't figure out how to stop it. This was that careful distance, that solicitous politeness she hid behind. Must be pure hell, doing everything within your power to hide from emotional attachment, yet driven by your angelic blood to be the very milk of human kindness.

"It's not every day a woman finds out she's pregnant after a one-night stand."

Gideon went utterly still. Rage exploded inside him so swiftly he barely kept himself from morphing into Temptation.

A one-night stand?

What part of never letting you go did you miss, darlin'?

Maggie drove him insane. She argued with him at every turn. She was, by turns, curious and courageous and intelligent. And she brought out these marrow-deep protective instincts he'd never experienced before. The woman set his blood on fire. She challenged him, making him—for the first time in his entire memory—actually and truly want to be a better person, not just go through the motions.

Not to mention, she was the only woman he'd been able to touch in an eternity. She thought what they'd just experienced had been nothing more than a one night stand?

She was in for a rude awakening.

"It's a little late for second thoughts now, isn't it, sweetheart?"

"I don't know about that," she snapped, giving him the evil eye. Seeming to have to work to calm herself, she added, "I just never pictured myself..." Her words trailed off with a slight frown.

"What? Pregnant with demon spawn?" God, he was being a bastard. He knew it. But he was too mad to give a damn.

"No," she said sharply, scowling ferociously. "Not that. And my child is not demon spawn."

A spark of relief kindled in his chest. It had been the first time she'd spoken possessively of the child they'd created. Maybe there was hope she might come to care for it after all.

A tiny part of him wondered if she could care for the child, could she also come to care for his father?

"So then it's just the fact that it's *my* kid that you find so distasteful," he pressed.

"I can't talk to you when you're like this." Standing up, she made to walk away. He shot a hand out grabbing her wrist.

"Then what is it? Explain it to me."

"Oh, I don't know," she drawled, heavy on the sarcasm. "I guess maybe I imagined when I finally did start a family it'd be with a husband at my side. With a man that—"

"That's just it, isn't it? With a *man*. Not with a *demon*."

"With a male," she said loudly, speaking over him. "One that might actually love me. Hell, right now, I'd settle for one that just plain cared for me. Not somebody who was only interested because I was knocked up with some relic in a stupid prophecy."

Gideon stared at her in stony silence.

Well, he'd be damned if he'd beg. He wasn't a fool, and he wasn't a glutton for punishment. At least, he never used to be. But damn it all, he still wanted her.

Maybe he was a fool after all.

Damning silence filled the room as they glowered at each other.

"You're an idiot," she finally growled. She jerked her wrist free and stormed from the room, slamming the door behind her.

Chapter Fifteen

"Xander and Kyanna will be here soon," Gideon told Maggie as he crossed the backyard and approached the gazebo.

"I'd better run inside and change," Maggie murmured. She rose from where she'd been clearing out one of the many flower gardens and dusted her hands on the knees of her jeans. She'd politely refused his offers to conjure the yard back into shape, insisting she needed something to do.

She studiously avoided looking at him as she hurried toward the house. She'd been doing a lot of that since this morning, avoiding him like the plague ever since she'd begged him to get her a pregnancy test and then sat for hours staring in shock at the little plus sign on the stick. His temper was coming apart at the seams. Much more of this and he was likely to snap.

He watched her scurry across the yard, as if fearful he might follow if she lingered. Swearing beneath his breath, he swung around to glower at the lazy river. But getting his temper under control was fast becoming more than he could manage. Not even the peaceful solitude, nor the gentle sounds of nature could soothe him as they once had.

He glanced over his shoulder at the gazebo where Maggie seemed to prefer spending so much of her time. The damned thing was all but falling apart. She'd insisted it was fine. That it had character.

It was a damned hazard. An accident waiting to happen. And she was—

He stopped, forcing a swallow.

She was pregnant. She didn't have any business putting herself in danger. With a swift, focused thought and a push of energy, Gideon conjured the gazebo back to its original whitewashed glory, complete with climbing emerald vines. She could get mad all she wanted—at least she'd be safe.

Hell, maybe that was what he needed to do. Piss her off on a regular basis. It might relieve him of some of this anger, and it might chip through that careful, cordial wall of icy politeness she'd erected between them.

No. Probably not the best idea. She was pregnant after all. He should be working to keep her calm, give her peace. Not plotting ways to make her blow a gasket.

Even as the thought occurred, a burst of pain shot through his head, and he could feel his energy waning. Made reckless by his frustration, he ignored the pain and extended himself further, depleting his energy just a bit more by conjuring a sturdy log swing, placing it in a golden patch of sunlight.

Sitting down, he tipped his aching head back, basking in the sun's rays. This would be a peaceful place for Maggie to read, or just to sit and enjoy the calm. He turned slightly in his seat, taking in the yard behind the house.

It was too soon just yet, but someday he'd put a swing set beneath the shade of that big maple. Maybe a jungle gym. Oh, and a sandbox too. Kids loved sandboxes, didn't they? Of course, he'd have to put up a fence. No little kid should be playing around a river.

Will he hate me as much as his mother does?

His shoulders sank, and he squinted against the bright sunlight. How had everything gone to hell so fast?

A shiver of awareness went through him. A new, familiar power had arrived, in the direction of the house. Xander was here.

Stirring himself, he drew his focus in, preparing to shimmer to the kitchen, only to catch himself at the last moment. Heaving a sigh of resignation, he pushed to his feet and slowly made his way up the gentle slope of the yard.

Gideon opened the back door to the kitchen and stepped inside. Heaving another sigh, this one of disgust, he closed the door with a rude thump. Xander had Kyanna perched on the edge of the counter, his narrow hips wedged between her thighs, one hand gripped tight on her ass. A mass of long blonde hair was wound around Xander's fist, and he tugged the woman's head back and to the side as he devoured the side of her throat. At the sound of the door closing, pretty blue eyes flew wide open, and Kyanna began pushing Xander away.

She was like a beautiful butterfly struggling against the inevitable force of the wind. She wasn't going anywhere until Xander decided to let her go. As if to prove the point, his hand still anchored in her hair, Xander held her head still until she stopped fighting and met his steady stare. The moment her struggles ceased, he sealed his lips over hers, patently ignoring Gideon's presence.

Xander, otherwise known as the Slayer and

formerly Lucifer's personal assassin, kissed the living daylights out of his woman. By the time he was through, Kyanna clung to his broad shoulders, fingers speared through his short, deep brown hair, as she made needy little noises in the back of her throat. Their audience was all but forgotten.

With a wholly male grin of satisfaction, Xander stepped back, balancing his woman with a hand on her shoulder until she found her legs once more. The side of her neck was bright pink, abraded from Xander's teeth and the dark whisker stubble covering the lower half of his face.

"Xander!" she hissed, red staining her cheeks as she remembered Gideon's presence once more.

"Yeah," Gideon drawled, plopping onto one of the kitchen chairs. "Thanks for that, by the way. I can never unsee that, you know."

"Welcome," Xander snarked. He sat down at the table and drew Kyanna onto his lap, one arm around her waist as he laced their fingers together on her thigh.

"First sign of trouble, and I'm shimmering Kyanna out of here," Xander warned pointedly, the rough rasp of his voice grating through the room.

Xander had once possessed a voice every angel in Heaven envied. The sound so pure and clear, so persuasive, he could make you do his bidding and believe it was all your own idea with a simple suggestion. When the angel Gabriel and the others had torn Xander's wings from him, they'd also mutilated his voice, forever cursing him with the abomination of sound he used now, which explained why he seldom spoke.

Kyanna twisted in his arms and jabbed Xander

square in the chest with a pointed finger. "Oh, no you will not. You will not interfere with me doing my job."

"Baby," Xander uttered warningly.

"Xander." Kyanna's her chin went up in mutiny. "You promised."

The fine lines around Xander's mouth tightened, but eventually he nodded.

"And you will not hover," she added, poking him again for good measure.

"That I did not promise."

She shot him a mock glare, but then relented, pressing a soft kiss to his lips. He captured the back of her head in retaliation, giving her another eye-glazing kiss. Just to prove some point, Gideon was sure.

"So where's the Halfling?" Xander asked, turning to Gideon.

"Her name is Maggie. Use it," Gideon snapped, earning a surprised look from Kyanna. Xander's expression remained placid, but a spark of interest glittered in the depths of his stormy gray stare. Conjuring a caramel macchiato, Gideon leaned back in his chair and propped his ankle on his knee. "She'll be down when she's good and ready."

Xander grunted, conjuring a can of soda for himself and a tall glass of iced tea with a wedge of lemon for Kyanna.

"Go ahead and say it," Gideon barked.

"Carly told us," Kyanna admitted, excitement bubbling from her. "About Maggie being able to touch you. So, it's true? I mean, not that I didn't believe Carly. But after all this time, Gideon! You can finally touch someone!"

Heaven forbid something should actually remain a

secret. Not in this group.

"How are things going between you?" Kyanna leaned closer, whispering conspiratorially.

Gideon gritted his teeth, reminding himself that Kyanna and Carly, now viewed themselves as his honorary little sisters, nosing into his business at every turn. Even as that reality chafed, the thought warmed him.

Before he could tell Kyanna to butt out, Maggie appeared in the doorway. For a moment, he could only stare at her, probably with that same stupid look of awe Mikhail had aimed her way that morning. She'd changed into a fresh pair of jeans, and a silky, patterned top that hugged her curves and fell in soft layers around her hips. She'd also pulled her hair up in some kind of a claw-shaped clip. A few tendrils had come loose, streaming down the side of her face and trailing over her neck.

She reached up and tugged the strand by her face behind her ear. From the corner of his eye, he caught the way Xander stiffened and stared hard at Maggie's belly.

"I'd say they're getting along pretty damned well," Xander growled, turning his head to give Gideon an arch stare. "Wouldn't you, Gideon?"

Gideon watched as Maggie made her way around the table, sitting down on the opposite side as him, vigilant not to meet his gaze.

"Not so much," he muttered.

Kyanna, as if sensing the sudden tension and seeking a way to dispel it, reached over and extended her hand.

"Hi!" she chirped brightly. "I'm Kyanna Hughes,

and this is my husband, Xander."

"It's nice to meet you," Maggie said, shaking Kyanna's hand. "Maggie Michaels."

Kyanna landed a sharp elbow to his middle when Xander made no effort to greet her. He grunted before thrusting out his hand as well, obviously not pleased he was being expected to extend himself this way. Eyeing Xander warily, Maggie accepted his handshake.

"We're still working on manners," Kyanna stage-whispered, earning herself a fierce scowl and a warning squeeze from her husband, who nestled her firmly back in his embrace.

"So you're the one who found me," Maggie said. "I don't know whether to thank you or…well, not."

"With this group, I'd say you pegged that right on the mark." Kyanna grinned impishly. "My mother actually found yours about the time she first got pregnant with you. They met a handful of times. My mother had begun to teach Clarisse some of the incantations to mask your powers so demons and angels wouldn't be able to locate you. But the last time she went back, Clarisse had disappeared. By the time Mom figured out what had happened to you, you were already in the system. I'm so sorry it took so long for me to find you."

Maggie shrugged. "It's okay."

Kyanna offered her a sympathetic smile. "I found papers in Mom's things. She filed a petition to have you placed with us, once she'd managed to track you down again that is. Records back then were a nightmare. But you'd already been placed with another family, the Hansen family, and the courts felt it wouldn't be in your best interest at the time to pull you out of the home."

Maggie blinked in surprise. "I don't remember meeting your mother. But that wouldn't necessarily mean anything. I'd bounced between so many foster homes, one more grown up in the bunch might not have made any impression. I didn't know that." Maggie paused for a moment, taking it all in. "About your mom searching for me, I mean."

Gideon clenched his hands beneath the table to keep from reaching for Maggie. She looked dumbfounded. As if someone had swept the rug out from under her. So she hadn't been as alone in the world as she'd thought herself all these years.

"Why did your mother never come for me later when I was removed from the Hansens' care?" Maggie asked in a small voice.

A fleeting look of sadness swept over Kyanna, but she quickly pushed it aside. "You'd slipped through the cracks in the system once more. By the time she found you again, you'd been placed in Stonebridge Academy. You were doing well there, had adjusted to the environment, and hadn't exhibited any…ah, nonhuman tendencies. She checked on you a couple times, put enchantments on the school itself, but decided to wait. She wanted to let you have a normal childhood, if possible. She didn't want to have to disrupt your life to tell you about…well, all of this, not until it was necessary."

Kyanna paused then, drawing a deep breath. "Mom died before you graduated. She'd already taught me all the enchantments and such, ever since I was old enough to speak. Other kids got fairy tales. I got the *Twilight Zone*," Kyanna said, smiling as she shook her head.

"I'm kidding! But seriously, while other little kids were reciting Jack and Jill went up the hill, I was reciting angelic incantations and spells. But Mom hadn't told me about you yet, and then she died. I suppose she thought she'd have more time, to prepare both of us. Xander and I were only recently able to track you through your teaching records."

Maggie nodded, lost in thought as she absorbed the information. Gideon sat in stoic silence, knowing she would not appreciate any offer of support or comfort coming from his side of the table.

Kyanna glanced from Maggie to Gideon and back, eyeing the distance between them, too perceptive by half. Clearing her throat, she pushed herself from Xander's lap.

"Maggie, why don't we go to the den and get comfortable. We can talk a bit more before we get started on the training."

Gideon pushed to his feet, filled with doubts. "You know, maybe this isn't such a good idea."

"You promised," Maggie said, frowning as she stood.

"That was before." His gaze dipped to her abdomen, lingering meaningfully before lifting to hers.

Her hands crept forward to shield her stomach. "All the more reason I should learn how to protect myself—protect *us*."

Kyanna gasped. Xander reached up and gently clasped her hand to quiet her.

"That's right, Kyanna," Gideon said. "We now have another relic. The Chosen One, to be exact."

Maggie aimed an angry finger his way. "You call my child that one more time, and I'm going to throw something at your head again."

"Again?" Xander asked, only to be shushed by Kyanna.

"*Our* child," Gideon corrected her, ignoring Xander's snort of laughter.

"Um, come on, Maggie," Kyanna coaxed as she held out a hand. "I'd say we have a little bit more to discuss now."

Maggie shot Gideon a fulminating stare, before taking Kyanna's hand and following her from the room. Xander barely waited until they were out of earshot. "What the hell were you thinking?"

"Obviously, I wasn't."

Xander stared at the door the women had just exited through for a long time. "Ah, damn it. Don't beat yourself up," he said at last, shocking the hell out of Gideon. He'd been expecting a royal ass chewing. Not wry commiseration. "If she's anything like Kyanna," Xander added, shaking his head, "you didn't stand a chance, brother."

Chapter Sixteen

"Good. Very good," Kyanna said as Maggie held her hands up, palms out, and concentrated really, really hard. "Now I'm going to have Xander try to push into your space."

"I'll do it," Gideon growled. Maggie tried really hard to ignore him. But just the tenor of his voice spiked hunger and hurt through her system.

And how embarrassing was that? Here she was, presented with the opportunity she'd been praying for since her twenty-first birthday, trying to pay attention to Kyanna, trying to memorize incantations and enchantments, and all she could focus on was the sound of Gideon's angry voice. And the mind-melting, warm, citrusy scent of him as he paced nearby.

She struggled to remember what Kyanna had told her.

Breathe in. She drew in a soul-deep breath. *Breathe out.* She released it in a controlled, long exhalation. *Focus on the scents around me. The fresh, crisp air, feel it on my skin. Smell the scent of pine nearby. The scent of lilacs, the freshly cut grass. Listen to the sound of the slow-moving river. The soft whoosh of breeze through the trees overhead and the rhythmic rustle of leaves. Listen to the birdsong.*

She couldn't do it. Not with Gideon stomping about, snarling like a rabid animal every time Xander or

Kyanna tested her shields.

"No, you won't," Kyanna said, her tone brooking no argument.

"Yes, I—"

"I said no, Gideon," Kyanna snapped, clearly at her patience's end. Truth be told, Maggie wasn't too far behind her. "Maggie needs training, not coddling. You won't push her for fear of hurting her. You'll pull your punches. I understand why, but in the long run, that's only going to hurt her. Do you think Stolas and his minions will treat her with kid gloves just because you lo—" Gideon growled low in his throat, and Kyanna quickly changed whatever it was she'd been about to say. "Because she's pregnant?"

"You're hovering," Maggie accused, her eyes closed tight against what she was sure was a very intimidating glower.

"Get used to it." Oh, he was furious now. She'd heard him angry before. But his voice held a new quality. A dangerous softness. One that instantly made the fine hairs on the back of her neck stand on end. Had she finally pushed him too far? Wearily, she squinched one eye open and watched him through the fringe of her lashes.

"I'm not going to let anything happen to you or our child, not even by accident," he promised in that same deadly soft voice.

Xander, of all people, cracked a huge smile. Maggie almost—almost—opened both eyes wide in surprise, catching herself at the last second. Remembering herself, that she was supposed to be concentrating on her shields, she held her pose.

"It's about time you found something to live for,"

Xander remarked.

Now Maggie looked at him, full on, puzzled by that last remark. "What does that mean? You make it sound like he—"

Gideon looked like he wanted to throttle someone. She wasn't sure which of them he'd like to get his hands on more. Xander, Kyanna, or her. Frankly, she didn't think he'd care either way, as long as someone was bleeding when he was done.

"Gideon?" Frustrated by her inability to focus on the enchantments, she reached over to pick up one of the daggers Gideon had brought outside for combat practice. "What's he—"

Maggie jolted, sucking a sharp breath in on a hiss as the dagger slipped from her hand. In an instant, everything and everyone around her disappeared. She caught flashes of images, light and sound and smell.

Sulfur filled the air, burning her nostrils. Terrible screams hurt her ears, tearing at her eardrums until the warm trickle of blood dripped from her earlobes. The heat was so intense she staggered back a step, sweat instantly pouring down her body.

She glanced around, spun around taking everything in at once. Rocks and crevices, dry arid land as far as the eye could see. Fire and shadows filled with creatures too horrible to imagine.

"I'll never submit," a hoarse woman's voice cried.

Maggie spun again. *There!* A large, wrought iron cage perched at the top of a spire of stone. All around the cage, creatures writhed and scrabbled. Hideous beings that clawed at the bars and pawed at the trapped woman.

No…not a woman. An angel.

Her wings—missing large patches of feathers, bloody and filthy—were wrapped protectively around her. Her reddish-colored hair hung in a dingy, matted knot at the base of her skull. Robes that had obviously once been pristine white were torn and bloodied, stained with soot.

"There she is," a raspy voice shouted. *Xander!* What was Xander doing here? Wherever *here* was? Maggie turned to watch the scene unfold.

But Xander wasn't alone. Gideon was there too. And Niklas and Mikhail. And two other demons she'd never seen before, one tall, blond, and knock-out gorgeous. The other had jet-black eyes, mocha-colored skin, and a goatee. The latter carried a long, ancient-looking sword with a huge bloodred stone set into the pommel and some kind of runes carved down the length of the blade. They swarmed the cage, beating back the ghouls.

A dark laugh came out of nowhere, seeming to echo through the valley. The remaining creatures melted back in fear. The six demons turned, moving to stand shoulder to shoulder, all preparing to fight as they formed a barrier between the caged angel and the new threat.

"Maggie!" Someone took hold of her shoulders and shook her. "Maggie, are you all right?"

Maggie blinked and sagged into Gideon's waiting arms. "I'm fine," she whispered.

"What happened?" Gideon swept an arm beneath her knees, scooping her off her feet.

"No! Put me down. I'm fine," she insisted, struggling.

He ground his teeth. "You have dark smudges

beneath your eyes, and you looked as if you were about to pass out again," he informed her. She struggled in his arms until he put her back on her feet, but he kept a careful arm around her waist.

"I had a vision."

Xander and Kyanna moved closer.

"You were there, Gideon. And you, Xander. Niklas and Mikhail too. And two others. One who…well, I imagine, looks much like a Norse god."

"Sebastian," Kyanna supplied, earning herself a peeved glare from Xander.

"The other one had dark skin, jet black eyes, and a goatee." She glanced back and forth between Gideon and Xander as she filled in the rest of the details from her vision, being as specific as possible. She didn't miss the look that passed between Xander and Gideon when she mentioned the sword.

"So Asher was there too," Gideon observed, stroking his fingers along his chin.

"We're going to have to call the others," Xander said.

Gideon nodded. "Do you suppose it's *the* sword? And if so, how the hell did Asher get his hands on it?"

Xander looked just as troubled as Gideon by this observation. "Who do you suppose the angel in the cage was?"

Maggie shrugged as everyone's attention turned to her. "I don't have any clue."

"It's time to call it a day," Gideon decreed at length.

"I'm not done training yet." Maggie stood firm, ignoring him, waiting for further instruction from Kyanna and Xander.

Gideon all but snapped his teeth at her. He turned to Kyanna, desperation leaking into his voice. "Can't you tell how tired she is? She's pushing herself too hard. We're all pushing her too hard, expecting too much."

"Stop hovering," Maggie told him as she tried to focus. "Help or go away."

"I have been helping," he shouted.

"No. You've been hovering," Xander corrected.

"And you haven't?" Gideon shot right back. "What was that earlier? When Maggie read that incantation wrong and Kyanna went flying? What do you call that? I've never seen you move so fast in your existence. Not even when that Ralsha Demoness decided she wanted you as her mate."

"What was that?" Kyanna asked, eyeing Xander. "What Ralsha Demoness?"

"I don't know what he's talking about," Xander said, cringing and shivering like something extremely unpleasant was crawling all over his flesh.

"Mmm-hmm," Kyanna said with patented disbelief and a *we'll-discuss-this-later* glare.

"I was simply taking proactive safety countermeasures and offering a bit of constructive criticism," Xander said, glaring at Gideon.

"'Proactive safety countermeasures', my ass," Gideon complained, getting right up in Xander's face. "Careful, Xander. You're starting to sound like the hot air bag you were trying to be a little while ago. If you can't take a little *constructive criticism*, don't be so quick to hand it out."

God, she couldn't take another second of this. She wouldn't be a bone of contention between Gideon and his friends. But neither would she live in ignorance because he was afraid she might break a friggin' nail.

"Damn it, Gideon! Enough!"

He glanced over at Maggie's furious outburst, clearly ready to argue his point. The words died on his lips as his eyes all but bugged from his head. He, Xander, and Kyanna all stared at her in similar shades of shock.

"What?" Frowning, Maggie glanced down.

She stood in the fighting stance Xander had taught her, her hands open at her sides. And hovering above her palms were twin, pulsing balls of white energy. Not exactly plasma balls, but remarkably similar.

Something they most definitely had not taught her.

Maggie screamed. She hopped back, shaking her hands wildly, but the balls would not be dislodged. If anything, they only grew.

OhmiGod! OhmiGod!

"Put them out! Put them out!" she cried, waving her arms frantically. One glowing orb broke free, slamming into a bush near the river. The bush erupted in blue flames, and another orb quickly reformed to take its place in her hand.

Gideon flew across the distance between them. He grabbed her wrists and slapped her hands together. "Breathe! Calm down."

The energy balls flashed and sizzled out.

"It's okay," he murmured against her hair as he dragged her into his arms, squeezing her tight. His heart thudded beneath her ear, keeping time with her own. "You're okay. They're out. Shhh. Shhh. You're okay."

He sounded as if he wasn't sure whom he was trying to convince. Her, or himself? Honestly, after that startling development, she didn't care. Maggie melted into him. Wrapping her arms around his waist, she buried her face in the soft fabric of his T-shirt and greedily sucked in the scent of him. She gratefully absorbed the protective warmth surrounding her.

What was that? What just happened?

"Is she okay?" Kyanna asked.

Gideon snarled. "What the hell do you think? She damned near set herself on fire. What the hell was that anyway?"

Slowly, Maggie eased back in Gideon's arms, though he wouldn't let her go completely. That was fine by her. Her legs were still shaking.

"I've never been able to do that before," she told the group, her voice little more than a whisper. "What was that?"

"I have no idea," Kyanna said, her eyes wide with wonder, her tone shocked.

"Angelfire," Xander rasped.

"Angelfire?" Gideon repeated, turning slightly to face Xander. He looked more than a little green around the gills. "Are you sure?"

"Pretty sure. I've only seen it once before. During the Great Fall. And it had been aimed at you, right before Mikhail deflected it."

A look of shock swept over Gideon's face, one that was quickly replaced by dawning understanding. And horror. Gideon's face lost all color before turning a sickly shade of gray. "After the Fall, Mikhail disappeared for decades," Gideon whispered, as if speaking to himself. He had to clear his throat before he could speak. "Mikhail didn't get the scars on his face from Ralsha venom, did he?"

Xander held his gaze but remained grim and silent.

Gideon swore.

Confused, glancing between the two towering demons, Maggie demanded, "What?"

"Your father can call forth Angelfire, Maggie," Xander said when Gideon looked incapable of speech. "And now, apparently, so can you."

"Angelfire." She whispered the foreign-sounding word, testing it on her tongue. "What exactly is it?"

"A select few demons, Xander included, can summon Hellfire," Gideon said, finding his voice at last. "Or, at least, Xander used to be able to. It's basically a superheated compound that will destroy anything. *Anything*." Gideon grimaced then, as if remembering something particularly unpleasant. His focus shot to Xander. "Mortikaï can summon Hellfire. He melted the Amulet of the Gods."

Maggie recalled the book shoved beneath Gideon's bed, and his fixation on the amulet. Was that what he'd been hoping to find? Had he been hoping to use it to break his curse?

Xander's brow furrowed, but before he could reply, Kyanna piped in, beating Maggie to the punch. "Yes, well, that's all very interesting. But what about Angelfire? I've never heard of it."

"That's because it's even more of an anomaly than Hellfire," Xander said, coming to stand behind Kyanna. He slipped his arms around her waist, drawing her back against his chest. "Angelfire works much the same as Hellfire. It's capable of destroying anything."

Maggie shook her head. She rested her fists against Gideon's chest, afraid to open them and lay them flat lest she accidently destroy him. "But I've never been able to do this before. Why now?"

Kyanna peered over her shoulder at Xander. "Do you think it has anything to do with the pregnancy?"

"Possibly. Could be she's channeling the babe's powers. Could be she just unlocked another of her own powers." Xander smirked. "Could be Gideon just pissed her off more than anyone else ever has."

Maggie shuddered, imagining a two-year-old capable of tossing about energy balls—*Angelfire*, she corrected—whenever he had a temper tantrum. Gideon smoothed a hand down her back, murmuring against her hair. As if sensing the direction of her thoughts, he leaned back, nudging her until she looked at him.

"We'll figure this out, Maggie. Together."

The look in his eye promised something far deeper, something she prayed she wasn't just imagining due to wishful thinking.

"Enough training for today," he said again, implacable this time. His focus skated to Xander. "I need you or Niklas to stay with Maggie for a few hours."

At first, Xander frowned, looking as though he intended to object. But then, with a meaningful glance from Gideon, he asked, "How long since you last—"

"Four weeks." Gideon cut him off.

"Four weeks since what?" Maggie looked back and forth between them.

If Gideon hadn't looked happy before, he looked downright thunderous now. Without a word of warning, the backyard shifted and fell away, only to be replaced by the bedroom they'd shared so intimately just last night.

As soon as they solidified, Maggie bent over at the

waist and gagged. It took every ounce of her self-control not to vomit all over the floor. Or his boots. She should have. It would have served him right for pulling such an underhanded stunt.

With a stifled curse, Gideon conjured a trash can and thrust it under her face.

"I'm sorry," he whispered, sounding truly contrite as he held her hair back from her face.

When her stomach finally settled, she allowed him to guide her to the bed and help her lie down. The room spun around her, and she broke out in a cold sweat. He sat down next to her, and gingerly blotted a wet cloth against her cheeks and forehead.

"I'm sorry," he said again. His face was pale, his expression pinched.

"No more shimmering," she pleaded softly. "Please, Gideon. It was really bad this time. Worse than the first time. I...I think it might not be a good idea right now," she said, slipping a hand protectively over her stomach.

He glanced down, swallowed and nodded. "No more. Unless it's an emergency." He smoothed her hair back. "Okay now?"

Maggie drew a testing breath. "I think so." She made to rise, but he gently pushed her back against the pillows.

"Rest for a little while. You're still white as a sheet." He was a fine one to be talking, because *he* certainly didn't appear to be in any better condition. Before she could object to his orders, he pressed a fingertip to her lips and offered her a rueful smile. "You can train again tomorrow. I won't get in the way this time, I promise. Kyanna's right. You need to be able to protect yourself."

She smiled weakly up at him.

He turned serious as he absently reached up and smoothed a lock of hair behind her ear. "I have to—" He broke off abruptly, biting the edge of his lip. "I'm going to be busy for a little while. I'm going to have either Xander or Niklas stay with you till I get back. Just for a few hours."

"Where are you going?"

He looked as though he wanted to crawl under a rock. Gideon licked his lips and glanced away.

"Gideon?"

He met her stare, his expression blanking right before her eyes. "I have to go."

"But—"

He leaned down, pressing a soft kiss to her lips, silencing her. His beautiful golden eyes were filled with remorse as they roamed her face. Without another word, he rose from the bed and strode toward the door.

"Gideon," she called, pushing herself upright. "Wait! Where are you going?"

But he just kept walking, stopping only to draw the door closed gently behind him.

Chapter Seventeen

Gideon drew his phone from his pocket and thumbed in a speed dial number. The phone rang several times, just long enough for him to nearly give up hope. Just as he was preparing to disconnect the call, a deep voice answered.

"She is well?"

Well, that was disconcerting. Frowning, Gideon said, "Maggie's fine." Shaking his head over Maggie's ability to bring out odd reactions in males, demon or otherwise, he raked a hand through his hair. "I need a favor."

A beat of silence. "What?"

"I need you to look somebody up for me. A human," he added, gritting his teeth as self-disgust boiled like acid in his guts. Gideon descended the grand staircase, making his way to the den.

After giving Mikhail the details, he disconnected the call, pushed the door to the study open, and strode inside, unsurprised to find Niklas and Xander had made themselves at home in the matching wingback chairs flanking the cold fireplace. A can of soda rested in Xander's hand, a beer in Niklas's. Gideon crossed the room and sank onto the padded leather chair behind his desk. He thought about conjuring himself his usual coffee but doubted caffeine would help at this point. His gaze drifted to the ceiling. Heaving a sigh, he conjured a crystal tumbler filled nearly to the brim with the strongest rotgut he could think of. He let his shoulders slump, weary to the bone.

Taking a sip, Gideon sucked in a sharp breath at the burn. His voice was a little hoarse when he finally asked, "Where are Carly and Kyanna?"

"In the kitchen having tea," Niklas supplied. "They figured you needed a little man time."

He should have guessed as much. Neither the Slayer, nor the Seer for that matter, often let their mates far from their sides.

Overprotective asses.

But that thought gave him pause, and he stilled, glass lifted halfway to his lips.

That was exactly what he was fast becoming.

If only things could have been different. If only the woman in question had chosen him, the way Carly had chosen Niklas. The way Kyanna had chosen Xander.

If Maggie had been given a choice, would she have chosen him? Willingly?

"See? Didn't I tell you?" Niklas asked, drawing Gideon out of his musings. What were they talking about? He'd lost track of the conversation he'd walked in on.

Xander nodded sagely, taking a long draw of soda.

"What?" Gideon asked.

"She's got you twisted up in knots." Niklas set his beer aside and laced his fingers over his middle, settling back in his chair more comfortably.

Gideon had watched Niklas twist in the wind over Carly. He'd seen the way Xander behaved around Kyanna. He'd even teased them about their predicaments. And here he was, in the same damned boat.

A boat that leaked like a sieve, smack in the middle of Shit Creek, and he with neither bucket nor paddle.

He wasn't fool enough to even try to deny it.

"You know, Slayer," Niklas remarked, a sly grin on his lips, his ice blue gaze dancing merrily. "I seem to recall some less-than-sympathetic comments someone made not that long ago about our own woman troubles."

"True," Xander said, nodding. He took another long gulp of soda and vanished the can. "Demons of lesser restraint might be tempted to rub his nose in his current situation."

"They might," Niklas agreed. "It's a good thing demons of our fine, upstanding, stature would never stoop to such deplorable behavior."

A deep chuckle rumbled through the room. "At least I don't have to worry about Kyanna frying my ass with Angelfire the next time she gets pissed off at me."

"No, you only have to worry about her locking you in your room and binding your abilities with angelic enchantments," Niklas crowed, earning himself a narrow-eyed glower from the now sober Xander.

Gideon snorted aloud. He was just petty enough to take a moment's enjoyment from his brothers' banter despite his own less than ideal circumstances.

"I wouldn't be laughing so hard over there. I didn't get my woman knocked up with the Chosen One," Xander snarked, shooting Gideon a gimlet stare.

"Only by sheer dumb luck," Niklas jeered. "At least Kyanna's friend had you, er, covered."

Gideon chuckled. He'd overheard Kyanna telling Carly the story not so very long ago. Kyanna's friend

Summer had the finesse of a hammer. When Kyanna had captured a wounded Xander, his clothing had been in a sad, sad state, having just come from a demon battle. Once he was inside the enchantments that had surrounded her antique shop and apartment, he had been unable to conjure fresh duds.

So, being the gracious hostess that she was—*cough cough*—Kyanna had phoned a friend. Summer, upon hearing Kyanna's request for replacement male attire, had promptly assumed Kyanna was having an out-of-character illicit affair and had sagely decided to look out for her best friend's interests, slipping a rather large box of condoms in amongst the clothing she delivered. Kyanna had been so mortified, she'd snatched the box from the palm of his hand and thrust it into the first cabinet she could reach. Her version of out of sight, out of mind.

Red actually stole into Xander's cheeks. "How did you find out about that?"

"Kyanna told Carly," Niklas said.

"And I overheard the telling," Gideon said, jumping in helpfully.

Xander harrumphed. "Yeah, well, you're not any better, Seer. You're rolling the dice here too." Xander grinned. "I can already see five or six little Carlys running around, wrapping you around their tiny little fingers just as their mother already has."

Expecting a snide comment, Gideon looked to Niklas. He was startled to find the Seer sitting there with a goofy grin plastered on his face and a faraway look of longing in his eyes.

And it got Gideon to thinking.

"I wonder what he'll look like. Suppose he'll have

Maggie's smile?" Where'd that come from? Great, now he was getting all gooey too.

"Won't it be pleasant if he gets his mother's termagant…excuse me"—Xander cleared his throat at Gideon's warning growl—"determined attitude along with that pretty smile?"

Niklas snickered.

A long stretch of silence filled the room. In the stillness, he became aware of the soft approach of familiar power. So subtle, so familiar now, he almost didn't pay any attention. Maggie was nearby. Just outside the den door, if he didn't miss his mark.

"Part demon, part angel, part human. Can you imagine what those midnight craving runs are going to be like?" Xander hitched a thumb in Gideon's direction. Niklas burst out laughing.

Hey! Wait a second.

"I'm sitting right here, you know?" Gideon growled.

But his mind shot ahead. He imagined Maggie, swollen with his child. He shifted in his chair to alleviate some of the tightness in his pants. Had it been the image that had shot lust straight to his gut? Or her mere presence, just on the other side of that mass of solid oak standing between them?

Or perhaps a stunning combination of the two?

Distracted by the growing erection steadily taking up more and more real estate in his pants, and the woman causing it, he lost track of the conversation once more until he heard Xander say, "That was a pretty smart move, by the way, Gideon."

He frowned. "What was?"

"We can't find the relic, so we—or rather, you

specifically—go out and make one. Strategy-wise, that was brilliant."

Gideon nearly groaned aloud when the soft pulse of Maggie's power behind the door spiked to white hot throb.

He should have put an end to the conversation about the baby earlier. Should never have let it get that far out of hand. Now he was kicking himself for not calling an abrupt halt the moment he realized she was close enough to overhear.

"Maggie, come in," he called.

Niklas and Xander exchanged guilty glances as the door slowly pushed open and a pale, rigid Maggie stepped inside the room. This time, when the silence stretched on, all three males cringed uncomfortably.

"Is that true?" she asked, her voice subdued, her posture ramrod stiff. "Did you get me…did you do this on purpose?"

Oh, Lucifer's balls!

Shit Creek had just developed some rather nasty rapids.

"No," Gideon said, hastily setting his drink aside and pushing to his feet. He, as well as Xander and Niklas, froze when she lifted a trembling hand, palm out, to stop him. Normally that wouldn't have been enough to keep him from going to her. But the pulsing orb of blue-white energy emerging from her palm gave him some serious second thoughts. At length, she drew a visibly shuddering breath, and the orb dissolved as she lowered her hand.

"No, Maggie, I didn't," he tried again, keeping his voice calm. Conscious of his engrossed audience, he cleared his throat and worked to focus solely on her.

"Touching you, kissing you—" He broke off, shaking his head. "I've dreamed of doing that, of being able to touch someone for so long, I guess I lost my head."

"So you weren't trying to get me pregnant on purpose?"

"No! I swear," he vowed, putting as much earnest conviction in his voice as he could.

"You just lost your head?"

"Right."

"Because you were overwhelmed by being able to actually touch someone else? *Anyone* else."

"Yes." He sighed, relieved she was finally getting it. He, and he alone, was responsible for the mess they were in. It was his fault he hadn't exercised better restraint. His fault he'd let himself get swept away in the taste and scent and feel of her.

"And it had absolutely nothing to do with me?"

"Yes! That's exactly right." *Wait.* Um, why did that feel like it had been a trick question? He ran the conversation back in his head and cringed. *Oh, yeah. Big mistake. Huge.* But he didn't quite realize just how huge until he saw the look on her face. "No! Damn it, Maggie, I didn't mean it like that. That's not—"

The cold stare she leveled him with froze the words in his throat. She turned without uttering another sound and left the room, closing the door quietly behind her. Too quietly. Gideon's gaze shot to the Niklas and Xander. Now they chose to be silent? As one, they began shaking their heads at him in mute disappointment.

Gideon dropped like dead weight onto his chair. He stared at the door, unable to comprehend how his situation could have gotten any worse than it had already been. Apparently, it had been quite easy. Step one, open mouth. Step two, insert foot.

A defeated groan seeped from Gideon as he slowly leaned forward and dropped his forehead on the hardwood desk with a jarring thud.

His sinking boat had just capsized.

And Shit Creek was awfully damned deep.

Chapter Eighteen

After listening to Gideon basically tell her she'd been nothing more than a convenient outlet for his pent-up libido, Maggie had locked herself in her room. It was bad enough he'd admitted to the fact without showing the least little bit of remorse. But to tell her so in front of his friends?

She'd never been so humiliated. And she'd been humiliated plenty in her life.

The gall of the man.

And to add insult to injury, he'd left her here without another word. Without so much as a goodbye. He'd hopped on a big black motorcycle and ridden away without a backward glance. She should know. She'd stood at the window like some angst-ridden heroine in a tragedy, watching him disappear round the bend at the end of the drive. He'd left her with virtual strangers. The very same strangers he'd humiliated her in front of.

Oh, they'd been kind. Kyanna and Carly had both come knocking softly at the door throughout the day, with pleading murmurs and offerings of food and tea. She'd refused to answer their inquires, let alone open the door. The men had avoided coming anywhere near her room. Their own version of kindness, she supposed. Well, she'd take what she could get at this point and be grateful for it.

Sitting on the side of the bed, she tugged uselessly at the hammered silver cuff. This mess had all started the moment she'd snapped this double-damned thing on her wrist. She should have taken her chances with those three demons. Physically, she might have been in more danger, but at least her heart wouldn't have been torn from her chest and trampled on.

The most pitiful thing of all, however, was that she had no one to blame but herself. She'd broken her own rule. She'd let someone get close—truly close—and she knew better.

Oh, she had good friends, Gail and Molly and Cori. Even Cecelia, in her own selfish way. And she always made a point of helping those that needed helping. After all, she'd been in need once too. Only she'd not had anyone to help her. Not until Stonebridge. She was only paying it forward.

She flirted briefly with calling Cori or Gail. Maybe Molly. But she couldn't draw her friends into the nightmare she now called life. She wouldn't knowingly put them at risk.

She stilled, going cold all over. Would she be able to go back? How could she return to her life now? She'd been offered a teaching contract for next year. But could she, in all good faith, surround herself with a classroom full of helpless children when a demon prince and his—according to Gideon and his friends—*countless* minions were gunning for her? Her hand crept to her stomach, tentatively settling.

A baby.

She was pregnant. She had a child to support now. The very idea left her slightly panicked. She'd never imagined herself a single mother. She hadn't planned this. Granted, she of all people knew life never went according to plan. But she felt vastly unprepared.

And at the same time, something kindled inside her. A flame that slowly began to burn, brighter and brighter. There was a baby growing in there. Her hand began to rub slow, gentle circles. Whether or not this child was the Chosen One, as everyone seemed to assume, they were overlooking one simple fact. This was a baby.

Her baby.

"We're going to be okay, kiddo," she whispered. "You and me. We're going to be okay. I'll figure something out, and I'll take really good care of you, don't you worry." Holding her free hand up, she concentrated very hard, then smiled wide as a pulsing blue-white orb of energy began to form. Slowly, she closed her fist, watching as the orb sizzled out. "I'm not going to let anyone hurt you."

She sat on a window seat and stared out over the river for what felt like hours.

Maggie's resistance finally crumbled when the scent of roasted vegetables and grilled chicken began to seep insidiously through the window. Her stomach grumbled, loudly. Standing, she made up her mind. No more hiding. She needed to eat, needed to keep up her strength. After all, she was eating for two now. She also needed to practice the incantations and see what other little surprises her powers were going to throw her way.

Maggie was halfway across the room when what sounded like a battering ram slammed against her bedroom door, cracking throughout the room like a gunshot. She nearly jumped out of her skin.

"Come out now or I come in and drag you out," a

harsh rasp ordered through the heavy oak door. "You are worrying Kyanna." Xander's tone implied he wouldn't tolerate anyone or anything causing his woman worry.

Swallowing the squeak of surprise, she drew in a deep breath and willed her pulse to slow.

"Maggie," Xander snapped, thumping the door again impatiently.

Maggie scurried forward, fearful he might actually break the door down before she could finish crossing the room. She wrenched the door open, but the sight of a furious Xander glaring at her made her forget whatever it was she'd been about to say.

"You will come down now," Xander barked. "Eat and practice. No more pouting because Gideon's too stupid to think before he speaks." Without another word, Xander disappeared in a wave of distorted air.

Maggie stood in the doorway, mouth hanging open, blinking.

Kyanna and Carly had spent the better part of the day cajoling and coddling her. And they'd only made her feel sorry for herself. But just like that, with a few unlikely words, Xander had managed to dispel her embarrassment, shifting the blame where it deserved to be.

On Gideon and his stupid mouth.

Huh? Who'da thunk it? Xander was actually pretty good at this comforting stuff.

Bemused, Maggie made her way to the kitchen.

As she stepped inside the room, Maggie glanced uneasily around. Carly sat on Niklas's lap, his arms snug around her as he nuzzled the side of her neck. Kyanna bustled near the counter, turning when she heard Maggie enter, a measuring cup in her hand. Xander sat at the table, balancing a lethal looking dagger as long as his forearm on the tip of his finger by the dagger's point. She offered Xander a tight-lipped nod of appreciation.

Kyanna caught the exchange. Casting a suspicious gaze at Xander, she asked, "Is that where you went? Tell me you didn't bully her into coming down if she wasn't ready."

"She was ready," Xander said, deadpan.

"You yelled at her, didn't you?" Kyanna crossed her arms and shook her head in obvious disappointment. Before Maggie could offer protest, Kyanna insisted, "Apologize."

Maggie thrust a hand up, frantically shaking her head. "Oh, no—"

"It's okay, Maggie," Kyanna interrupted, watching Xander. Xander stared back, unmoving but for the tiny tic that had begun in his cheek. "Tell her you're sorry for yelling at her, Xander. She's had a…a rough day. If she'd rather not have to deal with us, then—"

"Kyanna!" Maggie snapped in exasperation, gaining a startled look from both women. Both demons, of course, remained unfazed. "Xander didn't yell at me." Technically, he hadn't shouted. Just used a very…*ah*, very stern voice. "And I was ready to come down." Her attention skated to Xander, just long enough to connect meaningfully before she glanced back to Kyanna. "I was pouting." Somehow, she didn't think Kyanna would take it at all well that Xander had been the one to helpfully point out that fact. "But I'm done now. I still have a lot of work ahead of me." She offered the room at large a small smile. "And I'm hungry."

"Oh. Oh! Well, then," Kyanna said with a brilliant smile. She hurried to the oven, grabbed up a hot pad, and bent down to pull out a pan of dinner rolls. "We're just getting ready to eat, and there's food aplenty. Carly always cooks enough for a small army. Maggie, would you mind getting the lemonade from the refrigerator? Xander, the chicken should be done now. Would you mind?"

Maggie glanced at Xander one more time before she went to do as Kyanna asked. Xander met her glance and nodded his head ever so slightly. A slight crease formed in his cheek as the very edge of his mouth curled up a tiny bit. She hoped that was approval glinting in his eyes as he turned to head out the back door.

A short while later, as the small group sat around the table digging into the tasty food, Xander's phone rang.

Maggie watched as he flipped his phone to his ear and barked, "Yeah?"

His brow knitted in a deep frown as he stared absently at the salt shaker. "When?" Silence. "No."

More silence.

"Need backup?" Xander had transferred his attention to his plate. He listened for a moment more, then thumbed the phone off and shoved it into his pocket. He picked his fork up, took a bite of roasted potato, and chewed slowly.

"Well," Kyanna finally demanded on behalf of the room at large, "who was that? Sebastian?"

"Yeah," Xander said before scooping up another bite.

Kyanna growled, and the next thing Maggie knew, a wadded up linen napkin went sailing through the air to smack Xander in the face.

Xander looked up, his expression incredulous. "What happened to your precious table manners, Kyanna?"

"Stop making me pull teeth, demon," Kyanna snapped, glaring at her mate. "Is he all right? Did he find the Guardian's descendant? Does he need help?"

"Found her, and then lost her again."

"I'm sorry, who is Sebastian?" Maggie asked. Hadn't Kyanna mentioned him before? Had he been the blond in her vision? Everything was fast becoming a jumbled mess lately.

"Vengeance," Niklas supplied.

"He's really a very sweet guy," Carly rushed to assure her. "You'll love him. Great sense of humor. So considerate. Looks a lot like that guy who plays that Norse god in those movies based on the comic books."

Beside her, Niklas growled, and his eyes narrowed. "A Norse god?"

"Well, he kind of does look like one, actually," Kyanna agreed with a helpless shrug.

That earned a fierce scowl from Xander. "And you've seen so many of those, have you?"

"I don't think I'll be leaving you with Sebastian anymore," Niklas snapped in Carly's direction. "He doesn't need any more women in his harem."

Carly shot Maggie a mischievous grin. "Oh, I don't know. What do you think, Kyanna? If there was ever a harem to join, that would be the one to—"

She wasn't given the chance to finish. Niklas snatched her from her seat and dragged her across his lap. Holding tight to the squirming, protesting woman in his arms, he kissed her into submission. Kissed her senseless. By the time he was finished staking his claim, they were both breathing heavily and the room held a new kind of tension.

With one last searing look, Niklas deposited Carly unceremoniously back onto her own seat. Color rode high on her cheeks. She looked slightly dazed as she searched the table for something.

Niklas didn't even try to stifle his iniquitous smirk. He reached over and lifted Carly's hand—which was already clutching the fork in question—so she would finally notice it.

"In all fairness, Sebastian does actually look—" Kyanna gasped as she, too, was abruptly snatched up and found herself perched firmly on Xander's lap.

Maggie's mouth dropped open, only to snap closed as Xander gripped the back of Kyanna's neck in what looked like an inescapable hold. He dragged his wife closer, his gaze locked on hers. A wealth of meaning seemed to pass silently between the couple, and then Xander's mouth claimed Kyanna's. Not as Maggie had expected of the fierce warrior, all heat and force. Instead, Xander seduced Kyanna with an ever-lingering series of slow nibbles and nips. Gently, leisurely deepening each sweep until Kyanna moaned softly and wrapped her arms around his neck in submission, yielding all. Only then did he angle his head and sweep her into the fire.

When Xander eventually released Kyanna, she leaned back with a little whoosh of air and a disgruntled half frown, half smile. She sighed, shaking her head as she returned to her own seat.

Feeling like a voyeur, Maggie cleared her throat.

"So...ah, where was it that Gideon went again? He didn't exactly say." She forked up a piece of juicy herbed chicken, hoping to look nonchalant.

A death pall descended over the room. She frowned, glancing around at her companions. Had she just committed some terrible sin? She'd only asked a simple question.

Kyanna and Carly stared at each other, wide-eyed. Seemingly by mutual agreement, they both bent to their plates and shoved enormous heaps of food into their mouths.

Niklas shifted in his seat, toying with his fork.

"What?" Maggie glanced around the table. "Is it a national secret or something?"

A thought occurred to her, and she set her spoon down on the edge of her plate, the food in her stomach turning into a rock. What if Gideon had gone out to see how many other women he could touch?

"He left to feed," Xander rasped, calmly scooping up a heaping bite as though discussing the weather.

"Xander!" Kyanna mumbled around a mouthful of food.

Carly began choking. Niklas reached over to helpfully pound her on the back.

Maggie looked down at the small mountain of food on the table, frowning in confusion. Feed?

"She should know," Xander said to Niklas.

Niklas stared at him in silent contemplation. Then, "It's Gideon's place to decide if she needs to know."

"Know what?" Maggie asked, her focus bouncing between the two males as Kyanna and Carly fell silent. The strain around the table was thick enough to cut with a knife.

"His head isn't screwed on straight right now," Xander reminded Niklas, ignoring Maggie's question. "And what of the babe? What if it takes after its father?" he added. "She needs to know."

"He's right, Niklas," Carly said softly, reaching out to lay her hand over his on the table.

Niklas turned his hand over and laced their fingers together. He drew a deep breath and shot one last glance at Xander, who nodded.

"Maggie," Niklas began, and she braced herself, for the tone he used was not at all something one would associate with butterflies and puppy dogs, "demons don't feed like humans do."

She glanced at the half-empty plates in front of Xander and Niklas and frowned. What was he talking about? She'd been sitting there, watching both of them shoveling in food like there was no tomorrow.

"But you're eating the same things we are," she pointed out.

"Not *eat*. Feed," he clarified. "We take sustenance like this"—he waved his hand at the table—"to keep our physical bodies healthy and functioning. But we require more."

"You mean like a…like a vampire or something?"

"Sort of. But we don't exist on blood." Niklas looked to Xander, who nodded. "Well," he clarified, "most of us don't."

"Oh!" Kyanna gasped. Then, clutching her throat, she whispered, "Mikhail…"

Niklas and Xander remained stubbornly tightlipped, clearly refusing to discuss Mikhail. At length, Niklas resumed his explanation. "Our immortal souls were stripped from us when we fell."

"Like your wings?"

Nodding, Niklas added, "And our gifts."

"Like your voice?" she asked, turning to Xander.

Across the table, Carly sucked in a soft breath. But Maggie's gaze remained on Xander. He said nothing at first, simply stared at her as silence held reign. Fine lines appeared at the sides of his mouth as his lips compressed. She hadn't thought of how her question might affect him before she'd blurted it out. Now she could have kicked herself. She'd not intended to hurt him.

Maggie leaned forward, frowning in concern. Oh, she wished she could take the pain she'd carelessly caused away. Xander leaned back in his chair, a serene expression on his face.

Niklas shot forward in his seat. "Did you feel that?" He glanced from Kyanna to Carly to Xander. "Did anyone else feel that?"

"Feel what?" Kyanna frowned.

"That shot of…of…soothing warmth." Niklas shook his head, visibly grasping for the appropriate words. "Like…warm fuzzies."

Xander finally joined the conversation. Though his demeanor was still uncharacteristically tranquil, he said, "I did. Like a wave of peace washed through me."

"Did you do that?" Niklas asked, turning to Maggie.

"I…I don't know." She glanced helplessly at Kyanna. "Did I?"

Kyanna shrugged, baffled.

"Gideon would know, he'd be able to sense the push of power, but I swear I felt it. And it felt like it came from that side of the table," Niklas insisted, pointing at Maggie.

"It seems our Halfling is discovering new abilities right and left," Xander remarked, crossing his arms.

Uncomfortable with this new focus, Maggie turned back to Niklas. "Please...you were telling me about demons feeding."

"So, as we need human food to sustain our bodies, in order to keep our essence—our life force—strong, in order to maintain our powers, we must absorb human souls as well. But we're careful never to feed from the innocent. Only from those with evil intent, guilty of heinous crimes that would otherwise go unpunished by human law."

"And how do you *absorb* these souls?" she asked cautiously.

Xander glanced at Kyanna, his gaze troubled...guilty.

"We place our palms over the human's chest, and pull their soul through the connection, basically sucking it into ourselves." He glanced to Niklas, seeking extrapolation.

"That about sums it up."

"Doesn't sound very pleasant for the human. Is it painful?"

"Excruciating," Xander whispered, frowning down at the tabletop. Maggie watched as Kyanna reached over and gently squeezed his hand.

"So you're telling me that you and Xander...and Gideon...all of you...um, feed this way?" Maggie looked around the table for confirmation.

Xander nodded.

"And Sebastian," Niklas added, but then, almost as

an afterthought, he said, "Well, I don't anymore, I guess. I haven't had to since I bound my essence to Carly's soul."

"I don't either," Xander said. "Not after I stole half Kyanna's soul."

"Wait, what?" Maggie whipped around to gape at Kyanna. Kyanna seemed to realize she was rubbing the heel of her hand against her breastbone and quickly lowered her hand to her lap. She left her seat and crawled onto Xander's lap, gently touching his cheek.

"Don't, Xander," Kyanna said softly, shaking her head. "It was an accident."

He captured her hand, pressing a tender kiss to her palm.

Maggie stared at Kyanna for a moment, and then she remembered Niklas's comment about binding his essence to Carly's soul. She looked across the table to Carly. Both women seemed fine, healthy color riding high on their cheeks. Okay, one thing at a time. She had enough on her plate to deal with without touching on those revelations.

While it shocked her at first, oddly enough, the whole feeding thing wasn't bothering her nearly as much as it probably should have. Then again, she'd just found out this morning that she was pregnant. By a demon.

And now here she was, sitting at a table, surrounded by demons and their mates, calmly discussing the unconventional eating habits of her child's father.

God, could her life get any more messed up?

"There's something else you should know."

Dragging her attention back to Xander, she waited

for what felt like the other shoe to drop. Like ripping off the bandage, she told herself. Best to do it all in one shot and have the worst of it over quickly.

"Xander," Niklas warned.

"If he hasn't told her about feeding, do you think he'll be in any hurry to tell her about Michael?"

"No," Niklas allowed. "But—"

"She needs to understand why Michael hates Gideon so much, why he'll redouble his efforts to kill Gideon once he finds out about the babe. Gideon's going to need all the help he can get watching his back."

She glanced back and forth between the two demons as they seemed to be waging a silent debate.

"I don't understand. Why would the sperm donor—" Carly and Kyanna gasped and choked. Niklas and Xander elevated eyebrows to hairlines. "Excuse me, Michael... Why would *Michael* be trying to kill Gideon?"

Chapter Nineteen

"Gideon and Michael were like brothers, before the Fall," Xander rasped. He cleared his throat, and picked up his glass, taking deep gulps, grimacing in between.

Maggie couldn't process Xander's revelation, could only stare in shock.

As if by unspoken agreement, a grim Niklas took up where Xander had left off. "From the time we were all created, Michael and Gideon were like brothers. When Gideon chose to follow Lucifer, Michael took it as a personal betrayal. Every time there's been a confrontation since the Fall, Michael has made a point of going after Gideon with a vengeance. Now that you and Gideon…well, you're Michael's daughter. He's going to see this as another betrayal. A personal attack on Gideon's part. He's going to be gunning for Gideon with both barrels now. Despite the fact Michael is an angel, he can be one vicious SOB."

Maggie leaned back in her chair, her appetite gone.

"Maggie, I think there's something else you need to understand." Niklas leaned forward, pushing his plate away and bracing his elbows on the table.

"No more, please," Maggie said, shaking her head as she closed her eyes. "I don't think I can take any more revelations tonight."

"This isn't exactly a revelation. But you do need to understand one very fundamental thing about Gideon."

Maggie pressed her lips together. Resigned, she nodded, waiting for him to go on.

"Gideon may be a strategist at heart—and he's not afraid to fight dirty—but it's hot passion that drives him. Passion and a righteous rage, not the cold ruthlessness it would require to use a child as a pawn in this fight. That's why he loses control when he battles. He might believe himself capable of most anything. And he probably is when he's Temptation. But there's one line Gideon's never crossed, even in demonic form and mindless with battle rage. He has never hurt a child. And I would personally vouch that he never will." Niklas stopped to draw a breath, studying her face. "Something like that? Creating a child to use as a pawn? It never would have even crossed his mind."

Maggie bit her lip, her gaze skating away. Dear God, she wanted to believe him. But trust didn't come easy to her.

"Why did you say it like that? When he becomes Temptation? Isn't he Temptation all the time?"

Niklas frowned. "It's how he sees himself. Like there are two halves of him. There's Gideon. And there's Temptation. Two separate beings. I guess it's how he deals with the rage, separating himself from it. But he hates that side of himself, that part that loses control. And he fears it too. Fears what he might do to one of us…or do to you."

Maggie stared down at her plate, overwhelmed by all the revelations she'd learned that night.

****

Gideon slowly straightened, removing his hand from the now motionless chest of his last meal. His skin crawled, and he fended off a shiver. The bastard had been evil, pure putrid evil to the very recesses of his shriveled soul.

Nevertheless, the power pulsing inside Gideon, now that he'd fed again, was unbelievable. He felt like he could move a mountain. Hell, he felt as if he could conjure one without breaking a sweat. He popped his neck to one side, then the other, stretching the tight muscles in his neck. Tipping his head back, he let the meager beams of moonlight filtering down through the dingy warehouse skylights bathe his face.

He was slightly sick to his stomach, disgusted that in order to feel this good, he'd had to do something that despicable. An unfortunate side effect he'd been dealing with for longer than he cared to think about.

Shake it off. There's nothing for it. Besides, I need to be in top form, especially now. I have a woman and a child to protect. My woman. My child.

A wave of power shifted through the air somewhere nearby, followed closely by a second wave. Angels—Gideon knew instantly. Only an angel gave off that silvery resonance. Caution dictated he leave the area at once. Curiosity got the better of him. Why were angels there of all places?

He slipped out the small side door, and eased around the back of the building, slipping into the shadows of the alley.

"The child went missing in this neighborhood." A soothing male voice drifted to him.

Samuel, Gideon guessed. One of Michael's flock. Samuel had always been levelheaded, weighing all the facts—all the circumstances—rather than categorically meting out justice. After Kyanna had been discovered, Samuel had made several attempts at contact. But

Xander and the rest of the Fallen, hell even Kyanna herself, hadn't trusted the angel's intent.

A tiny grin tugged at Gideon's lips when he remembered the message Kyanna had demanded Samuel deliver to the rest of his compatriots when she'd thought an angel, namely the Archangel Gabriel, had killed Xander. She'd cussed like a sailor and threatened every last Heavenly being ten ways from Sunday with all manner of vile things. Bad old Lucy himself couldn't have done better.

For a moment, Gideon considered making his presence known.

"This is the same neighborhood in which several other children have gone missing, is it not?"

Michael, Gideon realized. He'd know that voice anywhere. He'd been meaning to have a little chat with the angel about a number of things, primarily about his daughter. About the fact Maggie was now his mate. And about the fact she carried their child. Michael's grandchild…and that realization gave him a moment's pause. How messed up was that?

Oh, hell. Might as well get it over with.

"It is." A moment passed, and then Samuel added, "Do you feel that? I sense…a demon presence."

Oh, this wouldn't be awkward, not at all. He drew a deep, bracing breath.

"Out slumming, are we?" he asked as he stepped from the shadows.

"Traitor," Michael hissed, dropping instantly to a battle stance, his attention never leaving Gideon. A flaming Sword of Justice appeared in his hand, crackling and whooshing through the air.

Samuel had stepped to the side, assuming a safe

distance from Michael's sword, to say nothing of his unfurled, lethal wings. Samuel did not summon his own sword. Instead, he frowned, and his eyes turned completely white, the way they did when he was "weighing" a soul.

Normally, Gideon would have had some witty bit of banter ready to poke at the angel. But he had too much on his mind, and matters were far too serious.

"Michael, we need to talk," he said, holding his empty hands up to show he meant no harm.

"Talk?" Michael sneered. "You've just murdered an innocent. I can feel the surging power inside you."

"He was no innocent," Gideon countered, scowling now but working to keep a level head. Getting into a pissing match with Maggie's father would get him nowhere.

"So you say," Michael accused, taking a determined step forward, angling his sword, obviously preparing to attack.

"The bastard I just drained was one of Maggie's foster dads."

Michael hesitated, all the blood seeping from his face.

"Yeah, that's right," Gideon said. "Maggie. You know, your daughter? Remember her?"

Michael shot an uneasy glance over his shoulder. But Samuel looked on, his expression carefully blank, as if he'd tuned the entire conversation out. Maybe he had. His eyes were still all white. The process usually only took a matter of seconds. By the saints, were Gideon's sins so numerous that he was still weighing him, even after all these minutes?

"How did you—"

"Doesn't matter how," Gideon growled. "The fact is I did."

Michael started forward once more, his demeanor even more dangerous than before. "If you hurt her—"

"Oh, don't even try to play the protective daddy card. You haven't earned it," Gideon said. "Do you have any idea what that bastard almost did to your daughter?"

Michael continued to advance, not really hearing a thing Gideon was saying, to Gideon's everlasting frustration.

Gideon was aware that Samuel had gone still, his eyes returned to normal, his rapt gaze bouncing between the two of them. Michael finally stopped advancing.

"His name was Randy," Gideon said, hurrying to explain, knowing he'd only have a small window of opportunity before Michael's hate got the better of his personal judgment. "He was one of the foster dads Maggie was placed with as a child. He was also a pedophile. One that came dangerously close to molesting Maggie when she was just a kid. Only reason he didn't succeed was because she managed to fend him off with a steak knife she stole from his own kitchen."

"You lie," Michael hissed. But Gideon could see the doubt creeping into his blue-green eyes and furious color bloomed in his cheeks.

"Samuel knows I speak the truth. But you're too blinded by your own hatred to plainly see what's before you. Weigh me for yourself."

Michael hesitated for a good long while, visibly struggling between doubting Gideon just on principle and his own inherent need to acknowledge the truth. Finally, he gave in to his nature. Easing forward, he peered hard at Gideon, his eyes turning white.

Shock, sick disgust filled Michael's countenance. When his burning stare returned to the present, to the corporeal demon before him, he demanded, "Where is Maggie now?"

"She's safe."

"With you?" Incredulous fury had taken over Michael's disgust. "With your legion of traitors?"

"Yes, with me and mine." Now his own hackles were rising. "You didn't exactly do a bang up job protecting her, now did you?"

"Michael," Samuel called soothingly. "I believe Gideon mentioned talking. I think it best we hear what he has to say."

The Archangel stared Gideon down, chest heaving, nostrils flaring, rage suffusing his features. In a flash, the flaming sword disappeared and Michael launched himself at Gideon, viciously pummeling him with bare fists. He caught Gideon in the mouth with one punch, in the eye with the next. Not to be outdone, Gideon blocked the next jab with his forearm, his other fist connecting with Michael's nose with a satisfying crunch. The two broke apart, circling each other.

"Damn it," Gideon huffed, dodging another blow. "Listen to me. Maggie is part of the Prophesy."

"The hell she is." Michael spat a mouthful of blood onto the ground, his fists bobbing in front of his face.

Spatters of blood flew, muscles were bruised and bone snapped as the two went at each other like prizefighters.

"She's a first-generation Halfling," Gideon

reminded Michael in between blows. His head snapped to the side from a brutal right hook to the jaw.

"No one knows about her. She's been hidden." Michael swung again, missing when Gideon wised up and ducked, driving a fist into Michael's ribs.

"Everyone knows about her, you stupid dipshit."

That gave Michael pause. Using the advantage, not caring that he was taking a cheap shot, Gideon slammed another fist into his stomach, driving the angel back and doubling him over.

"Stolas has the Sword of Kathnesh." Gideon propped his fists on his hips, fighting to suck in a breath around the searing pain in his kidneys from a couple of Michael's own cheap shots.

"That's a myth," Michael wheezed, hands on his knees, blood dripping from his nose.

"It's not."

"Have you seen it?"

"No."

"Then how do you know?"

"Because we have the Arc Stone."

Nearby, Samuel sucked in a sharp breath. In the fight, Gideon had forgotten the angel was still around. He angled now, so his back was to the warehouse. Easing to the side, he edged along the wall so the angels weren't blocking him from both sides. In theory, he could shimmer away, but he remembered all too well the toll shimmering took on Maggie. He would not do that to her again—not if he could help it.

"Stolas?" Michael straightened. Gideon took great pleasure seeing both Michael's eyes were beginning to swell shut, and that blood was still streaming from his broken nose. "But he's a prince. Lucifer's own grandson."

"If you think that lot has loyalty to any save themselves, then you're even more stupid than I thought."

Michael growled low in his throat and took a staggering step forward. A Sword of Justice ignited in his hand once more.

"If you kill me," Gideon said, shoving his wrist up in the space between them so the streetlight at the end of the alley glinted off the hammered cuff, "you'll kill her too. The cuffs are bound, and Mortikaï has the key."

Michael's flushed face turned a nice sickly shade of green. "You bastard," he hissed.

Michael vanished the sword and rushed Gideon again, tackling him to the ground. Gideon kicked Michael in the stomach, sending him flying overhead. The Archangel was on his feet in the blink of an eye, and charging into Gideon, shoulder lowered, head down. Gideon absorbed the blow, his breath leaving him in a whoosh. He let his fists fly, jabbing into Michael's lower back and sides. The two went tumbling along the filthy concrete and crashed noisily into a dumpster, sending a pack of rats scurrying into the night.

Another set of hands wedged in between them, tearing them apart. Samuel forced his body between them. He used his wings and his arms to restrain Michael as he stared hard at Gideon.

"Why have you done this?" Michael asked, eyeing first the cuff, then Gideon himself.

"At first, it was to keep her safe. To get around the curse so I could take her to safety."

"And now?" Samuel asked, his voice and his face

filled with strain as Michael raged and fought to get at Gideon.

Gideon straightened, watching Samuel struggle to hold Michael at bay. Though Samuel had just as much reason to hate Gideon and the others, he appeared to be willing to listen at least. Did they have an unexpected ally in the Heavens then?

Using the back of his wrist to wipe the blood from his mouth and chin, he eyed Michael. Telling himself he had nothing to feel guilty over, calling himself a rat-bastard liar for even trying to justify his actions that way, he lifted his chin, stare locked on Michael though he spoke to both angels.

"I've claimed Maggie as my mate," he said loud and clear, watching as Michael all but exploded with fury, his face turning purple.

Samuel, using his entire body now to restrain the Archangel, gritted his teeth and shook his head, looking to the skies as if praying for...for what? Divine intervention? Mercy on Gideon's blackened soul? The strength to keep restraining Michael in all his murderous fury? Protection for Maggie?

"I keep it now and always," Gideon added, "to protect my mate...and our child."

Just like that, time seemed to stand still. Michael froze mid-bellow, even forgetting to move, gaping at Gideon in incredulous silence. Samuel gave Gideon a strange look, one somewhere between shock and understanding, between horror and hope.

"Go," his unlikely ally finally said, positioning himself between angel and demon. In a burst of rage, Michael hit Samuel like a freight train with murder in his eyes.

"Go!" Samuel ground out as he used every bit of his strength to hold Michael back. He was fast losing the battle.

It went against every fiber of his being to run from a fight with Michael. But there were far more important things at stake than his pride now. Shooting the straining titans one last glance, Gideon turned and sprinted down the alley. He hopped on the big Harley parked at the end of the block, fired it up and sped off into the night.

Chapter Twenty

Maggie sat on the couch in front of the fireplace in Gideon's den, an open book in her lap as she stared at the flames crackling in the grate. All the things Xander and Niklas had told her bounced around in her head, unable to settle. But it all boiled down to immutable fact.

Gideon had to absorb souls to survive.

He was a dangerous, ruthless demon. But she never felt safer than when she was with him. He'd also given her the one thing she'd always wanted. The chance and the means to learn how to protect herself.

He'd given her far more than that, she reflected wryly, gently cradling her flat abdomen.

She connected with him more deeply than she'd ever connected with anyone else. But he had to absorb human souls to survive.

Could she live with that?

The sound of footsteps approaching the door drew her attention. Expecting to see Kyanna or Carly, though they'd told her they'd give her some space, she was surprised when Gideon entered the room.

He paused in the doorway the moment his gaze connected with hers. He seemed to draw in a bracing breath, his wide shoulders lifting as his muscular chest expanded. Then, without a word of acknowledgement, he dragged himself across the room to the elegant minibar in the corner. Maggie went up on her knees and twisted around, propping her elbows on the back of the sofa, to watch him.

He picked up a crystal decanter and poured a more-than-healthy amount of liquid the same burnt amber color as his eyes. She waited as he put the glass to his lips—the lower one cracked and swollen—and drained the glass in one long series of gulps.

Even now, knowing what she knew about him, she still wanted him. She watched his long lean fingers—his knuckles scraped and bloody—cradle the crystal, and she wanted those hands on her body again. She watched those seductive, abused lips as they parted to accept the amber liquid, and she wanted to feel them pressed to her skin once more. She wanted the wild abandon of his lovemaking more than she wanted her next breath.

More frightening, she wanted to snuggle into him. Wanted to lay her head on his chest, wanted to hear the steady thud of his heart. She wanted to feel his arms come around her and hold her tight. And she wanted, just for a little while, to let him shoulder the weight of the cares that were crushing her.

As he set the glass down to refill it, she studied the condition of his knuckles a little more closely. They were split and bruised. And his left eye was beginning to swell shut. Glass full once more, he took another sip, and grimaced. He finally crossed the room, and gingerly took a seat on the opposite end of the couch. She remained silent as he removed a throw pillow, noting that he seemed to be favoring the left side of his ribs.

Maggie took the rest of his appearance in now,

from head to foot, in the soft light of the fire. His hair was mussed more than normal. His clothing was torn in places and patched with dirt and blood.

He looked as if he'd been in a barroom brawl. She hoped, given the fact he was still upright and moving around, that he'd won.

But there was something else about him that was different. Something…more.

Despite the swelling and bruising, despite the caution in his movements, his skin was a healthy, glowing pink now. His eyes twinkled just a bit brighter. She knew, from what the others had told her, that absorbing souls strengthened his own essence, that—supposedly—it had no effect on his humanlike physicality. That he relied on normal human food for that.

All that aside, she was still convinced he looked different. He…glowed with good health, despite his battered appearance.

Disconcerting.

Frowning, she clasped her hands in her lap. "How bad's the other guy look?"

Gideon shot her a gimlet stare and grunted, taking another big gulp.

"Oh, for Pete's sake," she said, unable to help herself. She'd never been able to stand to see another suffering. Even if he'd probably brought it on himself.

Scooting over, she claimed possession of his free hand and drew it closer for inspection.

"I need a first aid kit," she murmured. She thought she'd noticed one in the bathroom cabinet upstairs in her—*his* room.

Before she could rise, a white box appeared on her

lap. Startled, she bobbled the case before grabbing hold of it and setting it on the couch between them.

"Thank you. But you could have warned me," she admonished.

Grunting again, he put the glass to his lips once more.

"So," she remarked as she opened the box and found what she needed. "Do you do this often?" She pinched her lips together when he started a bit as she applied antiseptic to his knuckles.

"Often enough," he assured her. The alcohol he'd consumed must have begun to kick in, because he actually leered at her now. "You gonna play doctor whenever I come home all banged up?"

She frowned her disapproval.

"Who were you fighting?" she asked. Gideon grimaced when she dabbed a little too firmly at his split lip.

"Your father."

In an instant, the things Niklas had told her about the relationship Michael and Gideon had shared came back to her. She fought the urge to cringe, hoping against hope that this particular fight hadn't been over her.

"My…oh. Why were you and Michael fighting?"

"I'll give you three guesses and the first two—" He broke off, glancing at her stomach. "Well, the first one, at least, doesn't count."

"Oh God," she said, dropping the folded cloth to her lap as she drew back. She felt slightly sick, though she didn't quite know why. Michael's reaction shouldn't matter to her. Not in the least. "You told him about the baby?"

Gideon nodded.

"And that we… That you and I…"

"Kind of hard to have one without the other, now isn't it?"

"Why does it bother me?" she asked in wonder, shaking her head, not really realizing she was speaking to herself out loud. She swiped the cloth up and began rubbing at the blood by his swollen eye, ignoring the way he cringed away. The big baby. Served him right. "I mean, it's not like he's ever been a real father, after all. He was never there when I needed him. Never there when I wanted him to be there. Why should it matter what he thinks?"

Only when Gideon grabbed her wrist did she realize she'd had him bent backward over the arm of the couch, cowering away from her as she'd angrily scrubbed at his face with the alcohol saturated cloth.

"Oh, I'm so sorry," she whispered, sitting back, horrified.

Cautious, he settled back in his seat and eyed her as if he feared she'd go after him again. "One good thing came of it. Samuel knows now."

"Samuel?" She held up a tube of triple antibiotic.

He eyed it for a moment, then glanced uncertainly at her. "That's all right, I heal fast. Thanks anyway," he said, shaking his head.

"Oh, good grief," she snapped, grabbing hold of his chin. But she was more careful now.

Before he could utter protest, she began gently daubing the ointment on his cuts. "Who is Samuel?"

"Samuel is an Angel of Justice. Technically, he's part of Michael's flock, but he's fair to the point of fault. He's more willing to listen to all sides of the story and take all the circumstances into consideration before he makes judgment."

"And he's on our side?"

As soon as the words *our side* left her mouth, she caught her breath. *Our side.* When had she cast her lot in with Gideon and his friends? Or was she just referring to herself and Gideon? Or herself and the baby? Or all of the above?

Oh, she felt sick all over again.

"He'll listen. But"—he motioned toward the sad shape of his face—"I didn't exactly have time to explain much. Michael had other ideas about the way we should spend our little bit of quality time together."

"I'm so sorry," she said again, catching her lower lip between her teeth as she smoothed her thumb over a nasty bruise forming on his jaw. "He shouldn't have hit you. Not over me."

"If it hadn't been over you, it would have been over something else." He snorted. But, as his gaze finally landed on her face, he must have seen something there that didn't sit well. "Hey," he said, sitting up a little straighter and drawing her hands into his lap. "This wasn't your fault. Michael and I…we have some issues that started long before you were even born." He frowned then, as if something had just occurred to him he'd not thought of before. Drawing a deep breath, he shook his head, focusing on her once more. "Not your fault," he said again.

"Oh, but—"

"Stop arguing with me."

"But, Gideon—"

Gideon leaned down, capturing her lips gently with his. Probably just to shut her up, she reflected for all of two seconds. And then her body took over, responding to his on a fundamental level. Her lips parted of their own accord, and her tongue tangled with his.

Gideon gave a deep groan and swept the first aid kit to the floor. His mouth firm on hers, he dragged her across his lap. He anchored one hand on her hip to hold her in place and tangled his free hand in her hair as he claimed her lips, slanting his mouth over hers again and again, tongue plunging, plundering, possessing.

Lost to a whirlwind of sensations, Maggie looped her arms around his shoulders and melted into him. Just as the hand on her hip began angling up beneath the hem of her shirt, the door of the den swung open.

"Maggie, I think I heard Gideon's motorcycle," Carly called as she swept into the room. "Oh! I'm so sorry!"

Maggie tore her mouth from Gideon's and glanced at the doorway, slightly dazed. She looked back at Gideon just in time to see him staring down where his hand rested on her abdomen. He flinched, and then she found herself rudely deposited on the sofa while he beat a hasty retreat behind his desk.

Mortified to have given in to his kisses so easily, humiliated to have been rejected—yet again—in front of his friends, Maggie struggled to her feet. Leaving the contents of the first aid kit scattered on the rug where they'd fallen, she walked with as much dignity as she could muster toward the door. She would not run.

But oh, how she wanted to.

"Excuse me," she said to Carly, edging around her as she headed for the doorway.

"Maggie, I—"

"I'm very tired," Maggie said, unable to meet the

woman's sympathetic brown eyes. "I think I'll turn in. I've had quite enough excitement for one day."

She slipped from the room, closing the door behind her. She paused for a moment just outside the room to collect herself, her dignity in tatters.

But she must not have gotten the door all the way closed, for she heard Carly softly admonish, "Why aren't you going after her?"

Despite her better judgment, Maggie found herself leaning toward the door, straining to hear his response. A ball of something hot and uncomfortable swelled in her chest making it difficult to breathe.

Gideon heaved a deep sigh she could hear all the way across the room and through a mostly closed door. "It's better this way."

Carly pressed, "Why are you working so hard to put so much distance between the two of you?"

"Who said it's hard work?"

Maggie heard the clink of glass and the slosh of liquid.

"Gideon, I love you like a brother, you know that. But right now you're behaving like a spoiled jackass."

Maggie's eyebrows shot up, and she clapped a hand over her mouth, silently cheering Carly on. There was a firecracker with a mighty bang hidden inside that tiny little body. Unfortunately, Gideon was behaving like a wounded bear.

"Sweet sentiments from candied lips," he remarked.

Maggie just barely restrained herself from leaning against the door in despair. Carly would give up now and Maggie would never hear his answer—the real one that actually mattered.

"Why?" Carly demanded with dogged determination, raising another notch in Maggie's esteem. "Maggie's got to be feeling pretty scared right now. Think about it from her perspective, Gideon. She can't go home, and it's probably best if she doesn't go back to the career she so obviously enjoyed. She has no family but for a father who can't, or just plain won't, acknowledge her. A very pissed off Archangel father, I might add. She's pregnant and surrounded by strangers. You're the one solid thing in her world right now, Gideon, like it or not. And you're pushing her away. Why?"

Maggie's head snapped back. Niklas's mate was human. And yet, Carly had managed to understand her far better than all these supernatural beings combined. Maggie would have died then and there of embarrassment if it hadn't been for the fact that she desperately needed to hear Gideon's answer.

A long beat of silence followed. She could hear the squeak of the chair behind Gideon's desk as he plopped down.

"Gideon, talk to me," Carly coaxed so softly Maggie almost didn't hear her. "What are you thinking?"

Maggie held her breath.

"I didn't give her a choice, darlin'. When I took her, I didn't give her a choice. Not when I took her from Portland, and not when I...when I claimed her. And not when I got her pregnant. I won't take her choice from her again."

"Is that it?"

"What do you mean, *is that it?*" Gideon demanded, incredulous. "Isn't that enough?"

"Oh, sweetie," Carly murmured. "I don't exactly see her beating you off with a stick." There was a shifting, shoes shushing over carpet.

Maggie realized the footsteps were coming closer. She spun around and scurried through the foyer, sprinting up the stairs, not stopping until she had the bedroom door closed behind her.

Wasn't there some old adage about eavesdroppers? Well, it seemed she'd just gotten a heaping helping of serves-her-right.

Chapter Twenty-One

Just as Maggie reached to turn the covers on the bed down, the bedroom door opened with no warning. She nearly jumped out of her skin.

An eerie sense of déjà vu hit her. Gideon stood in the doorway, staring at her in silence. His chest expanding, his shoulders lifting, his expression resigned. Embarrassed still from having listened in on his conversation with Carly, she resolutely turned her focus back to the covers, folding them down with careful deliberation.

"I'm tired, Gideon," she said, making sure her tone left no room for argument. She caught a faint whiff of Gideon's scent coming from the pillow as she plumped it. Unbidden, their intimacy returned to haunt her. Ducking her head so he wouldn't see the telltale heat filling her cheeks, she added, "All things considered, I think it best if you sleep elsewhere tonight."

"That's not gonna happen, Maggie."

Something off topic struck her. He'd called her Maggie. Kyanna and Carly were *darlin'* or *sugar* or some other such endearment. But not her. She was just plain old Maggie. Because the few times he'd called *her* darlin' had sounded far more like an insult than a compliment. And that didn't count. A little kernel of hurt settled in the pit of her stomach. Why, she couldn't figure out. She'd never liked the lovey nicknames to begin with. Yet that he felt so free to use them on others…stung.

That hurt gave her the courage to lift her chin and glare at him. "Well, you aren't sleeping here."

"This is my bedroom, darlin'," he reminded her. And there was that pissed off, insulting tone again. As if she needed the reminder.

Slowly, deliberately, he moved further inside the room and closed the door firmly behind him. He kept his gaze locked on her as he lifted the hem of his T-shirt. He whipped it over his head and casually tossed it into the corner.

The spit dried in her mouth.

But then—*finally!*—her pride decided to show its face. Where it had been for the last few days while she'd shamelessly thrown herself at him, she couldn't say.

"Fine. Then I'll find someplace else to sleep."

Back stiff, she stalked around the foot of the massive bed and made to walk past him, bracing herself for the moment he reached out to grab her. She even mentally rehearsed the techniques for breaking an attacker's hold, the same ones that Gideon himself had taught her. But as she walked by, he made no move to stop her.

Pride smarting at the latest blow, she kept walking, chin up, head held high despite the annoying burn of unshed tears rapidly forming. She made it all the way across the room in oppressive silence, bravely holding the tears at bay. She'd just use the bedroom Gideon had slept in her first night here and come back for her things in the morning.

She reached for the doorknob.

"I'll only follow you, Maggie," Gideon said on a deep sigh.

"What?" She whirled around, sure she hadn't heard him right.

"I said, I'll only follow you," he repeated, his expression reconciled.

"Why?" She shook her head, clutching the doorknob as she debated the wisdom of bolting. How far could she make it before he caught her? She'd wager not even to the stairs. And boy, wouldn't that be the last nail in the casket bearing her pride?

"Ward stones and spells aren't infallible."

"Ward stones?" She felt like an idiot, but she couldn't follow this sudden change in topic. What had ward stones to do with where he slept?

"Ward stones and spells have been breached before. I can't use Kyanna's enchantments. They would render me powerless, and I might need to fight. I'm sorry, but I'm not willing to risk your safety, not even for the sake of your pride."

Now that stung.

"You mean you aren't willing to risk your precious relic?"

His head snapped back as if she'd struck him.

In a heartbeat, he was across the room and in her face.

"Is that what you think of me, Maggie?" His breath was hot against her cheek. His furious stare burned her. "Really?"

Her first instinct was to step back. To yield. But she'd hit her limit. Caution might be the better part of valor. Right now, she was feeling much too reckless to care. Maggie stepped into his space, glaring right back.

How dare he play the innocent martyr here?

"But that's just it, isn't it? I don't really know you at all, now do I?"

"Do you honestly want to go there?" he snarled, bristling with aggression. His large hand covered her abdomen with such extreme gentleness that she shot back like she'd been struck by lightning. Safely out of reach. "Because I could vehemently argue to the contrary."

"Why didn't you tell me about how you feed?" she demanded, desperate to restore her defenses against this man. *This demon*, she reminded herself, however unfair she was being. "Why didn't you tell me about how you and Michael used to be besties?"

That froze him in his tracks. "Damn you, Xander," he hissed beneath his breath.

"*You* should have told me, Gideon." Maggie crossed her arms, aware she was standing there in little more than a thin nightshirt and panties arguing with a half-naked, very pissed off demon.

A muscle bunched and leaped in his jaw. He drew himself up, his presence taking up more space in the room than she'd thought possible.

"You're right. You don't know me," he informed her in a quiet voice. He took one more step toward her—a step of warning, a step of promise. "So let me sum this up for you in a nice tidy little nutshell. Whether or not you like it, I'm a demon. You're a Halfling. And, for the time being, you are under my protection."

He stopped speaking and drew a deep breath, glowering at her, all but begging her to argue. She couldn't find her voice. Could only swallow, her wide-eyed gaze locked on his.

"You are carrying my child. *My. Child.* Not some damned relic," he stated possessively, making her heart flutter. "There's also the little matter of these." He held up the wrist with the cuff on it.

"Take them off," she whispered. And even having said the words, she prayed he would deny her.

"No."

Her heart skipped a beat. "Why not?"

His lips compressed, and something odd flickered in his gaze.

Frowning, she pressed. "Why not, Gideon? Because without them you can't touch me? Because I won the catch-a-demon-lover raffle by default? Go me," she snapped, even as she watched him closely for a reaction.

He drew back, as if she'd somehow wounded him. And that made her feel an inch tall. Damn him. But then he blinked, and that odd light was back.

Guilt. That's what was written all over his face. Guilt.

Finally, he pointed at his neck. "Notice what's missing?"

Frowning, she glanced down at his bare, unmarked throat. She shook her head, meeting his gaze in confusion.

"I wore the key to these cuffs on a chain around my neck." He raked both hands through his hair. "Mortikaï ripped it off in the fight at your place. Now he has the key."

"Mortikaï?"

"Mortikaï is…" Something very dark and very ugly flickered over Gideon's face as he spat the name out.

"A mortal enemy. He was always jealous that I moved up in the ranks of Lucifer's army faster than he did. He was jealous of my powers. But he's lethal in his own right, and very dangerous. Remember the demon I told you about during practice? The one that can summon Hellfire? That'd be Mortikaï."

She nodded, waiting for him to go on. When he didn't speak, she prompted, "And without that key?"

He gritted his teeth, making the muscle in his jaw leap once more. "Without that key, these cuffs are never coming off."

He turned and stalked to the window. Pulling the drapes aside, he stared out into the night. Maggie watched the silvery light play over his muscles, gleaming here, falling away into shadow there, as she struggled to grasp how Mortikaï having the key to the cuffs would affect their situation.

"As long as he has the key to these cuffs, I'm not taking any chances. I won't risk him getting his hands on you. He could take them off, and then I wouldn't be able to—" He turned back, and a pallet appeared on the floor near the door. "I'll sleep there," he said.

The heat had drained out of him now, and he projected weary resignation. She didn't like seeing him like that. Someone like Gideon was meant to take control of a situation and bend it to his will. He was meant to be filled with spirit and charisma. He was meant to dominate.

"You can have the bed," he went on. "But neither one of us is *sleeping elsewhere*. Not tonight. Not any time in the foreseeable future. So, you better get used to my snoring."

Long moments passed as she stood there, hand on

the doorknob, head bent, searching her soul. As if she had any choice in this matter. Finally, with as much dignity as she could muster, she crossed the room once more and climbed onto the bed. Turning on her side, she pulled the covers to her ears. She'd been deliberately cruel, wanted to hurt him before he could hurt her. But the way he'd recoiled whenever she'd accused him unfairly haunted her.

She'd only managed to make herself feel even worse.

Another long moment passed before Gideon's footsteps faded across the room. The lights blinked off. Maggie could hear the shuffle of blankets as he settled on the pallet. And then a brutal silence descended.

Minutes or hours passed, she couldn't tell. But, oh dear Jesus, it felt like forever. Every time she moved, the rustle of sheets, the muffled squeak of the bed made her flinch.

It didn't sound as if Gideon was having any better luck falling asleep. Every time she moved, he shifted as well. Like they were in the same bed, moving in sync to accommodate each other. Sometime after the moon drifted past the slight part in the curtains, Gideon heaved a beleaguered sigh.

"You don't ever have to fear that bastard again." Gideon's soft voice cut through the darkness, making her jump.

What? Lost, she asked without thinking, "Who?"

"Randy," came Gideon's subdued, bitter response. "He'll never terrorize another young girl again."

Frowning into the dark, she couldn't piece this latest conversation together. Shaking her head, she gave up and asked, "Why not? What happened?"

The silence stretched on, heavy with innuendo.

Understanding hit her like a brick to the face. Bolting upright in bed, she gasped, "Oh my God! You *ate* Randy?"

He didn't answer. She sought his form in the deep shadows of the room. Gideon shifted on the pallet, and the whisper of moonlight revealed his movements as he laid his forearm across his forehead.

At first, she was too shocked to think of an appropriate response. And then the truth of it settled over her. Yes, he'd had to take a soul to survive. She'd thought she'd come to grips with that, until now. But she'd actually known this soul.

However, Gideon hadn't preyed on an innocent. And as a result, a depraved pedophile wouldn't be able to hurt helpless children any longer. Gideon had made sure of that.

How many kids had he saved by his actions tonight?

He had to have targeted Randy specifically. After all, what was the likelihood of stumbling upon—

Wait a second. Randy lived in a small town in the Midwest. They were in Tennessee. And Gideon certainly hadn't shimmered to Randy. If he had, she would have been the first to know.

"How?" she asked before she'd had time to sufficiently form the full question in her head.

He choked. Sitting up, he suffered through a mild coughing fit.

She waited until he calmed down, then clarified, "How did you get to him? He isn't exactly within driving distance."

"I had Mikhail find him and bring him to me at a

warehouse we use for…ah, questioning," he explained, lying back down.

"Oh." She fell silent. So Gideon had asked a friend for a favor, for her. She got the impression the small band often went out of their way to handle personal situations on their own. She wasn't sure how to feel about any of this.

"Good," she whispered, the words slipping from her without premeditative thought. Then that same small, vindictive part of her added loud and clear, "I'm glad."

Gideon remained silent.

"Thank you," she said.

"Lucifer's balls," he exclaimed, aghast, "don't thank me!"

"Why not?"

"Do you have to argue about even this?" he asked, clearly incredulous, though she couldn't understand why.

"You did something noble tonight, Gideon, and I just—"

"Noble? Noble!" he squawked. Gideon sat up and twisted to face her, a thin strip of moonlight bisecting his tormented face. "I killed a man tonight, Maggie. He might have been a rank, evil bastard, but he was still human. And I ended him. No, I took pleasure in ending him. And you wanna know what else happened? I'd just absorbed Randy's soul. His body was probably still warm, in fact. That's when your father found me. I'd just fed from a human, just like the monster I am. And then your father and I got into a brawl in the alley."

Shame twisted his features as he turned away and lay back down facing the wall now.

"You're not a monster, Gideon."

He remained silent. Ignoring her? Silently arguing? She couldn't tell, and it was driving her nuts. He couldn't possibly think of himself that way. He was not a monster.

Before she gave herself time to reconsider, she slipped from the bed and trod across the room. Dropping to her knees beside him, she reached out and touched his shoulder. Gideon's entire body went rigid.

Maggie pulled her hand back and clenched her fists in her lap. "I know you, Gideon." She caught the slight movement of his head, though he remained silent. Well this was one battle she was determined he would not win. "You were right earlier. I do know you," she insisted. "You're a lot of things…and not all of them necessarily very flattering…but a monster you are not," she firmly declared.

He continued to hold his tongue. Frustrated, she did the only thing she could think of. Easing down, she wiggled her way onto his pallet, molding herself to his bare back like a second skin. Oh, he was so warm.

But dear Lord, it was frigid down here. So cold in fact, that despite pressing tightly against Gideon's warm skin, in a matter of minutes, she was shivering. But she refused to be the first to yield.

"Damned stubborn, argumentative woman," Gideon muttered beneath his breath and rolled away. Before she could protest, he scooped her up in his arms and strode to the bed.

"Stay with me," she urged as he lowered her to the soft mattress. She locked her arms around his neck, forcing him to hover over her.

"I've taken your choices from you at every turn. I

won't force this on you too." He made to pull back, but she refused to let go.

"If you leave this bed, then that's exactly what you're doing." He paused, staring down at her with a frown on his shadowed face, and she pressed, "I want this, Gideon. I want you. I am making this choice."

"But you know what I have to do to survive now. How can you—"

"I can, because I know you."

He stared down at her for so long, she thought for a moment she'd lost the battle after all.

Desperate to get through to him, she gave him back the very words he'd once spoken to her. "We'll figure this out…together."

The edges of his mouth curled up, reminding her of the first time she'd seen him, standing across the nightclub, leaning against the bar, staring at her as if she were the only woman in the world.

He was looking at her like that again, right now.

Slowly, he lowered his head and captured her lips, branding her very soul. His lips were so very hot. His tongue swirled into her mouth, plunging and rubbing in a sinful mimicry of the sex act.

Without breaking the kiss, he shifted above her, slipping beneath the blankets, until he lay full length against her. Gideon got rid of their clothing with one of his little vanishing tricks.

Maggie's world narrowed. The pinpoint of her focus centered in this room, on this bed, in the intimate warmth of the two of them snuggled inside the warm cocoon of blankets. This was a world of sensation. A world of erotic, gentle caresses. Of soft sighs, and tender murmurs.

Gideon slipped a warm thigh between hers. The slightly coarse hair on his leg abraded her sensitive skin, sending delicious shivers through her. He slipped one arm beneath her neck, cradling her.

She splayed her fingers over his back, savoring the ripple of rock-hard muscles and controlled strength while she tangled her free hand in his hair. When she set her fingertips to tracing the gruesome scars on his back, he tensed.

"Do they hurt?" she whispered, there in the intimacy of the bed.

"No," he admitted, scowling.

"Then why do you tense when I touch them?"

"Because…because they're a reminder of the beast inside me. A reminder of my fall."

She continued to trace the scars. "That's not how I see them."

He frowned as he waited for her to explain, but his body was slowly relaxing into her touch.

"I see them as a symbol of your strength and the things you've overcome to be where you are now. Be what you are now. A being who's made mistakes and done everything in his power to correct those mistakes. And the beast inside you, as you call it, is a part of you. You need to learn to work with the rage instead of fighting it." She reached up, shushing him with a finger pressed to his lips. "Besides, without these scars, I wouldn't be able to be here with you like this."

He stared at her, long and hard. And then he smiled, a purely Gideon kind of smile.

His warm hand settled over her breast and he smoothed the rough pad of his thumb back and forth across her nipple. He stole her breath as he kissed her then, long and slow. Then he released her mouth, and Maggie gasped as his lips skated down the side of her neck. He edged down on the bed, lavishing every inch of her skin with soft caresses and erotic nibbling kisses. His hands moved to her hips, urging her over onto her back.

And when he settled his shoulders between her thighs, she sighed in pleasure. The last time he'd done this, he'd taken her with wild, reckless abandon. He'd utterly devoured her.

Now he took his time. Starting at her knees and working his way to the tiny bundle of nerves at the apex of her thighs, he nipped and nibbled. He licked and sucked. He nuzzled and teased. He drew it out into infinity. He leisurely savored as she slowly lost her mind.

Only after she'd drifted in a dreamy sensual haze, did he finally climb back up her body. Gideon's expression as he eased his rigid, thick length deep inside her, gentle but determined, was one she would hold close to her heart for the rest of her days.

And then he began to move.

They'd had sex before. She could honestly say she knew the difference now. What had happened between them before had been untamed, lust-filled, earth-shaking, mind-blowing sex.

Here and now, Gideon made love to her.

She'd never be the same again.

There would never be any going back, no changing her mind. No halves. No compromises.

For better or worse, as his body rocked over hers, as he surged inside her, Gideon laid claim to more than her body.

He laid claim to more than her heart. He branded himself upon her soul.

Chapter Twenty-Two

"Again," Maggie panted, wiping sweat from her brow.

Xander hurled another plasma ball at her, this one at her feet, and she leaped to the side, tumbling, rolling, coming up with a ball of Angelfire palmed and ready to launch just as they'd coached her. Xander vanished a split second before it would have set his hair on fire. He reappeared a foot away and made to kick her in the face, but she flung herself backward, rolled and shot to her feet, lobbing another ball of Angelfire on the fly.

This one left a scorch mark on Xander's forearm. But he wasn't done. He continued to attack, disappear and attack again, until Gideon finally called out, "Okay, that's enough."

Maggie had to give him credit. Though he'd flat out refused to stay away from practice—and he hadn't been able to bring himself to play the part of her attacker—Gideon hadn't argued this time when Xander had stepped into the role. And he'd kept his promise to not interfere once practice started.

He'd lasted much longer than she'd thought he would. Although, his lower lip looked nearly chewed to pieces, and he had bluish marks on his arms where his fingers had dug in to keep from leaping to her defense.

He'd given her far more today than she could ever thank him for. He'd given her the tools to protect herself. And he'd bolstered her self-confidence. Supported her, encouraged her even though allowing her to continually put herself in dangerous confrontations clearly went against every belief he held dear.

Xander acknowledged Gideon's dictate by extinguishing the flaming ball in the palm of his hand and straightening. "Your aim is improving. But shoot for the chest. It's a bigger target. You've done well," he told her before stepping back to make room for Gideon. Maggie beamed under the praise. And high praise it was indeed, considering the source.

Gideon stepped in front of her. He began touching her, turning her this way and that, obviously checking for injuries. His fingers skimmed a fresh bruise on her shoulder where she'd rolled over a rock. Maggie flinched before she caught herself. His expression turned thunderous.

"Don't," she warned, poking him in the chest. "I'm fine."

Gideon pinched his lips together. He didn't like it. Not one bloody bit. But he remained silent, and he nodded. Pleased, Maggie went up on tiptoe and pecked a kiss on his lips. As she settled back on her feet, he grabbed her up and planted another kiss on her, one designed to knock her socks off.

Mission accomplished, she thought fuzzily when he finally released her, leaving her swaying on her feet. Apparently satisfied at venting his thwarted frustration, he stalked off to confer with Xander. Shaking her head, a small grin tugging at her lips, she decided to let him off the hook for good behavior.

Maggie swiped more sweat from her brow and

plucked her damp T-shirt away from her body. Flapping it in the air to cool off, she watched Kyanna slip from Xander's arms. The stunning, leggy blonde snatched a bottle of water from a cooler filled with ice near the fountain and crossed to her side. Maggie tried not to be self-conscious, tried really hard. Usually, her weight was a nonissue for her. A take it or leave it kind of thing. What you see is what you get. She was very pragmatic that way. But her ego took a hit, nonetheless. How could it not? She felt short, pudgy and plain next to a woman who looked like Kyanna Hughes.

Oh, not that Kyanna had done anything to warrant this sudden attack of body envy. Quite the contrary. Kyanna had gone out of her way to be friendly and welcoming. The only shortcoming, Maggie was certain, was solely in her own mind.

"You've impressed Xander," Kyanna said as she offered Maggie the bottle.

Maggie eyed the tall warrior demon in question as she drained half the bottle in one long guzzle. "He's not holding back?" she asked, leaning a sore hip against the aged stone.

"Maybe just a little," Kyanna admitted, grinning as she plopped down beside her. "I don't think he wants to give Gideon a coronary, not just yet anyway. But Xander wouldn't tell you that you were doing well if he didn't truly mean it."

Maggie grunted and finished the rest of the water. Kyanna held out her hand for the bottle. Then, turning, she called, "Hey, baby?" As Xander glanced over, a dark brow arched, Kyanna tossed the empty bottle into the air. The bottle vanished. "Thank you," Kyanna chirped.

"You're welcome," Xander responded dutifully, earning a blazing smile from his wife.

Xander vanished without warning and reappeared directly in front of Kyanna. He swept her up into his arms and straight into a blazing hot, toe curling kiss. Maggie fought the urge to giggle and averted her gaze.

Laughing, Gideon joined them, his humor apparently improving now that Maggie was no longer a target for Xander's potentially lethal attacks.

"Get a room," he teased.

Kyanna finally managed to break the kiss, but she had to lean her forehead against Xander's chest and curl her fingers into the front of his shirt as she struggled to regain her composure. At last, still a little breathless, she pushed out of his arms. Maggie could tell, if given half the chance, Xander would have shimmered them away to finish what he'd started.

"I need to check on reports of a nest of Charocté in Denver," Xander told Kyanna, his own voice a little rougher than normal. "Will you be all right here for a bit?"

"Go," Kyanna said, giving him a quick squeeze. "Do your macho demon thing. But you better hurry," she added, trailing a finger down the center of his white V-neck T-shirt. "I feel like taking a bubble bath…and I might decide not to wait for you if you take too long."

Maggie blinked. She could have sworn Xander's eyes had just flickered red. *Hmm. Must have been a trick of the light.*

"Woman, if you start that bath without me, I'll turn you over my knee," he rasped.

"Promise?" Kyanna asked cheekily.

Xander growled. And this time, Maggie was

absolutely positive. His eyes had turned bright, flame red. Without another word, he disappeared in a now familiar distortion of air.

Kyanna turned back to Maggie. "That should give us a few hours—"

"Half an hour, at best, darlin'," Gideon corrected. "Charocté don't offer much of a challenge, at least not as much, oh, say Carpathï or Animagi. And let's face it, sugar, that was one motivated demon you just sent off."

Blushing, Kyanna laughed. "Then I guess we better get busy."

****

Gideon sat on the front veranda, leaning back on his elbows. He could relax now a bit. Maggie and Kyanna were only practicing simple charms. He watched as Maggie called forth a bubble of water from thin air, then caused it to float up and hover, shimmering in the golden glow of the late afternoon sunlight. The bubble popped, and crystal droplets sprinkled down over both giggling women. Maggie's skin glowed with vitality, her face alight with excitement.

She took his breath away.

He could hear the murmur of the women's voices as they spoke quietly back and forth, Maggie asking questions, Kyanna instructing and praising. Maggie was a quick study, picking up the finer points of angelic magicks like she'd been doing it all her life. He felt his own chest puff just a bit every time she easily mastered what Kyanna often warned might be a difficult enchantment. She was gifted. And smart.

And he was starting to sound like a sap, but he just didn't care. The woman amazed him at every turn.

His first inkling that something might be wrong came in the form of an odd wave of power quivering through the air. At first, he thought it was Maggie and Kyanna, one of the many angelic enchantments that often caused a demon's skin to crawl.

A huge black void appeared out of nowhere, opening up about ten feet from the women. It seemed as though time stood still yet leaped ahead a thousand years all at once. Gideon was off the veranda and sprinting across the yard before the next heartbeat.

Everything swayed toward the vortex, foliage, grass, even the very air seemed to be pulled inside. The cooler overturned. Cubes of ice and bottles of water, the cooler itself went skidding across the lawn before the whole mess was sucked up inside the black void. Maggie and Kyanna screamed as they were dragged backward.

Maggie managed to grab hold of the lip of the old stone fountain with one hand. She hung horizontal above the ground, the vortex pulling relentlessly at her. Her other arm was stretched back, and she clung tenaciously to Kyanna's hands. Kyanna, who'd been closer to the vortex, floated precariously in the air, her feet all but disappearing into the void; the only thing keeping her on this side of the portal was Maggie.

"Hold on!" he shouted.

The closer Gideon got to them, the more he could feel the terrible pull of the vortex. His boots began skidding across the grass, until he was no longer running toward them, but skating along, trying to keep his balance as he angled for the fountain. He collided with the aged stone hard enough to severely injure the ribs Michael had already bruised. Thank God the thing weighed nearly a ton, or both women would have been long gone by now.

Frantic, Gideon scrambled around the massive center tiers until he could reach for Maggie. She was hanging on by the tips of her fingers now. Terror closed his throat, trapping any words of instruction inside. He had to hurry. Her wide, terror-filled eyes sought his, pleading with him. She wouldn't be able to hold on much longer. She screamed, but the vortex sucked even that away.

Throwing caution aside, he leaped for her. His fingers brushed hers, but it wasn't enough. Before he could get a grip, her hand slipped from the fountain, and both women tumbled into the void, disappearing before his eyes. The whole thing had happened in less than a minute.

"No!" Gideon screamed.

He launched himself from the fountain, aiming for the vortex. But the vortex slammed closed, and Gideon landed facedown on the grass.

Everything in him rebelled. No. She couldn't be gone.

Oh God! Oh God, Maggie! No.

Though it was a desperate struggle, he forced himself to focus on the house. He shimmered into the den, his wild-eyed gaze swinging around.

Alone. He was alone.

He shimmered to the bedroom.

Alone again.

To the farm.

Alone.

Bellowing, he went to his knees, his fists gripping his hair. His mind raced, but panic had him by the throat. *Maggie! Maggie!* He had to get her back.

Get it together. You're not going to save her like this.

Forcing himself to his feet, he shimmered back to the plantation. With trembling hands, he yanked his phone from his pocket and began dialing.

Within minutes, Xander, Mikhail, Niklas, and Carly arrived. But those minutes were the longest of his life.

"Where the hell *is* she?" Xander exploded the second he materialized. He had Gideon by the throat in the blink of an eye, slamming him into the kitchen wall. "Where's Kyanna?"

Guilt kept him from fighting back.

"I don't—" He gasped for air as Xander's fingers bit mercilessly into his flesh. "I don't know."

Niklas and Mikhail leaped forward, peeling a straining, feral Xander off him. Head pounding, chest filled with terror, Gideon sucked in one breath after another.

"What happened?" Niklas, ever the voice of reason, asked, turning to face Gideon once Xander had backed off a bit.

"Maggie and Kyanna were practicing charms by the fountain," he summed up succinctly, fearing their time was running out. "I felt an odd wave of power in the air, and a split second later this huge void opened up right beside them. The pull of this thing…it was unreal. It sucked them in and then snapped closed before I could jump in after them."

All four demons glanced at each other. Niklas yanked his phone out and dialed a number. He cursed after a moment, then shoved the phone back in his pocket.

"Sebastian isn't answering."

"Can't you shimmer Maggie back?" Carly asked, pointing to the cuff. "Won't that work?"

Gideon shook his head. "I tried. When I shimmer, I get there alone. Whatever this vortex is, wherever it brought her...or whoever has her, something's blocking it." As soon as the words left his mouth, understanding dawned. There was another possible explanation. One he hadn't thought of until that moment. There could be another reason the cuffs weren't working. What if she wasn't wearing it anymore?

Mortikaï had the key to the cuffs. If she was no longer wearing her cuff, then Mortikaï had to be involved. He remembered what Mortikaï had done to the Amulet of the Gods, and a wave of nausea rolled through him.

"She might not have the cuff on anymore," he finally managed to get out.

"What do you mean?" Xander demanded.

"Oh no!" Carly interjected, understanding dawning in her soft brown eyes as her gaze went to Gideon's bare neck.

"You think Mortikaï has her?" Niklas asked.

Carly turned to Xander. "Can't you sense Kyanna? Through your connection? Can you feel her?"

If possible, Xander looked even more upset than before. "I can't feel her," he snarled. The demon looked like a wounded animal. A vicious, lethal predator a hairsbreadth from slaughtering everyone in sight.

Gideon didn't feel much better.

Mikhail asked, "The vortex opened by the fountain?"

Gideon nodded, leading the group out the back door.

He watched as Mikhail paced off the area, a fierce frown of concentration furrowing his scarred brow. Gideon opened himself up, wide open, like a raw, exposed nerve.

Nothing but lingering remnants of pure evil.

He followed Mikhail's movements hopefully, praying the Demon of War might have some trick up his sleeve to help them find the women.

At last, Mikhail stopped in his tracks. "I can see the path, but the way is not clear. There is too much interference. I can't get a lock on the destination."

Xander exploded, his skin began to turn demonic red and his fangs began to grow. His fist smashed into the fountain in a shower of dust and crumbled rock. The massive fountain crashed to the ground in pieces.

"But there is a path, right?" Carly pressed, turning in Niklas's arms to look up at him. Ever since hearing of the vortex, Niklas hadn't let her out of arm's reach, as if fearful she, too, might be snatched away. "There has to be someone who can follow the path, isn't there?"

"Asher," Niklas said at once, his voice hopeful. "Asher might be able to."

The phone was already in Gideon's hand.

"Yo," Asher answered.

"We need your help," Gideon barked, skipping over the pleasantries.

"What kind of help?" Asher asked, his voice neutral.

"A vortex opened up and sucked Kyanna and Maggie into it. We need to know where they went, and how to get there."

"Maggie who?"

"My mate."

"Ah, the Halfling."

How did Asher know what Maggie was? Suspicion rode him, but Gideon pushed it aside. He'd deal with that all later. Right now, he just needed to get Maggie back safe and sound.

"The vortex, Asher," he snapped impatiently. "Can you trace it?"

"A vortex, huh?"

"Yeah."

"Did you try to follow it back to the origins?"

"Yeah, Mikhail did, but he said there's too much interference. And I tried to jump into it right after them, but it snapped shut before I could get inside."

"Hmm."

"That all you got?" Gideon demanded, growing more desperate by the second.

"Where?"

Gideon gave him the coordinates, not caring that he'd just willingly revealed the location of his home to one of the most dangerous, sketchiest demons Hell had ever spat out.

Before Gideon could end the call, Asher appeared a few feet away.

"I think Mortikaï may be involved," Gideon began, but Asher held his hand up to silence them. He began pacing through the area, scowling in concentration, just as Mikhail had.

Gideon held his breath, aware everyone else present was doing the same. At length, Asher stopped on the exact spot the portal had opened up.

He stood, utterly still, arms out, palms up, face turned to the sky for what felt like an eternity. Finally, he turned to Xander and Gideon, his expression grim.

"Mortikaï might be involved as you suspect, I can't say, but he doesn't have the power to open a vortex. Especially not one this powerful, and not one on protected land."

"Then who?" Xander snarled.

Asher's gaze went back and forth between Gideon and Xander. Gideon could see the gleam in the mercenary's eyes, but he didn't care. He'd pay any price to get Maggie back. And he knew Xander would do the same for Kyanna.

"The one who took your mates will make a fierce enemy." He paused, as if considering how much it would cost for him to burn that bridge.

"Who is it?" Niklas pressed.

Asher met his steady gaze dead on. "Ashïek."

"He was already our enemy," Niklas pointed out. "Or rather, Sebastian's. That bastard's had a hard-on for Sebastian since day one. Won't be happy till Sebastian's head is mounted and hanging on the wall of his trophy room."

"Yes," Asher replied. "Well, he wasn't my enemy. And if I help you, he will be."

"Can you find the origins of the vortex or not?" Xander hissed, clearly out of patience.

"I already have." Asher considered them in turn. "How badly do you want them back?"

"Anything," Gideon whispered hoarsely. "I'll do anything to get her back, promise anything."

"I don't have to ask about you, do I?" Asher remarked with a sly grin, turning to Xander.

"In a heartbeat," Xander said anyway.

"State your terms," Asher prompted, all business now.

"Take us to our mates," Gideon blurted. He had to get to Maggie, had to make sure she was okay. From his peripheral vision, he saw Xander nod agreement.

Asher's eyes turned pure bottomless black; not a speck of white remained. An ancient, aged scroll appeared before Gideon. A blood contract. An identical scroll appeared in front of Xander.

"My terms now. Someday, I'm gonna ask a favor of you. From both of you. This will be your second, Xander. You're both gonna give me exactly what I want, no qualifications. No questions asked."

A heavy silence fell over the group. Niklas and Xander both glanced warily at each other. Mikhail's frown deepened. Gideon had always wondered why the mercenary had never tried to collect on the outrageous contracts Lucifer had taken out on the Fallen.

Now, he understood.

Asher was collecting debts. And whatever he intended to cash them in on was far bigger than anything he stood to gain by currying favor with the Dark Prince.

Gideon was too worried about Maggie to care. Conjuring a dagger, he slashed his palm and slapped his bloody handprint to the ancient parchment. From the corner of his eye, he saw Xander do the same.

"Agreed," they echoed in unison.

The ancient parchment absorbed the blood, sucking it up like a living thing, then vanished.

"Take us to our mates," Gideon demanded once more.

"Just remember what you've bargained for," Asher said, and his smile made Gideon's blood turn to ice in his veins.

****

"Master," the Charocté called from the dungeon hallway.

Stolas growled low in his throat at the interruption. The red-haired Halfling flopped limply beneath him. He'd had her but a week, and already she'd lost her spirit. "I told you I didn't want to be bothered," he roared, glaring over his shoulder toward the door.

"Apologies, master. But Dimiezlo insisted you would want to know."

Cursing, Stolas rose from the pallet on the floor, the Halfling he'd been mating forgotten. He conjured himself clean and shimmered straight to the Great Hall. Dimiezlo was waiting.

"This better be good. I was in the middle of something...pressing."

"I received a message a short while ago. Together, Mortikaï and Ashïek managed to open a portal onto land protected by the Fallen. Mortikaï's captured Temptation's Halfling, and the Slayer's mate as well, the Guardian."

"Where are they?"

Dimiezlo looked decidedly uncomfortable. "Mortikaï tricked Ashïek into allowing him to hold the females. Then he secreted them away the moment Ashïek stepped from the room and he changed the terms of his fee."

Stolas growled low in his throat. "What does he want?"

"He said he wants Temptation. He said you can

have the Halfling, the Slayer, and his mate. But he wants Temptation."

"Done," Stolas immediately agreed. A small price in the grander scheme of things.

Dimiezlo ducked his head, cringing. "He also wants the sword."

"The sword," Stolas snarled. No need to ask which sword. Only one sword mattered. This was exactly why you had to be so careful of who you allowed to have certain information.

"No. He won't get the sword. No Halfling's worth that price."

"He said if you wouldn't bargain with the sword, then perhaps...perhaps Lucifer might be interested to know you have it." Dimiezlo gulped, groveling.

Stolas glowered at the cowering minion. Mortikaï had just signed his own death contract.

"Where is Mortikaï now?"

"He's gone into hiding. But I have Hunters after him. They've already locked on to his shimmer trail. It's only a matter of time."

"A matter of time! If he's threatening to go to Lucifer, then I'm out of time." Stolas moved his hands up, clenching his fists, then threw his arms wide open. Dimiezlo went flying through the air. He flipped end over end, stopping only once he was pinned against the far wall. The Animagi clawed at his neck, his red face taking on a purplish hue. "Do you remember what I told you would happen if this went badly?"

"Please," Dimiezlo gasped, his eyes bulging. "Please, Master. I will fix this." He gasped again, flailing. "I will kill him myself and bring the Halfling to you. I swear it."

"No. You will take me to him. And I will see that he is eliminated myself. The moment the Hunters notify you that they've located him, I want to know." Stolas smiled then, evil power seething to the surface. "And you've forgotten one little detail."

Dimiezlo forced a swallow, too fearful to speak.

"Now you suffer for failing me." Stolas's gaze went to the horns atop the minion's head.

"No!" Dimiezlo pleaded now, reeking of the kind of raw terror Stolas savored like the finest of feasts. "P-please, M-master. Anything else. Anything. But n-not that. Not the—"

Stolas began to slowly, viciously twist the minion's horns until they started to crack. Dimiezlo's screams echoed in his ears.

Chapter Twenty-Three

Asher held out his hand, palm up. Gideon immediately slapped his palm onto Asher's. Xander's hand came down on top of his.

"Wait," Niklas barked, stepping forward.

Mikhail advanced as well. "We all go," he growled, reaching for the point of contact.

"Two contracts, two passengers," Asher said, and the world spun away from the trio locked together by hands and blood contracts, leaving Niklas, Carly, and Mikhail behind.

A dank cell materialized around them, a scene straight out of a medieval nightmare. Water trickled down the solid, grungy rock walls. The scents of mildew and refuse filled the air. A sputtering torch rested in a wall mount near a low, rust stained, iron reinforced door with a tiny window slot.

"Ky!" Xander shouted. He sprang away from them and fell to his knees beside the prone woman.

Kyanna's hands were bound at the wrists behind her back, and her ankles were tied as well. A strip of duct tape covered her mouth. Her clothing was filthy and torn, and her left eye was all but swollen shut. Otherwise, she appeared unharmed, and mad as hell.

"Thank Christ!" Xander whispered brokenly.

He dragged his mate into his arms and squeezed her tight. His face went lax on a look of profound relief.

She began squirming and mumbling beneath the tape. Xander turned her in his arms and gently pulled the tape from her mouth before he vanished her bonds.

"Gideon!" she exclaimed, twisting toward him. In the torchlight, her face was streaked with tears and dirt. Her long blonde hair was tangled and matted, sticking to her face and neck. "He dragged Maggie away."

Gideon dropped down beside her. He instinctively tried to take the hand she reached out to him in his, but his passed right through hers. "Do you know where they took her?" he asked. "Did you see what they looked like?"

"Just one," she corrected. "A big guy, bald, pointed ears, deformed face. His skin was gray, lumpy. God, he smelled...smelled like death. He came in the cell and Maggie and I, we fought him. Maggie almost got him with Angelfire. The minute we started the incantation to freeze him, he backhanded her, knocked her against the wall, and then he punched me.

"I don't know what happened after that," she cried. "When I came to, I was already tied up, and she was gone. A little while ago...oh, God, Gideon." She paused, sobbing now, looking as if she wanted to be sick. "A little while ago, I...I heard her screaming. Over and over. And then she went silent. Gideon, I don't know if—I'm so sorry, I couldn't stop him."

Fear nearly paralyzed him. "Where did the screams come from? Could you tell which direction?"

"That way, I think." She motioned to the wall on the left. "But everything echoes in here. It's hard to tell."

"Get her out of here," Gideon said then, meeting Xander's steely gray stare.

"Will you be trapped here? I don't even know where we are," Kyanna said.

Gideon shook his head. "This isn't Hell. Mortikaï must have set up this lair Earth side. I can still shimmer us out if need be."

Xander's face was grim. Gideon could tell he desperately wanted to get his woman to safety, and Gideon didn't blame him one bit. But Xander was also a warrior at heart and leaving a comrade behind to face unknown odds didn't sit well either.

"Go," Gideon insisted.

"Gideon—"

"This wasn't your fault, Kyanna," Gideon assured her. "And now, thanks to you, I at least know for sure who I'm up against."

He'd never done a damned thing to deserve the target Mortikaï had put on his back. But this time bastard had crossed the line. He would pay with his life.

Asher had been anything but passive while the three had been talking. A loud thunk, and a slight screech echoed in the room. Turning, Gideon watched as Asher rose from his knees by the door.

"Come on, we gotta go before somebody comes to check on that sound," Asher urged.

"Take her home," Gideon ordered Xander one last time. He waited until Xander and Kyanna, locked in each other's arms, disappeared in a distortion of air, before he took off after Asher. He was forced to crouch to get through the small doorway, and then he crept through the narrow hallway.

They went door to door and pried the tiny windows open to look inside each cell. Demon after demon in varying states of decay were chained to walls and bones littered the filthy floors. But no Maggie.

Then, three doors down, Asher hissed to get his attention and motioned him over. Abandoning the window he'd been working on prying open, Gideon rushed to Asher's side.

"She's in there." Asher pointed to the door.

Gideon didn't need to hear any more. He put his shoulder to the door and shoved with all his might. It opened with a wail, and he burst inside the room. Maggie hung from bloodied wrists that were chained to the wall. She was limp and unconscious. Duct tape bound her fists closed. Her head was flopped slightly forward.

Through the curtain of her hair, he could see the beginning shadows of bruises, and the trickle of blood at the corner of her mouth. Her T-shirt was torn at the collar, and one shoulder seam was split. Both knees of her jeans were ripped, revealing bloody, skinned knees.

"Maggie!" Gideon flew across the room.

He reached for her.

Pain exploded in his skull, and blackness descended.

****

Gideon groaned. His head rolled on his shoulders, feeling like a thumb somebody had smashed with a hammer. He tried to move his arms and was met with the clank and rattle of iron from somewhere above his head. Gideon forced his eyes open despite the screaming pain trying to claw his brain out through his ears. He blinked woozily until he could focus on the woman hanging from chains on the opposite wall.

"Beware the demon you call friend," a deep voice said from the doorway.

Brenda Huber

Gideon's head swung toward the voice, and he glared at the two demons standing across the room.

"Guess everyone has a price. Asher's always been very clear about his, haven't you?" Mortikaï asked Asher, though he didn't wait for an answer. Turning back to Gideon, he went on, "For instance, all your capture required was his weight in gold. Well, he got that, and plenty more as a bonus for helping me locate your mate as well, and the Slayer's. She'll make a tidy little bow for the package, won't she?"

So he didn't know Xander had escaped with Kyanna yet. Good. That might buy him a little extra time. But then he puzzled over why Asher had let Xander and Kyanna go. His head throbbed so hard it was tough to reason it all out.

"Did you know, Temptation, that the price on your Halfling's head is nearly as large as the one on yours? Different interested parties, of course. But quite profitable, all the same."

"Bastard," Gideon snarled at Asher, jerking at his wrists. The chains rattled but held. "We had a blood contract!"

"One I fulfilled," Asher pointed out, unperturbed. "The contract stated I had to take you to your mate, nothing more, nothing less." He nodded toward Maggie, who was only now beginning to stir. Dear Jesus, what had they done to her that she would remain unconscious through all this noise?

"You're here, aren't you?" Asher asked. "And she is your mate, isn't she? Contract satisfied. You—and the contract—stated nothing about making sure the two of you made it safely back." Asher shook his head. "You should be more careful about what you're signing, Temptation."

"I'll take out another contract," Gideon immediately prompted.

"No," Asher said after a moment, "I don't think so. After all, I got everything I wanted from the last one. And you don't look as if you're in any position to…ah, uphold your end of any bargain you might make right now." He offered Gideon a strange smile then. "Remember, Gideon. Everything happens the way it happens for a reason." His gaze moved to Maggie, dipped knowingly toward her lower abdomen, then shot back to Gideon and narrowed. "Besides, you wouldn't thank me if I change the way things end."

And then Asher shimmered away, leaving Gideon shaking with fury. His focus went back to Maggie. Her eyes fluttered open, and she moaned, scrunching them closed again.

"Oh, and in case you're wondering," Mortikaï added, drawing Gideon's burning stare, "shimmering won't do you any good. Well, it won't do her any good, at least. Nifty little trick with the cuff, by the way."

It was then that Gideon finally noticed the bit of silver Mortikaï twirled around his finger. Holding it to the light, Mortikaï admired the ancient runes carved into the cuff.

Just like he'd done with the Amulet of the Gods, Mortikaï summoned Hellfire. Gideon strained against the chains with all his might, but they wouldn't budge. Before Gideon's horrified eyes, the cuff on Mortikaï's palm melted into a ball of silver, and then liquefied and dripped from Mortikaï's hand to puddle on the floor at his feet. As if sensing its partner's fate, the cuff on Gideon's wrist clicked open and fell uselessly to the floor.

The ramifications were too much for Gideon to bear, and something inside him shattered.

"Oops! My bad." Mortikaï sneered. "Guess you're back to being cursed."

Gideon snarled. His body vibrated with rage. It clawed inside him, shaking him, ripping through him, demanding to be released. The only thing keeping him sane in that moment was knowing that if he lost control, in that tiny room, Maggie wouldn't stand a chance.

"I know your secret, Temptation," Mortikaï taunted, crossing his arms. He leaned negligently against the doorframe. "Your rage controls you. And your rage is the only thing that will get you out of those chains. But you won't risk that, will you? You won't risk going demonic with her so close." Mortikaï straightened, shaking his head. "Pitiful."

Gideon refused to rise to the bait. His worried eyes were busy sweeping over Maggie, searching for signs of serious injury. She was fully awake now, supporting her weight on trembling legs. She did not speak, but her eyes filled with tears as she looked between Mortikaï and Gideon.

"Ah, well, it'll be worth it to see how this plays out. Either you stay chained up, and watch Stolas come for his merchandise. Maybe he'll get rid of the bastard you already planted in her and plant one of his own. Then again, maybe he'll keep it and raise it himself. Now doesn't that just give you warm fuzzies?" Mortikaï laughed, dark and gut deep.

"And if you do decide to let the rage take over and break those chains, so I'm out a bit of gold." He shrugged carelessly. "I'll get to watch you rip your own mate to shreds. The pain that will cause you—once you regain your senses, of course—will be well worth it."

Chuckling, Mortikaï turned and left the room.

"Are you okay?" he asked Maggie, devouring her battered face with his eyes.

Huge tears rolled down her cheeks, but she shook her head. "You shouldn't have come, Gideon. I'm bait. He used me to get to you."

"No, Maggie," Gideon argued. "He wants you every bit as much as he wants me. Besides, I promised you I'd keep you safe." He gave a vicious jerk on the chains and got nothing but a smarting wrist. "I'll figure something out. You're sure you're okay? Kyanna said she could hear you screaming."

"How is Kyanna?" Maggie asked, frantic. "Mortikaï hit her so hard—"

"She's okay. She's just fine, I promise. She's with Xander. He'll take care of her."

Maggie sagged in relief.

"Why were you screaming?" Gideon pressed. Afraid to hear the answer, yet terrified of not knowing. And blaming himself all the while. He should have taken better precautions. But he'd been too arrogant. And look what had happened. She'd quite literally been snatched away right under his nose.

Maggie turned her head and closed her eyes. A single tear slipped down her cheek.

Gideon was utterly destroyed. "Oh, God, Maggie! Did he—I'm so sorry I wasn't here to stop—" He couldn't even finish the thought in his own head, much less say it out loud. What she must have suffered. He'd take it all upon himself if he could.

"No!" She turned back in a rush, her eyes wide and

sincere. "Oh, no, Gideon. Not that. I swear! He didn't…he didn't touch me like that."

"Then why—" He shook his head, confused.

"He put his hands on my head, and he showed me things, inside my head. Thoughts, nightmares, visions, my worst fears, I don't know what they were. But they were horrible. You, and the others, all dead…by my hands. He forced me to choose between my baby and you all. Forced me to…to… One by one. And then the whole world burned to ash, because of me. Because I wanted to protect the child I carry." Weeping, she hung her head and let the tears fall.

His heart twisted, and he fought the chains again. He wanted to go to her, to hold her, to comfort her and tell her he would make it all better. But he couldn't do that, not anymore, could he?

The cuffs were gone.

Even if he could get to her, he'd never be able to touch her again. He tried to shimmer across the room, but his bonds held.

"Maggie," he said, anguished. "Maggie, don't cry."

"What if those visions were right, Gideon? What if—despite whether we get out of here or not—what if this child is evil? What if it doesn't matter what we teach it, or how much love we give it?" She sobbed, her doubt-riddled, tear-drenched gaze meeting his. "What if it's just inherently evil and brings about the destruction of the world?"

"That's not going to happen, Maggie. Do you hear me? That is not going to happen!" Gideon gave up jerking at the chains, and instead, his whole body strained toward her. "We will smother that baby in so much love that any seeds of evil will wither and die before they can take root. We will show him the world, together, so that he cherishes it. We won't let him go bad. You won't let him go bad. Just like you kept his father from giving up."

That seemed to calm her. She wiped her cheeks against her shoulders and drew a deep breath. "We have to get out of here."

"I can't break these chains," Gideon told her. "Not in human form. I think they might be *thulmate*."

"What's that?"

"It's a special metal forged specifically for Charocté Demons, to keep them bound and submissive. While in human form, I don't have a hope in Hell of breaking them. Even in demonic, I'm just not sure."

Maggie licked her lips. "Can't you just shimmer us out of here?"

"No. The chain's been reinforced with some kind of dark magicks. I can't shimmer at all."

"If it's because I got sick before—"

"No." Gideon twisted his wrists around. "The cuffs are gone. Even if I could shimmer, I won't be able to take you with me."

"Then you have to turn," she urged.

"What! No!" He shook his head, unwilling to even consider it. "I won't risk it. It's too dangerous," he stated. "I could end up killing you myself."

"There's no other way, Gideon. You have to turn."

Chapter Twenty-Four

"Jesus, Maggie! Didn't you hear a thing I just said? No!"

"Listen to me, Gideon," she argued. "We will both die if you don't at least try. All *three* of us will die."

She watched his gaze dip to her belly, and she took hope. Something fierce and protective had kindled in his eyes at her words. But then he shook his head, and that light in his stare dimmed.

"Damn it, Gideon! Don't you give up on me! You don't have that luxury anymore. You're going to be a father, do you hear me? A daddy." He looked up at her, and the emotions she saw there were so raw, so exposed, she nearly faltered. But too much was at stake to back down.

"We need you, Gideon. I can't protect us." She wiggled her bound fists. "I can't fight like this. I can't stop them the next time they come back. I need you to keep me safe, Gideon. I need you."

She wanted to tell him the rest, but she was too afraid. Too afraid he'd use it as an excuse to shut her escape plan down for good. Too afraid he might not say it back.

"Please, Gideon. I know you won't hurt me, won't hurt *us*. You have to try."

She watched the battle of emotion sweep through him. He didn't trust himself. That was the bottom line.

No matter how much she trusted him, he didn't trust himself.

Okay then, what else was there to lose? If she didn't do something drastic, they might never get out of this hole alive. What could possibly be more drastic than telling him her true feelings?

"Then you better know something else," she threw out there, reckless now. "I love you, you big jerk. I stayed with you because I love you. I believe in you because I love you. Now get that through your thick skull."

Gideon gazed at her, stunned. Not even the theatrical clapping from the doorway broke through his openmouthed shock.

"Brava, Halfling, brava," Mortikaï jeered. "Now wasn't that moving?"

Mortikaï stepped further into the room and approached Maggie. The stench of him was enough to make her gag.

"Ah, such lovely sentiment." He trailed his fingers through her limp, sweat soaked hair as if it were the finest silk. "It stirs the blood, does it not, Temptation?"

"Get your hands off her," Gideon snarled, fighting his restraints with renewed fury. Blood ran from the fresh wounds on his wrists.

"You know, I've been thinking," Mortikaï went on, ignoring Gideon's rabid tirade. Maggie turned her head away, seeking desperately to avoid the aroma of wasting corpse that wafted from his putrid flesh. He trailed a grotesque finger down the line of her jaw, down her neck, and hooked a ragged black claw in the torn collar of her T-shirt. "Why should Stolas have all the fun?"

A scream ripped from her throat before she could muffle it as he used that claw to rip the front of her shirt wide open, leaving a trail of crimson seeping from her skin. Behind Mortikaï, Gideon roared, his face contorting with rage. Mortikaï was too busy staring at her exposed breasts with salacious intent.

"Such a shame to let all this go to waste before Stolas gets his claws into you. I'm told he's not very careful when it comes to the females he beds. In fact, most don't even survive."

Mortikaï reached out, his gaze rapt on the flesh he was about to fondle.

Maggie cringed.

Gideon exploded.

One minute Gideon was there, blond haired, amber eyed, handsome Gideon. And the next moment, his body morphed into a nightmare. One she remembered all too well from the night he'd taken her to her home. One that fought with a mindless, killing rage. And she was directly in his path.

The chains snapped like strings, and Gideon charged Mortikaï. Mortikaï ducked to the side with an evil grin. As if this was exactly what he'd been after all along. He swung a beefy fist, and Maggie could tell he had every intention of drawing this fight out. Of putting her in as much peril as possible.

But there was one thing he had miscalculated. He'd underestimated Gideon's fury and his relentless drive to protect what he deemed his.

Gideon was all over him in a heartbeat. All his ferocious rage focused solely on the demon now fending off blow after blow.

Maggie could do nothing more than hang on the

wall and watch in mute shock as Gideon brutally ravaged Mortikaï. Mortikaï slipped in a puddle of blood and went down on one knee. Gideon was moving too fast for Maggie to tell if any of it was his.

Gideon knocked him the rest of the way down, and then sat on his chest, pinning him to the floor. The air around Mortikaï began to shift, just the slightest bit, just as Maggie had come to recognize it did when a demon was about to shimmer.

Gideon gave a mighty roar and plunged his fist deep in the cavern of Mortikaï's chest. Mortikaï froze, eyes wide, mouth agape on a garbled roar. Smiling a grisly, serrated-teeth-filled smile, Gideon ripped the still beating heart from Mortikaï's chest.

A wave of nausea hit Maggie, followed swiftly by dizziness at the sight of Gideon's blood-soaked fist clutching the organ in the air. But he didn't stop there. He tossed it aside like rubbish and clamped both hands on either side of Mortikaï's head. With a brutal twist, Gideon liberated Mortikaï's head from his twitching body.

Gideon roared in triumph, holding the head in his hands. He stood there a long moment, staring at the thing as though admiring a trophy.

Maggie sucked in a shuddering breath, unable to drag her attention from Gideon's bloody hands. The sound drew his attention. His head snapped around, and his stare zeroed in on her like a heat seeking missile.

"Gideon," she whispered. Clearing her throat, she forced herself to speak slowly and soothingly. "Gideon, stop. You have to calm down."

He lowered his head and began stalking toward her, her imminent death glittering in his black eyes.

"Gideon," she squeaked. Her words tumbled over each other, faster and faster, in her desperation to get through to him. "It's me. Remember me, Gideon. Maggie. Your mate."

He hesitated, just for a moment, his head cocked to the side. But then he shook it off and advanced again.

"Gideon! Snap out of it. I'm your mate! You don't want to hurt me. The baby! Remember the baby! Feel my belly, Gideon! Feel his power. Feel your baby!"

He paused again, less than two feet away now. His eyes narrowed, as if he were trying to make sense of what she was saying. His gaze lowered to her chest, zeroing in on her bare breasts, before dipping lower.

At last, he lifted his hand. His very large, very lethal, very bloody hand. And he laid it against her belly. Part of her wanted to cringe away, but she knew if she did it would be the end for her. The rage would take over, and he'd kill her without knowing what he was doing. Not until it was too late to make a difference.

And so she forced herself to remain still as the blood of his fallen enemy soaked her skin.

Finally, those black eyes rose, meeting hers with a lucidity she hadn't seen since the moment he'd morphed into this being.

"Mag-gie," he growled, his voice guttural and layered. "My Mag-gie."

She sagged with relief and sobbed aloud. "Yes," she said, nodding. "Your Maggie."

He eyed her dubiously for a moment. But he continued to touch her belly, and she took hope.

"Cut me down, Gideon," she prompted.

His brow puckered, and he looked up at the chains

binding her to the wall. He looked back down at her, and suddenly, he was leering. A look he'd perfected in human form, to be sure. But his interest was more than obvious.

Her eyebrows shot up. "No, Gideon."

Oh, he didn't like hearing that. Not at all.

"Stolas is coming, remember?"

Just like that, his gaze went flat, and the rage took over once more. She'd lost him. Scrambling to figure out how to bring him back, she bit her lip.

Gideon began to turn away, his body crouching to a fighting stance, his scowling face eagerly searching for another foe.

"Gideon!" Nothing. Desperate, she yelled, "Temptation!"

His head whipped around.

"Mag-gie," he growled.

"Yes!" She could have cried with relief. At least they weren't going to have to re-establish her identity. But time was slipping away, and she had no idea how long she had before this Stolas guy showed up.

"Cut the chains," she ordered, praying that was the right tone.

He looked at the chains once more, then, as if giving a mental shrug, he reached up and jerked them free of the rock.

Not stopping to think about how he might react, Maggie threw herself into his arms. Sobbing, she peppered his chest and neck with kisses. He stood utterly still, frozen like a hunk of granite. He wasn't even breathing.

And then, so slowly it broke her heart, he eased his arms around her, holding her like she was made of

311

glass. Laughing, leaning slightly back, she tenderly caressed the side of his face.

"Take me home," she said firmly.

"Home," he repeated. "My Mag-gie."

"Home," she confirmed, smiling as the air around them distorted, and the dank, bloody cell fell away.

Suddenly, they were in the bedroom of the plantation. The nausea wasn't quite so bad this time. But it still took her knees from under her.

Gideon, still in demonic form, swept her up and laid her upon the bed. As he reached up to touch her face, he must have noticed the blood on his hands. He began to pull away from her, but she quickly grabbed his hand and tugged him back. She cupped his cheek as she searched his face.

Her Gideon was in there. She could just see glimmers of him. It was time for him to come home too.

"I love you, Gideon." She smiled when he blinked rapidly, frowning. "I. Love. You. No matter what you look like. No matter which form you're in. I love you, and I always will."

He looked down at her, wonder slowly turning his black eyes amber. Right before her eyes, he began to change back into human form. Once he was there with her, really there, he started, grabbing her hand up in shock.

"Maggie!" He gasped, tugging her into a bone-jarring embrace. "Maggie, oh, my sweet Lord! I can touch you! Look," he said, pushing her away to show her their wrists sans the cuffs, only to jerk her right back into his arms. He squeezed her so tight she had to struggle to gain enough room to breathe.

"Why? Why can I touch you?" He pushed her back, gripping her by the shoulders as he stared hard at her. "What am I saying? I don't care! I can touch you, nothing else matters."

Maggie giggled at his exuberance—she couldn't help it—and wrapped her arms around his neck.

Someone discreetly cleared his throat from near the doorway. Maggie glanced over, and felt Gideon stiffen in her arms. In the blink of an eye, Gideon was across the room. He had Asher by the throat and slammed him up against the wall.

But he was still too close to the rage, and Maggie feared she might not be able to talk him down this time. She leaped from the bed and rushed to Gideon's side. She wrapped both hands around his straining bicep and pulled. "Breathe, Gideon. Calm down. Just take a deep breath and calm down."

"Bastard!" He slammed Asher's head against the wall again.

"Curse," Asher gasped, struggling to loosen Gideon's hold. His mocha skin rapidly took on a mottled reddish hue. Somehow he managed to pry a sliver of breathing room and sucked in a pained breath. "Your…curse…broken," he gasped again.

Eyes narrowed in suspicion, Gideon released him after one last good thunk against the wall. He herded Maggie behind him, and demanded, "You got five seconds to explain yourself. Then I'm gonna rip your head off for putting Maggie in jeopardy like that."

"Your curse is broken."

"How?" Maggie asked, edging around Gideon.

He pushed her back, echoing, "How?"

"All this time you've been searching for some*thing*

313

to break your curse. You should have been searching for some*one*." He rubbed at his throat. "A woman worthy of you. A woman who loves you unconditionally. A woman you learned to control the rage for." He paused, eyeing them meaningfully. "A mate you would willingly die for."

Maggie froze. Was Asher saying what she thought he was saying? Could it be possible that Gideon actually loved her too?

"All those times I came to you…commissioned you to search for… Why the hell couldn't you just have told me that?"

"Some things have to happen just the way they happen," Asher replied with a mysterious smile.

"You had no right to endanger my mate like that." Though the tone was calmer, somewhat, there was still enough heat to scorch paint from the walls.

"I just made sure you had the proper motivation."

Gideon growled low in his throat and made to lunge at him again. Maggie quickly grabbed at him. She smoothed her hand up and down his broad back. His muscles were like solid rock beneath her hand. "Gideon, it's okay. Everything worked out. Calm down."

"You see?" Asher arched his dark eyebrow, and his deep brown eyes followed the movements of her hands over Gideon as if her actions were only confirming the brilliance of his plan. "Even now, she soothes you."

Asher reached into his pocket and drew out a small gold pendant on a chain. He offered it to Maggie. "This is for you."

She glanced at Gideon, who frowned but nodded, before stepping around him to accept Asher's offering.

He laid the circular adornment flat on her hand. She studied the delicate filigree and the dainty stones.

"You must wear it at all times," Asher cautioned her, his expression deadly serious. "The pendant will protect you and the child you carry. It will prevent any more portals from opening up within at least a hundred meters of you.

Frowning, not sure if she should believe him, she turned a questioning gaze to Gideon. Before she could open her mouth, Gideon snatched the pendant from her hand and had it clasped around her throat.

Well. I guess that answers my question.

Shaking her head, fighting a laugh at Gideon's superstitious reaction, she turned back to Asher as Gideon's arms slipped around her waist.

"Thank you." She smiled at the handsome demon.

He grinned, lifting the edges of his finely trimmed goatee. "A demon and a Halfling. Normally, I'd say that's a recipe for disaster. But that little one gives me hope. And he deserves a fighting chance. One I never got." Asher winked at Maggie, and then disappeared, leaving Maggie and Gideon frowning at each other, baffled.

****

Stolas glanced around the dank room, took in the broken chains on the walls, the splashes of blood and the headless body at his feet.

They were gone. The Halfling, the Slayer, his mate, and Temptation. And Mortikaï was already dead, depriving him of even that small pleasure. This situation was fast spinning beyond his control.

Damn it. Damn it all. He drew a deep breath. He had to keep his head. The Halfling may have eluded

him. This time. But he wasn't out of the game. Not yet.
He still had one more ace up his sleeve.

Chapter Twenty-Five

Gideon used the toe of his boot to keep the log swing gently swaying. He couldn't ask for a better, more relaxing evening. The soft shushing of the river and the occasional muted warble of birdsong lulled his senses. A whisper of a breeze rustled the leaves overhead. The sun was just setting, casting a warm golden hue over everything.

And Maggie was nestled in the protective circle of his arms, her head snuggled in the crook of his shoulder.

No, it didn't get any better than this.

"How are you feeling?" he murmured against her hair.

"I'm fine, Gideon. Stop fussing." She patted his chest.

He opened his mouth to argue that it was his right to fuss, when a shiver of awareness skated down his spine. *Angel.* His senses screamed the warning, even as he urged Maggie up, preparing himself to fight.

"What? What is it?" Maggie whispered, her gaze scanning the tree line and the grounds. Angelfire formed in the palm of her hand, and she moved into position at his side.

God, he was proud of his woman.

"Angel," Gideon warned, hovering protectively near his mate.

317

"I mean no harm," Samuel said, separating himself from the foliage across the way.

"Hell's bells," Gideon muttered beneath his breath, "what'd Asher do? List this place as a point of interest on Google Maps? Anybody else shows up here uninvited, and I'm gonna kick his ass."

"May I come closer?" Samuel asked politely, his voice deep and gentle.

He could feel Maggie relaxing beside him and made a mental note to speak to her later about caution around angels.

"Why are you here?"

"I have come to speak with you about the Prophesy," he said. "I vow, by all that is holy, I will not harm your mate or your child."

"Or Gideon," Maggie quickly prompted, earning herself an approving smile from the angel.

"Or Gideon," he amended.

Samuel was one of the few angels that still referred to the Fallen by their given names rather than traitor or another derogatory demon epithet. Eyeing him with suspicion, Gideon nodded his assent. Though he didn't believe the angel would break his vow, and Samuel appeared relaxed, his wings tucked smoothly behind him, Gideon couldn't help but maintain his battle-ready wariness as the angel approached. He slipped a cautious arm around Maggie.

"I have consulted the ancient scrolls of our brethren," Samuel began. "And what I have found is…disconcerting."

Maggie's hand tightened apprehensively on his arm. "How so?"

Samuel clasped his hands in front of his waist. His

white shirt stretched taut across his broad shoulders, and the sunlight glinted in his ginger hair. "The scrolls containing the Prophesy have been tampered with; some were blatantly damaged."

Gideon's eyebrows shot up at that. He remembered the massive marble building housing endless rows of scrolls and texts, tomes and charts. Each piece held with the highest, hushed reverence, catalogued, maintained, and protected by the Custodian.

"How is that possible?"

"We do not know. But we did find an obscure reference to the Prophesy, and a name."

"Why are you telling me this?" Gideon asked.

"I have tried, as I'm sure you are aware, to make contact with Xander and his mate. Unsuccessfully. I believe you might be more willing to listen." Gideon caught his gaze straying to Maggie's belly. "I think I begin to understand what the Fallen are trying to do."

"And what is it that you think you understand?"

"You seek to recover the relics, not to use them, but to hide them away and keep them from the hands of those seeking to…upset the balance. I am not the only one puzzled by your behavior."

Gideon tilted his head. Could this be the break they were looking for?

He knew he courted ridicule, or flat out confirmation they'd never gain forgiveness, but he lifted his chin and rolled the dice. If there was even the slightest possibility of gaining something—anything— that might aid them in their quest, then he'd throw his pride to the wolves if he had to.

"We know we were wrong," Gideon said. "When we chose to follow Lucifer, we made a mistake. One we all regret. We seek to make amends for our actions. We know we cannot make right the wrongs we have inflicted, but we strive to earn forgiveness, all the same."

Maggie squeezed his arm, and that small show of support buoyed him, insulating him from anything harsh Samuel might have to say.

"Your actions have not gone unnoticed," Samuel remarked at last. "And you should not forget that you have allies."

That took Gideon aback, and he nearly forgot to press for answers. "What is the name you spoke of earlier?"

"The scroll was damaged, but the last legible sentence read, 'The balance of the worlds will be weighed in the hands of Rehsa'."

Gideon had never heard the name before.

Samuel nodded. "I will continue to search for the name in the Library, and should I find more, I will be in contact."

"Ah, thank you. We'd appreciate any help you are willing to give us."

Samuel nodded his head. Then he stepped closer and held his hands out to Maggie, though his gaze included them both. "May I?"

Gideon kept his arm around Maggie, but he nodded. Gideon watched as Samuel's long sun-bronzed hands enveloped Maggie's. The angel closed his eyes for a moment, and then a radiant smile blossomed on his face.

The angel then made the sign of the cross over Maggie, and another over the child that grew within her womb, speaking low and soft as he blessed mother and child. That simple blessing lifted an oppressive weight from Gideon's shoulders. One he hadn't even realized he'd been carrying.

Samuel released Maggie and stepped back, clasping his hands before him once more.

"I will return when I have more information. Perhaps at that time we might discuss the sanctity of holy matrimony?" The angel turned to walk away, but then paused, shooting Gideon a grin over his shoulder as he added, "Your glow suits you nicely."

Gideon's eyes rounded, and his mouth fell open.

A glow? Did he mean…

Only a soul—a true soul—caused a being to glow.

Had he finally earned his back?

Chuckling, Samuel crossed the yard, and with every step slowly faded until he vanished.

"Wow," Maggie whispered. "That was…surreal. Was I just blessed by an actual angel?"

"Yes, love, you were," Gideon said, turning her into his arms. He'd wait till later to tell her his own good news, to explain the comment about his glow.

But then he caught the strange look on her face.

"What's the matter?"

She frowned up at him and shook her head. But he caught her chin on the crook of his finger when she made to look away.

"What?" he urged.

She drew a deep breath and cleared her throat. "Do you realize that's the first time you've ever used an endearment when speaking to me and really meant it? I mean, aside from when we first met, you know, before we…" She arched her eyebrows suggestively.

He frowned down at her. What was she talking

about?"

"You just called me *love*," she prompted. "You call Kyanna and Carly *sugar* or *darlin'* all the time. I mean, you've called me those things before too, but always…only when you were irritated with me. And that sounds really childish and jealous," she added, shaking her head.

"No, it doesn't," he said, pinching her chin between his thumb and finger, forcing her to look up at him. "*Sugar* and *darlin'*, are just…well, they're just things I say. They don't mean anything at all." He grinned down at her. "And you're right. When I called you those names before, they were more of a… Well, let's just say they weren't exactly complimentary."

She pursed her lips ruefully at him.

He took a moment to figure out exactly how to explain. "I don't call you those things because you mean more to me than that, more than some easy nickname a guy might use so he doesn't have to trouble himself with names. Names are important. And every time I say your name…" His voice trailed off, and he tilted his head. His eyes widened in sudden self-awareness. "Every time I say your name, it's like me telling you I love you. Your name is the only endearment perfect enough for you."

Tears overflowed and slipped down her cheeks.

Oh, crap, I screwed it up.

He opened his mouth to apologize. To tell her he was an idiot. To plead with her not to cry.

But she wrapped her arms around his neck and kissed him senseless. He couldn't remember what he'd been about to say. Couldn't remember what they'd even been talking about. Hell, he couldn't even remember his own name.

And he sure as hell didn't care that his place had become Grand Central Station for every angel and demon who felt like dropping by.

Gideon lowered his woman, his mate, his Maggie to the grassy riverbank. He took his time stripping her, one article of clothing at a time. And he sampled and savored every inch of precious skin that he bared. And when he finally moved over her, when he finally slid deep inside her and felt her welcoming silken flesh close around him, he realized this was what he'd been praying for all along.

He'd finally found his Heaven.

Epilogue

Sebastian stepped inside the quaint little coffee shop located in picturesque Port August, Michigan. The scent of freshly ground coffee beans mixed pleasantly with the aroma of cinnamon and spice. He paused just inside the door under the guise of letting his eyes adjust to the change in lighting. But he spent that moment scanning the plentiful crowd. Filling the long, narrow shop were dozens of small, bistro-style tables. There had to be at least thirty people in here, and he began to feel the first fragile flutters of hope.

She has to be here.

He was looking for a woman in her early thirties. Five nine, slim, almost boyish build. She had long, straight brown hair she habitually kept restrained in a tight bun, and she wore old lady, cat eye rimmed glasses. He'd been able to piece that much together over the course of too many stops to keep track of throughout this infernal town. Not to mention the other false leads he'd followed throughout Michigan.

And through his fruitless search, he'd swear he'd now made the acquaintance of nearly every bloody person in Port August. He'd met the dean of Redmond College where Professor Mackenzie lectured. He'd also met the post mistress, the clerk at a small fresh food market, the proprietor of the hardware store, the checker at the grocery store, the gas station attendant, the newspaper reporter and the professor's next door neighbor Jill, all of whom seemed to know Professor Mackenzie on a first name basis.

Oh, yes, and a nice young bank teller who'd offered her own number should he decide to give up chasing after the good professor.

But he'd not managed to catch so much as a glimpse of the hard-to-pin-down professor herself.

He strode to the counter and pasted a charming smile on lips that had gone stiff with the repeated effort. He'd drained the well of his nearly legendary, endless supply of patience. If one more person—just one—told him he'd just missed the ever-elusive Professor Phoebe Mackenzie, he wouldn't be held responsible for his actions.

A pretty young woman stepped up to the counter to greet him. "Welcome to Perk It Up! What can I get for you?"

"I was hoping you could help me find somebody."

Her provocative gaze drifted over him, and a suggestive brow arched. "Anyone in particular, or are you taking applications?"

Somehow, he managed not to roll his eyes and groan aloud. *Not again!*

Sebastian clenched his hands at his sides to stifle the burning sensation that signaled a plasma ball was about to form. He drew a deep breath and informed her, "Someone specific. I'm looking for Professor Mackenzie. Phoebe Mackenzie."

"Oh, sure," the woman chirped, bobbing her head hard enough to make her unruly curls dance. "She's one of our best customers. Comes in every morning for her usual. And again in the afternoon. In fact, you just—"

"Missed her," he finished. If he gritted his teeth any harder, he'd have a mouthful of coarsely ground powder. Oh dear saints, he didn't want to ask. "Did she say where she might be headed next?"

"Oh, you bet she did. She's off to the airport. I saw her ticket when she dug through her bag for change," the girl added in a conspiratorial whisper. "Was in a rush too. Trying to get all her last-minute errands done before taking off, I imagine."

"What?" The burning sensation in his palms grew to near unbearable levels. Much more and he'd be throwing sparks.

"Well, sure. She's headed to Mexico, Cam-something-or-other. Big archeological dig, I guess."

Sebastian ground his teeth. Why in God's name had the dean not mentioned this crucial little tidbit when Sebastian had spoken to him before?

"Did the professor mention *when* her plane was leaving?"

"No." The clerk stared at the clock on the wall, as if it might answer. "Can't say as she did, though she seemed in an all fired hurry, so I'd guess sooner rather than later. Oh! Oh! I don't know if it'd help you or not. But I did happen to notice the flight number on her ticket. I have a head for that kind of thing, you know." The woman rambled, beaming at him as she rearranged the small plastic bins holding silverware. "Numbers just stick with me."

"That would be exceedingly helpful," Sebastian prompted. He caught himself visualizing lighting a fire under the annoying clerk's feet to get the information out of her a little faster, maybe even just burning the whole place down.

No! That's not the way we operate, not anymore, he reminded himself.

Sternly.

And he forced himself to wait patiently, breathe in, breathe out, while the woman recited the flight information like she was reading it off the ceiling.

The second he had the information he needed, Sebastian spun on his heel and rushed out the door without another word.

By now, he was pretty comfortable with the lay of the land, having gotten directions based on local landmarks at nearly every stop. He'd begun to doubt anyone even knew a street name here. Everything was either "turn left at the big oak at the end of old man Mosby's lane", or "hang a left at Beal's Garage", or "go on straight a few blocks past the fire station". He'd not been to the airport just yet, so he had to rely on vehicular transportation rather than simply shimmering. He stomped on the accelerator and prayed he wouldn't hear the phrase "you just missed her" ever again in his longer-than-your-average lifetime.

After screeching into the airport parking lot fast enough to summon Homeland Security, he erupted from the car. Sebastian didn't bother to close the door behind him. He sprinted across the cracked pavement and burst into the small terminal.

The building appeared empty but for a lone man standing behind a long counter littered with brochures, pens, magazines, and newspapers. Sebastian hurried to the counter and recited the flight information, asking which runway the professor's flight was departing from.

"Oh, I'm so sorry—"

"Please, please, do not tell me I just missed her!"

The balding little man behind the counter looked at him oddly. "Well, I'm sorry, but you have." He hitched a thumb over his shoulder toward the window behind him. A small plane was taxiing down the runway. Sebastian looked over just in time to see the front wheels leave the ground. "In fact, there she goes now."

Sebastian watched as the plane soared into the air. He let out a really, *really* long breath. His palms sizzled. The little man behind the counter took a cautious step back, his eyes wide as saucers.

Keeping his temper in check took far more control than he was comfortable admitting. Sebastian turned and stalked from the building. Halfway across the parking lot, his phone began to ring. Frowning, he pulled the device from his pocket.

Xander? He closed his eyes and groaned aloud. *Damn it.*

Sebastian gritted his teeth, teetering on the edge of saying fuck it and smashing his phone rather than taking the call. But his conscience—or whatever meager shreds of decency he had left—got the better of him. Something had to have gone wrong in a big way if Mr. I'd-Rather-Be-Tortured-Than-Talk-On-These-Damned-Things was heating up the airwaves. He so didn't have time to deal with any more shit today.

"Yo," Sebastian barked into the phone. "Listen, man. Right now isn't a good time to—"

"Stolas has Mikhail."

A word about the author…

Brenda Huber lives in Iowa with her husband, her two children and her very spoiled dog Sam. You can learn more by visiting her on her website:
www.brendahuber.webs.com
or following her on Facebook:
http://on.fb.me/1F4VsNc

~*~
Look for these titles by Brenda Huber

Now Available:
Mine
Cravings
Shadows
Queen's Chess

Texas Series
Texas Bride
Texas Blaze

Chronicles of the Fallen
The Slayer
The Seer
Temptation

Coming Soon:
Vengeance

*Don't miss these other titles in Brenda Huber's
Chronicles of the Fallen Series!*

THE SLAYER
Chronicles of the Fallen, Book 1

The darker side of his nature just can't let her go.

Born of heaven, forged in hellfire and damnation, Xander roams the earth as an unlikely protector of the innocent. Grudgingly embroiled in a demon uprising, Xander must help his brothers-in-arms recover four Sacred Relics rumored to be Lucifer's downfall.

The stakes are simple. If he fails, a new regime will assume control of the underworld and the boundaries between hell and earth will crumble. If he succeeds, long-awaited salvation could be his. But when a beautiful innocent is caught in the crossfire, the price of redemption could be too steep.

Kyanna Hughes is a hereditary Guardian, sworn to protect a sacred Relic at all costs. From the cradle, she was taught to hate all things demon, but her unwanted attraction to Xander turns everything she's been taught upside down.

The danger she faces involves more than her heart. For Kyanna is not only a Guardian, but a keeper of secrets so dangerous, that to keep them out of demon hands even the angels in heaven would see her dead…
Warning: Contains a demon with a notoriously single-minded determination to save the world, and a sworn enemy for whom he will risk eternal damnation. And so begins the journey of six fallen demons and the women who capture their hearts…

THE SEER
Chronicles of the Fallen, Book 2

Not even the fires of Hell will keep this demon from his mate.

All whisper his name in fear, for *The Seer* was the right hand of Lucifer, the Collector of Souls. Condemned by Heaven, a fugitive from Hell, Niklas's only hope for salvation lies in protecting the innocent from demons bent on ravaging mankind

After uncovering a plot to overthrow Lucifer, Niklas and his compatriots scramble to retrieve crucial Sacred Relics before the plot's mastermind gets to them. For if Lucifer falls, so too shall fall the barriers between Earth and Hell.

Carly Danner's life is turned upside down when she stumbles upon a demon summoning, plunging her into a dangerous realm of temptation and forbidden love. Left with no choice, she must trust the most unlikely of protectors, a darkly sensual demon with a fearsome reputation.

As the tangled web of desire and betrayal draws her deeper, Carly walks a blurred line between good and evil. And Niklas must decide if redemption is worth losing the woman who stole his heart.

Warning: Contains a demon willing to put the world at risk for the love of one woman, and an innocent human who would sell her soul to save the demon she can't live without. And so continues the journey of six fallen demons and the women who capture their hearts.

Thank you for purchasing
this publication of The Wild Rose Press, Inc.

For questions or more information
contact us at
info@thewildrosepress.com.

The Wild Rose Press, Inc.
www.thewildrosepress.com